DODGERS

Praise for *DODGERS*

'Dark, edgy and riveting and, for all that, deeply, humanly
serious, *Dodgers* is white knuckles for the mind. I love this book
and will closely follow Bill Beverly forever hereafter'
– Robert Olen Butler, Pulitzer Prize winning author of
A Good Scent from a Strange Mountain

'An excellent book … Imagine the young corner boys
from *The Wire* on a road trip across the USA'
– James Brown, *Sabotage Times*

'Akin to William Gibson in its staccato blizzard of sentences,
each as taut and tight as a drumhead, and reminiscent of James
Ellroy in its sense of social injustice and of a life and upbringing
etched caustically across the pages. A compelling debut'
– Luke McCallin, author of *The Man from Berlin* and
The Pale House

'Not only is the fast-paced and masterfully plotted *Dodgers*
one of the greatest literary crime novels you will read in your
lifetime, Bill Beverly has also created, in the teenage boy, East,
one of the most unforgettable and heartbreaking characters ever
encountered in American fiction' – Donald Ray Pollock, author
of *Knockemstiff* & *The Devil All the Time*

'Propulsive, brutally honest and yet unexpectedly tender,
Dodgers is one of the best debuts I've read. I was absolutely
gripped by the voice, the world of East and his brother, and
surprised at nearly every turn. I audibly gasped at the end'
– Attica Locke, author of *Black Water Rising* and *Pleasantville*

'Reading *Dodgers* is like having the veil lifted from your eyes: the world is more vivid, more intense, more exquisite, and more terrifying than you ever knew. Bill Beverly is a conjurer, a poet of the dark arts, and his novel is a spell: when he sends his young drug-world protagonist on a deadly errand in the alien landscape east of LA – that fat swath of America known to him only by its names and its shapes on maps – it is you who makes the journey, who is the stranger in a strange land, a watcher who now feels the eyes of others wherever you go, and who must pay the devastating tolls of crossing boundaries. Hypnotic, breath-taking, bruising, beautiful, important, true – choose your adjectives, this is a great novel,
– Tim Johnston, author of *Descent*

'In *Dodgers*, Bill Beverly delivers with honesty and empathy as he takes us into the hope-killing shadow of LA's street-level drug kingdom. His prose is a perfect match for young East's life-altering journey; spare, clear-eyed and with the cutting edge of flint. Beverly leads us into the heart of a young man molded by circumstance and, much as Richard Price's *The Whites*, gives a view that will change the way you look at the world'
– Susan Crandall, national bestselling author of
Whistling Past the Graveyard

'The sentences will snare you, and the story keeps you hooked – a thrilling cross-country journey that takes on the poetry and resonance of myth' – Adam Sternbergh, author of *Shovel Ready* and *Near Enemy*

'Bill Beverly's wild and auspicious debut takes off from page one and never lets up. *Dodgers*, a kind of modernized and urban take on Theodore Weesner's *The Car Thief*, is lightning-quick

and world-wise, full of pitch-perfect dialogue and criminal misadventure. Most importantly, it's a lot of fun'
– Tom Cooper, author of *The Marauders*

'*Dodgers* transcends genres. Its main character East, is part Kerouac's Sal Paradise, part Wright's Bigger Thomas, and even part Salinger's Holden Caulfield. The hero's journey is an American story' – Ernesto Quinonez, author of *Bodega Dreams*

'*Dodgers* is a wickedly good amalgamation of *Adventures of Huckleberry Finn* and *Clockers* that stands firmly on its own as a remarkable debut. A harrowing road trip into the heart of America that will shock you, move you, and leave you marveling at its desolate poetry. A real accomplishment: a book that makes you see the familiar through new eyes. It will stick with me for a long, long time' – Richard Lange, author of *Angel Baby* and *This Wicked World*

'Bill Beverly's gritty and propulsive debut novel, *Dodgers*, is more than a riveting read; it is a stunning literary achievement. Our hero, East, a fifteen-year-old hit man, drives across America on a deadly mission, from the mean streets of LA to the heart of the country. East is a character as memorable and as haunting as any I've met in contemporary fiction. And he's not alone in that van, but there is room for one more. So hop in, but strap on your seatbelt and hold on to your hat. The road's a little bumpy – and more than a little terrifying – up ahead' – John Dufresne author of *No Regrets, Coyote*

'A terrific novel, urgent, thrilling, and dangerous from start to finish. In East, Mr Beverly has created a character who stays in the mind after the book is finished, an Odysseus straight out of

Compton. His venture into the unknown lands of the American Midwest has a classic, mythic shape and scope. And the writing throughout is lovely, economical and exact. You could read this for the sentences alone' – Kevin Canty, author of *Into the Great Wide Open*

'I knew before I'd gone very far into Bill Beverly's superb first novel that I was about to lose some sleep, since putting it down seemed to be beyond me. To say it's a page-turner doesn't do it justice, though it certainly is. It's also much more. His characters are vivid and real, and yes, sometimes they'll break your heart. The world they inhabit – no matter where they may be at a given moment – all but leaps off the page. It's a winner. So is its author' – Steve Yarbrough, author of *The Realm of Last Chances* and *Safe from the Neighbors*

'From the moment we encounter East, a mostly silent kid who "didn't look like much," we are initiated into his gaze on the malfunctioning world, a kind of concentrated, exquisite hypervigilance that is both his burden and his gift. It is this quality of attention that makes *Dodgers* such an intense read – inescapable, inevitable, impossible to set aside. We can no more turn off East's vision – and the sense of urgency that comes with it – than he himself can, and we are along for the ride. The truth-telling and pared-down purity of voice here are reminiscent of Denis Johnson, as if this novel were not written but channelled. This is a beautiful, extraordinary book' – Wendy Brenner, author of *Large Animals in Everyday Life* and *Phone Calls from the Dead*

DODGERS

BILL BEVERLY

NO EXIT PRESS

First published in the UK in 2016
by No Exit Press,
an imprint of Oldcastle Books Ltd,
PO Box 394, Harpenden,
Herts, AL5 1XJ, UK
noexit.co.uk
@noexitpress

This is a work of fiction. Names, characters, places, and incidents either
are the product of the author's imagination or are used fictitiously,
and any resemblance to actual persons, living or dead, businesses,
companies, events or locales is entirely coincidental.

A CIP catalogue record for this book is available from the British Library.

ISBN
978-1-84344-856-3 (Hardcover)
978-1-84344-857-0 (Trade paperback)
978-1-84344-778-8 (B format paperback)
978-1-84243-779-5 (Epub)
978-1-84243-780-1 (Kindle)
978-1-84344-781-8 (Pdf)

2 4 6 8 10 9 7 5 3 1

Typeset by Avocet Typeset, Somerton, Somerset
in 12.5pt Minion Pro with Din display
Printed and bound by CPI Group (UK) Ltd, Croydon, CR0 4YY

This book is for Olive, who gave me a new life

And giving a last look at the aspect of the house, and at
a few small children who were playing at the door, I sallied
forth… my course lay through thick and heavy woods
and back lands to town, where my brother lived.
James W. C. Pennington, *The Fugitive Blacksmith* (1849)

Every cheap hood strikes a bargain with the world.
The Clash, 'Death or Glory'

I

THE BOXES

1

The Boxes was all the boys knew; it was the only place.

In the street one car moved, between the whole vehicles and skeletal remains, creeping over paper and glass.

The boys stood guard. They watched light fill between the black houses separated only barely, like a row of loose teeth. Half the night they had been there: Fin taught that you did not make a boy stand yard all night. Half was right. To change in the middle kept them on their toes, Fin said. It kept them awake. It made them like men.

The door of the house opened, and two U's stumbled out, shocked by the sun, ogling it like an old girl they hadn't seen lately. Some men left the house like this, better once they'd been in. Others walked easy going in but barely crawled their way out. The two ignored the boys at their watch. At the end of the walk, they descended the five steps to the sidewalk, steadied themselves on the low stone wall. One man slapped the other's palm loudly, the old way.

Again the door opened. A skeletal face, lip-curled, staring, hair rubbed away from his head. Sidney. He and Johnny ran the house, kept business, saw the goods in and the money out with teenage runners every half hour. Sidney looked this way and that like a rat sampling the air, then slid something onto the step. Cans of Coke and energy drink, cold in a cardboard box. One of the boys went and fetched the box around; each boy took a can or two. They popped the tops and stood drinking fizz in the shadows.

The morning was still chilly with a hint of damp. Light began to spill between the houses, keying the street in pink. Footsteps approached from the right, a worker man leaving for work, jacket and yellow tie, gold ear studs. The boys stared down over him; he didn't look up. These men, the black men who wore ties with metal pins, who made wages but somehow had not left The Boxes: you didn't talk to them. You didn't let them up in the house. These men, if they came up in the house and were lost, someone needed them, someone would come looking. So you did not admit them. That was another thing Fin taught.

Televisions came on and planes flashed like blades in the sky. Somewhere behind them a lawn sprinkler hissed – *fist, fist, fist* – not loud but nothing else jamming up its frequency. A few U's came in together at seven and one more at about eight, crestfallen: he had that grievous look of a man who'd bought for a week but used up in a night. At ten the boys who had come on at two left. The lead outside boy, East, shared some money out to them as they went. It was Monday, payday, outside the house.

The new boys at ten were Dap, Antonio, Marsonius called Sony, and Needle. Needle took the north end, watching the street, and Dap the south. Antonio and Sony stayed at the house with East, whose twelve hours' work ended at noon. Antonio and Sony were good daytime boys. The night boys, you needed boys who knew how to stay quiet and stay awake. The day boys just needed to know how to look quiet.

East looked quiet and kept quiet. He didn't look hard. He didn't look like much. He blended in, didn't talk much, was the skinniest of the bunch. There wasn't much to him. But he watched and listened to people. What he heard he remembered.

The boys had their talk – names they gave themselves, ways they built up. East did not play along with them. They thought East hard and sour. Unlike the boys, who came from homes with mothers or from dens of other boys, East slept alone, somewhere no one knew. He had been at the old house before them, and he had seen things they had never seen. He had seen a reverend shot on the walk, a woman jump off a roof. He had seen a helicopter crash into trees and a man, out of his mind, pick up a downed power cable and stand, illuminated. He had seen the police come down, and still the house continued on.

He was no fun, and they respected him, for though he was young, he had none in him of what they most hated in themselves: their childishness. He had never been a child. Not that they had seen.

A fire truck boomed past sometime after ten, sirens and motors and the crushing of the tires on the asphalt. The firemen glared out at the boys.

They were lost. Streets in The Boxes were a maze: one piece didn't match up straight with the next. So you might look for a house on the next block, but the next one didn't follow up from this one. The street signs were twisted every which way or were gone.

The fire truck returned a minute later, going the other way. The boys waved. They were all in their teens, growing up, but everyone liked a fire truck.

'Over there,' said Sony.

'What?' said Antonio.

'Somebody house on fire,' said Sony.

The smoke rose, soft and gray, against the bright sky. 'Probably a kitchen fire,' East said. No ruckus, nobody burning up. You could hear the wailing a mile away when someone was burning up, even in The Boxes. But more fire engines kept rumbling in. The boys heard them on the other streets.

A helicopter wagged its tail overhead.

By eleven it was getting hot, and two men crashed out of the house. One was fine and left, but one lay down in the grass.

'Go on,' Sony told him. 'Get out of here.'

'You shut the fuck up, young fellow,' said the man, maybe forty years of age. He had a bee-stung nose, and under his half-open shirt East saw a bandage where the man had hurt himself.

'You go on,' said East. 'Go on in the backyard if you got to lie down. Or go home. Not here.'

'This *my* house, son,' said the man, fighting to recline.

East nodded, grim and patient. 'This *my* lawn,' he said. 'Rules are rules. Go back in if you can't walk. Don't be here.'

The man put his hand in his pocket, but East could see he didn't have anything in there, even keys.

'Man, you okay,' East said. 'Nobody messing with you. Just can't have people lying round the yard.' He prodded the man's leg lightly. 'You understand.'

'I *own* this house,' said the man.

Whether this was true, East did not know. 'Go on,' he said. 'Sleep in back if you want.'

The man got up and went into the backyard. After a few minutes Sony checked on him and found him asleep, trembling, fighting something inside.

The fire's smoke seemed to thin, then came thicker. Trucks and pumps droned, and down the street some neighbor children were bouncing a ball off the front wall. East recognized two kids – from a neat house with green awnings, where sometimes a white Ford parked. These kids kept away. Someone told them, or perhaps they just knew. For the last two days there had been a third girl playing too, bigger. She could have grabbed every ball if she'd wanted, but she played nice.

East made himself stop watching them and studied the chopper instead where it dangled, breaking up the sky.

When he glanced back, the game had stopped and the girl was staring. Directly at him, and then she started to come. He glared at her, but she kept advancing, slowly, the two neighbor kids sticking behind her.

She was maybe ten.

East pushed off. Casually he loped down the yard. Sony was already bristling: 'Get back up the street, girl.' East flattened his hand over his lowest rib: *Easy.*

The girl was stout, round-faced, dark-skinned, in a clean white shirt. She addressed them brightly: 'This a crack house, ain't it?'

That's what Fin said: everyone still thought it was all crack. 'Naw.' East glanced at Sony. 'Where you come from?'

'I'm from Jackson, Mississippi. I go to New Hope Christian School in Jackson.' She nodded back at the neighborhood kids. 'Them's my cousins. My aunt's getting married in Santa Monica tomorrow.'

'Girl, we don't give a fuck,' said Antonio, up in the yard. 'Listen to these little gangsters,' the girl sang. 'Y'all even go to school?'

Probably from a good neighborhood, this girl. Probably had a mother who told her, *Keep away from them LA ghetto boys,* so what was the first thing she did?

East clipped his voice short. 'You don't want to be over here. You want to get on and play.'

'You don't know nothing about what I want,' boasted the girl. She waved at Antonio. 'And this little boy here who looks like fourth grade. What are you? Nine?'

'Damn,' Sony cheered her, chuckling.

Somewhere fire engines were gunning, moving again; East stepped back and listened. A woman and a daughter walked by arguing about candy. And the helicopter still chopping. It tensed East up. There were too many parts moving.

'Girl, back off,' he said. 'I don't need you mixed up.'

'*You're* mixed up,' said the girl. She put one hand on the wall, immovable like little black girls got. A fighter.

'This kid,' East snorted. The last thing you wanted by the house was a bunch of kids. Women had sense. Men could be warned. But kids, they were gonna see for themselves.

A screech careened up the flat face of the street, hard to say from where. Tires. East's talkie phone crackled on his hip. He scooped it up. It was Needle at the north lookout. But all East heard was panting, like someone running or being held down. 'What is it?' East said. 'What is it?' Nothing.

He scanned, backpedaling up the lawn.

Something was coming. Both directions, echoing, like a train. He radioed inside. 'Sidney. Something coming.' The helicopter was dipping above them now.

Sidney, cranky: 'Man, what?'

'Get out the back now,' East said. 'Go.'

'*Now?*' said Sidney incredulously.

'*Now.*' He turned. 'You boys, get,' he ordered Antonio and Sony. Knowing they knew how and where to go. Having taught them what to do. Everyone on East's crew knew the yards around, the ways you could go; he made sure of it.

The roar climbed the street – five cars flying from each end, big white cruisers. They raised the dust as they screeched in aslant. East thumbed his phone back on.

'Get out. Get out.' Already he was sliding away from the house. *His* house. Red Coke can on its side in the grass, foaming. No time to pick it up.

Sidney did not radio back.

How had this gotten past Dap and Needle? Without a warning? Unaccountable. Angry, he slipped down the wall to the sidewalk. The smell of engine heat and wasted tire rubber hung heavy. The other boys were gone. Now it was just him and the girl.

'I told you,' he hissed. 'Go on!'

Stubborn thing. She ignored him. Staring behind her at the herd of white cars and polished helmets and deep black ribbed vests: now, *this* was something to see.

Four of the cops got low, split up, and gang-rushed the porch. Upstairs a window was thrown open, and in it, like a fish in rusty water, an ancient, ravaged face swam up. It looked over the scene for a moment, then poked out a gun barrel. East whirled then. The girl.

'Damn!' he yelled. 'Get out of here!'

The girl, of course, did not budge. The *pop-pop* began.

East hit the sidewalk, crouched below the low wall. Beneath the guns' sound the cops barked happily, ducking behind their cars like on TV. Everyone took shelter except the copter and the street dogs, howling merrily, and the Jackson girl.

East fit behind a parked Buick, rusted red. His breath fled him, speedy and light. The car was heat-blistered, and he tried not to touch it. Behind him the air was clouding over with bullets and fragments of the front of the house. Cop radios blared and spat inside the cruisers. The gun upstairs cracked past them, around them, off the street, into the cars, perforating a windshield, making a tire sigh.

The girl, stranded, peered up at the house. Then she faced where East had run, seeing he'd been right. She caught his eye.

With a hand he began a wave: *Come with me. Come here.*

Then the bullet ripped into her.

East knew how shot people were, stumbling or crawling or trying to outrace the bullet, what it was doing inside them. The girl didn't. She flinched: East watched. Then she put her hands out, and gently she lay down. Uncertainly she looked at the sky, and for a moment he disbelieved it all – it couldn't have hit her, the bullet. This girl was just crazy. Just as unreal as the fire.

Then the blood began inside the white cotton shirt. Her eyes wandered and locked on him. Dying fast and gently.

The talkie whistled again.

'God damn you, boy,' Sidney panted.

The police in the back saw their chance, and three of them aimed. The gun in the window fell, rattling down the roof. Just then the four cops on the porch kicked in the door.

'You supposed to warn us,' crackled Sidney. 'You supposed to do your job.'

'I gave you all I got,' East said.

Sidney didn't answer. East heard him wheezing.

He got off the phone. He knew how to go. One last look – windows blown out, cops scaling the lawn, one U stumbling out as if he were on fire. *His* house. And the Jackson girl on the sidewalk, her blood on the crawl, a long finger pointing toward the gutter, finding its way. A cop bent over her, but she was staring after East. She watched East all the way down the street till he found a corner and turned away.

2

THE MEET-UP WAS A mile away in an underground garage beneath
a tint-and-detail shop with no name. The garage had been shut
down years ago – something about codes, earthquakes – but you
could still get a car in, through a busted wall in the lot below some
apartments next door. Nothing kept people away from a parking
space for long.

East took the stairs with his shirt held over his nose. The air
reeked of piss and powdered concrete. Three levels down he
popped the door and let it close behind him before he breathed
again. A few electric lights still hung whole and working from
a forgotten power line. Something moved along a crack in the
ceiling, surviving.

East wondered who'd be there. Fin had hundreds of people in The
Boxes and beyond. After things went wrong, a meet like this might
be strictly chain-of-command. Or it might be with somebody you
didn't want to meet. Either way, you had to show up.

Down at the end he saw Sidney's car: a Magnum wagon, all
black matte. Johnny reclined against it, doing his stretches. He

squared his arms behind his head and curled his torso this way and that, muscles bolting up and receding. Then he bent and swept his elbows near the ground.

Sidney stood away in the darkness with his little snub gun eyeing East's head.

'Failing, third-rate, sorry motherfucker.'

East went still. They said that down here people got killed sometimes, bodies dropped down the airshaft into the dark where nothing could smell them. He looked flatly past the gun.

Sidney was hot. 'I don't like losing houses. Fin don't like losing houses.'

'I ain't found out yet what happened,' East said simply.

'Your boys ain't shit. Who was it?'

'Dap. Needle.'

'Someone's stupid. Someone didn't care.'

East objected, 'They know their jobs. That was my house I had for two years.'

'*I* had the house, boy,' Sidney spat. 'You had the yard.'

East nodded. 'I was there a long time.'

'Best house we had in The Boxes. Fin loves your skinny ass – you tell him it's gone.'

It was not the first gun East had talked down. You did not fidget. You showed them that you were not scared. You waited.

Just then, Sidney's phone crackled. He uncocked his gun and stuck it away. Behind him, Johnny wagged his head and got off the car. Johnny was a strange go-along, dark black and slow-moving where Sidney was half Chinese, wound up all the time. Johnny was funny. He could be nice; he handled problems inside the house, kept the U's from fighting with each other. But you did not want to raise his temperature.

'Sidney don't relish the running,' Johnny laughed. 'In case you wasn't clear about that.'

East breathed again. 'Did everyone get out?'

'Barely. They got some U's. No money and no goods.'

'Who was shooting out?'

'I don't know, man. Some old fool, shotgun in his *pants*. We was grabbing and getting. I guess you could say he was too.'

Sidney put his phone away. He turned, fuming. 'Someone *did* get shot.'

'I know it,' said East. 'Little girl.' He could see the Jackson girl, the roundness of her face, like a plum, a little pink something tied in her hair.

'In the news it ain't gonna be no little girl,' said Johnny. 'Gonna be a very big girl. It's a little girl when *your* ass gets shot.'

This had been a bad time. Fin's man Marcus had been picked up three months ago. Marcus kept bank, never carried, never drove fast or packed a gun, quiet. He had a bad baby arm with seven fingers on his hand. He knew in his head where everything came from and where it went, where it was – no books, nothing to hide. Twenty-two years old, skilled, smart: Fin liked that. But they had him now, no bail. No bail meant the PD could just keep asking him questions till they ran out of questions. Since then, everything was getting tight. One lookout picked up just loitering – they kept him in for three days. Runners getting scooped off the street, just kids, police rounding them up in a boil of cars and lights, breaking them down.

Some judge wanted a war, so everything had gotten hard.

They rode the black wagon south unhappily. Sidney coughed wetly, like the running had made him lung-sick. He wiped his gargoyle face. 'Don't look at the street signs,' he snapped.

'Man, who cares? I know what street this is,' said Johnny. Something went *pumma, pumma, pum* in the speaker box, and the AC prickled hard on East's face. He closed his eyes, like Sidney said, and didn't look out at the street.

Losing the house – it was going to be on him. He owned the daytime boys; he owned their failure. He'd run the yard for two years, and he'd taught the lookouts, and until today everyone said he'd done it well. His boys knew their jobs; they came on time, they didn't fight, didn't make noise. He could not see where it'd gone wrong. That girl – he shouldn't have talked to her for so long. Maybe she would have wandered off. He could have let Antonio muscle her a bit. She wound up dead anyhow.

What could he do? That many cops come to take a house, they're gonna take it.

A pair of dogs went wild as the car slowed, but East didn't open his eyes. Some of the neighbors' dogs likely were Fin's. Most people would keep a good dog if you gave them the food for it. And the cops looked where the dogs were. You didn't keep dogs where you stayed.

'Don't look at the house numbers.'

'Man, how I'm not gonna see what house it is?' countered Johnny.

They parked down the street and walked. A little girl on a hollow tricycle scraped the sidewalk with her plastic wheels. The day had turned hot and windy. When Sidney said, '*Hyep*,' they all turned and mounted two steps up toward a flat yellow house.

FOR SALE, said a sign. Someone had blacked out the real estate agent's name.

Answering the door was a short, stark-faced woman East had seen once before somewhere. On her hair she wore a jeweled black net. Her mouth was thin and colorless, slashed in. She showed them in, then retreated, into a kitchen where something bubbled but gave no smell.

The room was empty, bare, brown wood floors. The drawn blinds muted the daylight into purples. A lonely nail on the walls here and there told of people who'd lived here once. There were two guns there too, Circo and Shawn. East had seen them before. It was never good, seeing them.

'Everyone get out your house when it happen?' asked Shawn. He was a tall kid, like Johnny.

'Little bitch didn't even give us a heads-up,' flared Sidney.

East ignored it. It wasn't Sidney he had to answer to now. He wondered how much about it everyone knew.

Shawn wiped out the inside of his cheek with a finger and bit his lips unpleasantly.

'Gonna need me in Westwood tomorrow?'

'Depends. See what the day brings,' said Sidney. 'Miracles happen.'

Shawn laughed once, more of a cough. He patted the bulk in the pocket of his jeans approvingly.

A security system beeped, and down the hall a door opened – just a click and a whisper of air. The woman exited the kitchen softly, on bare feet, and turned down the hall. She slipped inside the cracked door and shut it. A moment later it beeped open again. East watched the woman. She had a spell about her, like her time in this world was spent arranging things in another.

She pointed at East, Sidney, and Johnny. 'You can come,' she said calmly.

East had been in rooms like this before, where guns had talked vaguely amongst themselves. Until today, the day he'd lost the house, he'd found it exciting. Today he was glad to be summoned away. He caught a scent trailing from her body as he followed, and inhaled. Usually if he got this close to a woman, it was a U, heading in or out. Or one working the sidewalk, or stained from the fry grill. This woman was perfumed with something strange that didn't come out of a bottle. He held his breath.

The net in her hair glistened: tiny black pearls.

The system beeped again as she unsealed the door.

Fin's room: unlit except for two candles. He sat in a corner, barefoot and cross-legged atop a dark ottoman, his head bowed as if in prayer, a candle's gleam splitting his scalp in two. He was a big man, loose and large, and his shoulders loomed under his shirt.

This room had a dark, soft carpet. A second ottoman sat empty in the center of the room.

Fin raised his head. 'Take off your shoes.'

East bent and scuffled with his laces. In the doorway behind them appeared Circo, a boy of nineteen with a cop's belt, gun on one side and nightstick on the other. He stuck his nose in, looked around, and left. *Good.* The door beeped as the woman pulled it shut behind her.

Johnny took a cigarette out.

'Don't smoke in here, man,' Fin said.

Johnny fumbled it back into the pack. 'I'm sorry.'

'House is for sale.' Fin wiped the back of his head. 'Purchase it if you like. Then you can do whatever you want.'

The three boys arranged their shoes by the door.

Dust curled and floated above the candles. Fin sat waiting, like a schoolteacher. When he spoke, it was with an ominous softness.

'What happened?'

Sidney answered, grievous, wheezing. 'No warning, man. Paying a whole crew of boys out there. When the time came, no one made a call. Didn't shout, didn't do shit.'

'I did call you,' East protested.

'When there was police already banging on the door.'

So Sidney was here to saw him off.

'Why didn't they call?' Fin said it quietly, amused, almost as if he were asking himself.

Sidney jostled East forward unnecessarily. This meant him: this was his *why*.

'There was a lot going on,' East began.

Fin, quizzical: 'A lot?'

'Fire trucks. House fire,' East said. 'Lots of noise. The ends – Needle, Dap – maybe that's what they was thinking: police going to the fire. Maybe. I mean, I ain't spoken to them yet, so I can't say.'

'I think your boys know to call when they see a police.'

'Oh, yes, they know,' East said. 'Oh, yes.'

'And why ain't you talked to them?'

'Something goes wrong, stay off the phone,' East answered, 'like you taught.'

Fin looked from East to Sidney and back.

'Was there a fire for real?'

'I saw smoke. I saw trucks. I didn't walk and look.'

'Maybe it don't matter,' said Fin quietly, 'but I might like to know.' He gave East a hard look and then veiled his eyes. East felt a beating in his chest like a bird's wing.

A minute passed before Fin spoke again. 'Close every house,' he said. 'Tell everybody. Submarine. I don't want to hear *anything*. I hate to say it, but people gonna have to look elsewhere a few days.'

'I got it,' said Sidney. 'But what are we gonna do?'

'Nothing,' Fin said. 'Close my houses down.'

'All right,' said Sidney. 'But how is it this little nigger fucked up, and *I'm* not getting paid? Johnny neither?'

'I taught you to save for a rainy day,' Fin said. 'And, Sidney, I taught you not to say that word to me. You know better, so why don't you step out. You hear me?'

Sidney fell back and grimaced. 'I apologize for that,' he said, and he turned to pick up his shoes.

'You too, Johnny. You can go.' Fin sighed. 'East, you stay.'

'You want us to wait for him?'

'No,' Fin said. 'Go on.'

East stood still, not watching the two boys moving behind him. When the door beeped open and they left, the woman was there, outside, barefoot, waiting. She brought in a tray with two steaming clay cups. She stood mute, and something passed between her and Fin, no words, borne like an electrical charge. Then she placed the tray with the two cups on the empty ottoman.

Quietly she eyed East and then turned and left through the same door. *Beep.*

'How you doing?' Fin said. 'Shook up?'

East admitted it. He was aching where he stood. Tightened up more than ever. His knees felt unstrung. 'Yeah.'

'Sit.'

East lowered himself to the second ottoman stiffly and sat beside the steaming tray in the dusky room. Fin spread his shoulders like a great bird. He moved slowly, top-heavy, as if his head were filled with something weightier than brains and bone.

Fin was East's father's brother – not that anyone had ever introduced East to his father. Others knew this; sometimes they resented East for it, the protective benevolence he moved under. But it shaped their world too, the special care that was given him, his house, his crew. When East was a child, Fin had been an occasional presence – not a family presence, like the grandmother whose house held a few Christmases, like the aunt who sometimes showed up in bright, baggy church clothes on Sunday afternoons with sandwiches and fruit in scarred plastic tubs. Fin was a visitor when East's mother was having hard times: to put a dishwasher in, to fetch East to a doctor when he had an ear infection or one of the crippling fevers he now remembered only dimly. Once Fin took East to the Lakers, good seats near the floor. But East didn't understand basketball, the spitting buzzers and the hostile rows of white people in chairs, and they'd left long before the game was decided.

But since East had grown, Fin was the quiet man in the background. East had never had to be a runner, a little kid dodging in and out of houses with a lunchbox full of goods or bills. He'd been a down-the-block lookout at ten, a junior on a house crew at twelve. He'd had his own yard for two years, directing and paying boys sometimes older and stronger than he was. Not often in that time had he laid eyes on Fin, but often he'd felt the quiet undertow of his uncle's blood carrying him deeper into the waves.

Did he want to do this? It didn't matter: it would provide. Did boys respect him because he could see a street and run a crew more tightly than anyone else, or because he was one of Fin's favorites? It didn't matter: either way he had his say, and the boys knew it. Was this a life that he'd be able to ride, or would he be drowned in it like other boys he'd kicked off his gang or seen bloody or dead in the street?

It didn't matter.

'Try it,' Fin said.

East touched a cup, and his hand reared back. He was not used to hot drinks.

'Not ready yet?' Fin reached for his cup and drank soundlessly. The steam rose thick in the air. 'Now tell me again why that girl got shot.'

East saw her again, her face sideways on the street. Those stubborn eyes. He could still see them. 'I tried,' he said, and then his voice slipped away, and he had to swallow hard to get it back. He stared at the tea, the steam kicking up.

'I tried to make her go away,' East said. 'She been down the street all weekend playing ball and just came up that minute. Then the police. You couldn't tell her nothing.'

'I see. Just her bad luck, then. Her bad timing.'

'She was from Mississippi.'

Fin sat and looked at East a long time.

'You know that girl hurts me more than the house,' Fin said. 'We got houses. We can move. Every time we move a house, we bring along the old and we pick up the new. It's that girl that costs us. It's that girl that goes down on my account.'

'I know.'

'She died.'

East swallowed. 'I know,' he said.

Fin agitated his cup and stared down into it. 'Get up and lock that door,' he said. 'I don't want nobody walking in on us, what happens next.'

East stood. He stumbled in the carpet's pile. The lock was a push-button, nothing more. East pressed it gently.

Fin's dark eyes followed him back to the cushion.

'So you're free now. Had a house. Had a job. Lost the house. Lost the job.'

East hung his head, but Fin waited on him to say something. 'Yes, sir.'

'You wondering what comes next?' Fin smacked his lips. 'Because maybe nothing comes next. Maybe you should take some time.'

Take some time, East thought. What they said when they didn't want you anymore.

'There is something you might do for me,' Fin said. 'You can say yes or no. But it's quiet. We won't talk about it. Not now, next year, not ever. You keep it till you die.'

East nodded. 'I can keep quiet.'

'I know. I know you can,' Fin said. 'So: I want you to go on a drive. At the end of that drive, I want you to do something.' He curled a foot up and pulled on it. Fluid joints, a slow movement. 'Murder a man.'

East drew in his shoulder and carefully dried his mouth on it. A spark fired in his stomach; a snake curled.

'You can say yes or no. But once you do, you're in. Or out. So think.'

'I'm in,' East said automatically.

'I know you are,' said Fin. And he drank down the rest of his tea, then shook his head twice, a long shudder that might have been a laugh or might have been something else entirely. East felt Fin's gaze then and swallowed the hard beating inside him.

'Be ready tomorrow, nine o'clock. You're gonna clear out straight. So bring clothes, shoes. That's all. No wallet. No weapons. We gonna take everything off you. Bring your phone, but you can't keep it. No phones on this trip. And no cards – we'll give you money. You hear?'

'All right.'

'Keep your phone on, and Sidney will call.'

'Sidney ain't too pleased with me right now.'

'Sidney ain't got no choice,' Fin said. 'Okay? Be some other boys too going along. They a little older, more experienced. You might not feel you fit in. They might wonder too. Especially after today.' He swabbed the moisture from the inside of his cup with his fingers. 'But I think you got something they need.'

This praise from Fin warmed him.

'Gone five, six days. You got a dog or a snake or something, find someone to feed it.'

East shook his head.

'Good,' said Fin. 'Then we ain't talking about nothing in here. Just catching up. Stay a minute and drink your tea.'

East picked up the heavy cup. He wet his tongue. The tea

tasted old, like dust at first. Like something collected from the ground.

'You like this?'

East didn't, but he tried not to show. 'What is it?'

'No name. It's good for you, though,' said Fin. 'That woman, she owned a tea shop. Then she fell into some things. I helped her. She knows business. She knows about bringing in off the docks. And she knows how to brew.'

East nodded. 'She's from China?'

'Half Thai. Half everything else,' said Fin lazily. 'How's your mother?'

East coughed once. 'She's all right. She got a little sick, but she's better.'

'House holding up?'

'Holding up,' said East. 'Hold up better if she cleaned a little.'

'You the man of the family,' said Fin. 'You could up and clean it. Stop and see her before you go.'

'Yes, sir. All right.'

'All right,' Fin said. 'This is a big favor, man. This is not easy, what you're doing. I want you to know that it is important to me.' Fin's hands clasped his feet and stretched them, twisted them. Like bones didn't matter, like they could be shaped any way you wanted. 'I will remember it was you that did it,' Fin said again. He put his cup down with East's. The two cups touching made a deep sound like the bell of a grandfather clock.

'Boy, go,' Fin said. 'Not a word. Nine o'clock. Sidney will see after your crew, take care of them. Don't worry. Stay low.'

East stood. He felt childish in his white socks.

Fin brought out a thick fold of bills. He counted out twenties – five hundred dollars. He handed it over without looking at it.

'Some for your mother there.'

'All right.'

'One more thing you want to know. Your brother, he's in. He's part of the trip.'

East nodded. But a little pearl of anger splattered inside his chest: his brother. Babysitting. Not that his brother was any baby.

'Maybe you ain't gonna like it. Figured I'd give you a night to get used to the idea.' Fin rubbed down his feet, popped a toe. 'You know why he's going.'

East put the money away and laid his hand over his pocket. 'Yeah, I know.'

A bad street. Dogs bashed themselves against the fences. Televisions muttered house to house through caged doors and windows. East was the only person moving outside. He stepped up to a porch and unlocked the door.

In the living room, in a nest of dull air, his mother lay watching a game show. She looked older than her thirty-one: runny-nosed, fat and anemic at the same time. She drank from a plastic cup, a bottle of jug wine between her knees.

East approached from behind. She noticed, but late.

'Easton? What you doing here?'

Her fierceness, as always, was half surprise. She sat up.

'Hello, Mama,' East said. He looked sideways at the game show.

'You come and sit down.'

He sat beside her, and she smothered him in a hug that he received patiently, patting her arm. She did not turn down the TV: it made the windows hum. When she released him, her nose had grown wet again, and she was looking for somewhere to wipe it.

'I thought I might see you. I made eggs and bacon.'

East stood up again. 'I can't eat. I just came by to check.'

'Let me take care of you,' she reproached him.

East shrugged. The TV swerved into a commercial, even louder. It made him wince. He split off half the fold of bills Fin had given him, and she took it without resistance or thanks. The money curled unseen in her hand.

East said, 'Nice day. You see it?'

'Huh?' his mother said, surprised again. 'I didn't get outside today. Maybe. Where's Ty? You see him?'

'I ain't seen him. He's all right.' He retreated to the kitchen, a little preserve behind a white counter littered with empty glasses. He could see her craning her neck, tracking him.

'He ain't been to see me.'

'He's doing fine. He's busy.'

'He my *baby*.' Her voice rose frantically.

'Well, he's doing fine. He'll come around. I'll tell him.'

'East,' she commanded, 'you eat some eggs. They're still in the pan.'

Let me take care of you.

When he flicked the switch, one of the two fluorescent tubes on the ceiling came to life. The kitchen was a wasteland. East bagged what could easily be thrown out. With a napkin from a burger bag he smashed ants. The eggs on the stove were revolting – cold and wet, visible pieces of shell. He turned away.

His mother had gotten up. She stood in the doorway.

'Easton,' she breathed, 'you gon stay here?'

Embarrassed, he said, 'Mama, don't.'

Proudly she said, 'There's sheets on your bed.'

'I can't tonight.'

'I ain't seen either one of you,' she sniffed.

Like every minute weighed a ton. 'Mama, let me get this trash out.'

'Whyn't you have some eggs?'

'Mama,' he pleaded.

'Don't neither my boys love me,' she announced to something on the opposite wall.

East dropped the bag of garbage. He found a fork in the congealed eggs, hacked out a mouthful, and shoveled it in. Sulfur. He tried to chew and swallow, eyes closed, and then turned to his mother. Eggs still milled around the sills of his teeth, horrible.

'You see.' His mother beamed.

East's room was small but neat: twin bed with pillow, two photos on a shelf. A carpet he'd pulled up because he didn't like the pattern and laid back upside down. A little dust but no clutter. He shut the door, but the TV noise still buffeted him. He picked shirts, socks, and underwear out of the pressboard dresser and stuffed them into a pillowcase. He looked around for a moment before the door opened.

His mother, weary on her feet but still pursuing, stood in the doorway.

'Any of Ty's clothes here?' he asked.

She let out a sickly laugh. 'Ty's clothes – he took them – I ain't seen – I don't know what Ty wear.'

'Shirts? Anything?'

Two years younger, but Ty had left first. Even the room they'd shared for ten years – Ty barely ever seemed to live there. No toys, no animals, nothing taped to the wall. Like it was never his.

She zeroed in. 'You going somewhere? You look like a tramp.'

'Me and Ty need clothes for a few days.'

She hummed, casual but knowing. 'In trouble?'

'No.'

'Suitcases in the closet. But they old.'

'I don't need a suitcase,' East said.

He stopped and waited stock-still till she retreated. After a moment he heard the squeak of the couch springs: she was down. He was alone. He checked the block of wood he'd mounted inside his bed frame, underneath: tight. He loosened it with the thumbscrew. He left his ATM cards there, then tightened it back down.

At the door he said, 'I'll be back in a few days. Come see you then. Come and stay with you.'

'I know you will. I know you gon come back,' his mother cooed. He took out the remaining money, peeled off three bills, and gave her the rest.

'I know you ain't in no trouble,' she begged. 'My boys ain't.' He tilted his face down, and she kissed him goodbye.

Down the street, freed from the shout of her TV, East heard the silence hiss like waves. He walked north until he entered an office park of sandy gray buildings nine stories high. Two of them stood in a sort of corner formation, and East walked around them. A faint hubbub of raucous people drinking came from somewhere in the darkness.

A narrow sidewalk led behind the air-conditioning island. The concrete pad full of AC units lent cover as East bent at the last building's foot. His fingers found the makeshift metal stay wedged between the panes of a basement window. The window fell inward, but he caught it before it made a sound. Quietly, twisting his body in one limb at a time, he crawled through.

The basement crawl space, dim behind dusty windows, was clean, its packed-dirt floor higher at the sides than in the middle. It was empty save for East's things and a faucet in one corner. It didn't turn on, but it wouldn't stop dripping either, and East had placed a wide stainless-steel bowl beneath it; there was always water, clear and cold. He tossed his bundle down and put his face over the bowl, watching his reflection swim in upside-down from the other side.

He drank. Then he washed his face, his hands, the caves of his armpits.

The spot where he slept was a pair of blankets, a pillow he'd bought at a roadside mattress store, and a large, heavy cardboard box the size of a washing machine. The air conditioners hummed all day, all night, washing out the hubbub and street noise. But that was not enough. East paused, stretched, then knelt on the floor beside the box. His hole. He tipped the cardboard up one side and straightened the blankets on the floor beneath it. He smacked the pillow straight and put his bundle of clothes down at the foot of the blanket. Then he slithered beneath and let the box drop over him. Like a reptile, a snake, calmest in the dark. Even the sound of the air conditioners vanished. Nothing. No one.

He breathed and waited.

3

NEAR EAST'S UPTURNED BOX lay his pad of blankets and pillow. His shoes waited together in the shallow dirt, next to the old pillowcase full of clothes. Through the basement windows, early light crept in, the palest blue.

Sleeping through the night wasn't what he was used to. A long time, he'd been standing yard midnight to noon. He cleaned his teeth with the cold clear water brimming in the steel bowl. He cleaned his gums, fingers stretching his face to strange masks. He washed his arms again and his neck and face. He lowered his pants and washed his flanks and all around his balls, and shivered in the morning chill.

He checked his phone – Antonio, Dap, Needle, Sony. Nothing. The house. He needed to go back and see. It was ten minutes' walk out of the office park to the house. East crossed the main street where the awnings were going up, taquerias and rim shops, the outer crust of the neighborhood. Then in, past the houses where everything was waking up, men hopping down their steps with cups and bags and keys, jumping into cars. Joggers and dog-walkers, old women smoking in their doorways.

A few blocks deeper, the cars turned older and were packed less tightly at the curb. The row houses sat blind behind plywood doors and windows – just a few at first, then more. Then two out of three. This was The Boxes.

He turned onto his street. This spot was where Dap kept one end's lookout. But he hadn't called. Needle watched the other end, five blocks down. He'd called too late. Sidney said back before cell phones was better: you knew who you could get in touch with and who you couldn't. You never sat and worried why somebody didn't answer his phone.

Two old gray women stood clucking on the shelf of their lawns. Most days when they rattled out to judge the morning, he'd been there for hours, eyes and skin already tuned to the movements of the day. But this morning they had the drop on him.

As he neared the house, he studied it sideways: brown face bullet-pocked, splintered, upper windows open like eyes. Smoke still seemed to hang. Now the door was just a sheet of plywood, bolted on. Yellow police tape stickied the yard side to side.

He ducked under to check. Power cords, recharging cables, all gone from the porch. So he had maybe an hour of battery left. Well, they'd be taking his phone. He gazed around the yard, but it told him nothing.

A patch on the sidewalk was still unmistakably bloody. He tried not to look. The Jackson girl's face was right near the top of his mind and he did not want to be seeing it, inside his head or anywhere else.

A man in a suit came walking past. Every day he walked by wordlessly, but today he nodded at East and thundered, 'Good morning.'

East nodded back.

'They caught you, didn't they, boy?' The man was jolly. 'Shut you right down.'

East ignored him, but the man kept on, made cocky by yesterday. 'I see you got a pillowcase. Got your life in there?'

East shrugged and walked faster. He could have broken off a stick and beaten the man, bruised him, made him shut up and run. And for what?

He tried his phone in the open air, tried Dap, tried Needle. Neither of them answering. He left brusque messages: 'Call me.' But he'd trained his guys: if we run, stay off the phones. Now he was crossing that up.

It was ninety minutes before he needed to show up. He'd get a walk and eat breakfast. He picked his way south through The Boxes. Birds and small bugs stirred among the trees, buzzing like phones. Three little girls were out early, playing chalk on the sidewalk, colored *tizas* as big as their wrists.

A cough from a porch was directed at him. 'Hey, man. Hey,' the voice came down.

East looked, then stopped. It was a man, maybe thirty-five, maybe forty, a U who'd come to his house some days. The man sat drinking out of a tall paper cup.

'What you need?' East said.

It was strange what he knew and didn't know. He knew this man, his secret hours. He remembered when he'd first showed up in the evening hours, still with a neatly made face, a thick gold band. Then he'd come more often. East remembered when he'd lost his job, and he'd marked the passage of drug time across the man's face, the thinness he'd taken on and the way his eyes now had that light to them, that ingenious, failing light.

The man's name was the one thing he didn't know.

'What you doing now?' the man said.

'Nothing.'

'Where am I gon go?' asked the man indignantly.

East shrugged. He heard again what Fin had said. *Submarine. People gonna have to look elsewhere.* He knew a house a mile away, one that wasn't Fin's. But you didn't talk about other houses you knew. You didn't connect the dots.

The man coughed three times and spat out a large, silvery thing. 'You don't *know*? Unacceptable, man.'

East lowered his eyes and got walking again.

'Boy, don't deny me,' the voice came, following him.

At eight, Sidney called him, told him where to go. A mile away – down off the south end of The Boxes. 'Make sure you bring clothes for a couple days.'

'Fin told me,' East said.

'Course he did,' sneered Sidney. Then East's phone died.

He bought a glazed doughnut to eat as he walked, then pulled down an orange off a low branch. He turned it in his hand as he walked, a small, heavy world. It was ripe, but he waited to eat it.

In the alleyway behind a line of stores, Michael Wilson was telling East about his car. Michael Wilson had the police interceptor and new glows down front and back and underneath. With a second battery Michael Wilson could run his system all night, loud as a club, and still crank it up and drive it away.

Michael Wilson was twenty – long body, long teeth, big brown eyes he liked to keep behind silver shades. Always laughing. Always telling a story. He had been a guy who came around The Boxes, sometimes keeping an eye, sometimes delivering a payday or food. He was an up-and-comer. He had gone away to college, UCLA, and East hadn't seen him since. He'd been a lot of noise to start with, and now he impressed himself even more.

Michael Wilson was shucking peanuts out of a blue plastic

bag, tossing the nuts into his mouth, flipping the shells over his shoulder onto the pavement. Michael Wilson worried that the other guys might be stupid. Said he didn't have time to be riding with no one stupid, because stupid didn't stay cooped up. Stupid infected everyone. Little gangsters always thought they had a code, when really what they had was a case of stupid. East nodded, and he pretended to listen, because Michael Wilson was going to be a part. *But God damn,* he thought.

For the longest time it was only the two of them. East checked his phone – dead. He shook his head. 'What time you got?'

'Like nine,' said Michael Wilson.

'What is *like nine*?'

'It means almost nine. Approximately nine, motherfucker.'

East sighed. 'Let me see your watch.' He grabbed Michael's wrist, eyed the watch's gold hands, the shining stones. 'That's eight fifty-four. Not *like* anything.'

'It's like nine, old man,' Michael said.

A couple of raggedy cars and a blue minivan shared the early light. Bulky air conditioners rusted on raised pads, muscular posts sunk in concrete to protect them from the drivers. Most of the stores were dark. One Chinese restaurant belched its fryer smells, and the women peered out at the boys and smoked in the safety of their doorway.

The next to arrive was a pumpkin-shaped boy in a green shirt. He waddled slowly, carefully; fat made his face young, his gait ancient. He breathed hard, excited, scraping his feet as he came. 'Whew,' he said. 'Michael Wilson. What's up.' They grabbed hands. Then Michael recognized him.

'I remember you. Walton? Wallace?'

'Walter.'

Michael laughed at himself. 'I remember you was up in those computers. A little science man.'

'I remember you was going to college. You in charge of the laughing and lying, I guess.'

'You in charge of the eating,' said Michael Wilson. 'Where's your bag at?'

Michael Wilson had things in a glossy contoured bag with a gym name on it. It looked like a new shoe. East had his pillowcase and his orange.

'I got no fuckin bag,' Walter said. 'I had no idea. I been all weekend at my uncle's in Bakersfield. They picked me up off the street fifteen fuckin minutes ago.'

East eyed Walter. The *fuckin*. A soft boy sounding hard.

'I don't know what they told you. We gonna be gone for days, son,' Michael Wilson said.

'I'll get some clothes on the road, I guess.'

'If we can find a tent store,' smirked Michael Wilson. He went to touch East's hand, but East looked the other way. *So*. There was a whole connection that came before. He leaned against the loading dock and studied the other two.

'You got the rundown? What the plan is?'

'No, man, they gonna tell us. They doing that here.'

'And I heard you was at your leisure,' the fat boy addressed East.

East looked up. 'At what?'

'I said, I heard you was out of a job.' Walter leaned against a post and addressed Michael Wilson. 'This the boy whose house got shot up yesterday. They said there's three others coming,' he explained, 'so I asked who.'

Michael Wilson cracked open a peanut and tossed the shell at East. 'You lose your house? What you doing now?'

East swept his hand. 'This.'

'Moving up,' said Michael Wilson. 'What about you, Walt?'

'Everything,' Walter said. 'A couple days back they had me running a yard. Substitute teacher.' He addressed East with a certain friendly contempt. 'I used to work outside like you. Few years ago.' He giggled.

East couldn't contain himself. 'What you do now?'

'Projects,' Walter said. 'Research.'

'*Research?*' said Michael Wilson. 'How old are you, fat boy?'

'Seventeen.'

'How about you, East?'

East looked away. 'Fifteen.'

The car arrived next. It was a burly black 300. Floating slow, the way cops sometimes did, all the way down the alley. At last the windows rolled down to reveal Sidney and Johnny.

'God damn, man,' crowed Michael Wilson. 'Could have walked here faster.'

East saw that Michael laughed almost every time he talked. It wasn't that he thought everything was funny; it was like his sentence wasn't finished yet without it.

Sidney scowled at Michael Wilson and got out. He wore all white, a hot-day outfit. Johnny wore black jeans and no shirt.

'Where is the last one?' said Johnny.

'I don't know, shit,' said Michael Wilson. 'Number one is right here.' Cackling.

'We ain't going over this twice,' said Sidney. 'What time is it?'

'Nine oh-five,' said Michael Wilson.

'Fuck him then. He's late. Let's go on.'

'I'll get him,' Johnny said. 'Fin said four boys, we gon have four boys.' He fell back and started working his phone.

The fat boy scratched his face. 'Who we waiting on?'

'My brother,' said East calmly. There was a way to stick up without putting your neck out. Dealing with Ty – *Maybe you ain't gonna like it,* Fin had said – would take plenty of neck.

'Oh. Ty,' Sidney said. 'That child cannot listen anyhow. So let's start. Just sit his ass in the back with a coloring book.'

Sidney booted up a tablet on the back of the black car and swept his finger through a line of photos. A solid-looking black man, maybe sixty, a whitish beard cut thin. Broad, hammered-looking nose, a fighter's nose. Sharp eyes. In the pictures, he looked tired. His clothes cost good money: a black suit, a tie with some welt to it.

Sidney looked over their shoulders. 'Judge Carver Thompson,' he said. 'When Fin's boy Marcus goes up on trial, he's the witness.'

'Carver Thompson,' said Michael Wilson. 'If that ain't a name for a legal Negro, I don't know what is.'

'Don't worry about his name. He used to be an asset to us. Now he ain't.'

'That's why you going to kill him,' said Johnny softly.

East looked around at the other boys. Michael Wilson nodded coolly. Looked like he knew. Walter didn't. Something falling out in the fat boy's throat, gagging him. East watched with satisfaction. *Little science man. Fuck you,* he thought.

'Why this gonna take five days?' said Michael Wilson, quick on the pickup. 'Why we ain't doing it already?'

Sidney put a road map down on top of the trunk. 'Because here's where we at.' He tapped Los Angeles. 'And this man is way – over – here.' He swept his hand across all the colors on the long stretch of land till he tapped on a yellow patch near a blue lake.

'Wisconsin?' said Michael Wilson.

Walter said, 'What's a *black* man doing in Wisconsin?'

'I guess a nigger likes to fish.' Sidney shrugged. 'Also likes to stay alive.'

'How we gonna get there?' said Michael Wilson.

Now Walter's face turned cloudy. 'Oh, shit. Oh, shit,' he said, 'I know what you're gonna say next. No flying, right? We about to drive all that?'

'Correct,' said Sidney.

'You're tripping. That's a thousand miles,' Michael Wilson said.
'Two thousand,' said Walter despairingly. 'That's why we ran them
documents. Right? That's what you been setting up.' He opened
his hands, a little box, in front of Sidney.

'Crazy,' said Michael Wilson. 'We ain't gonna drive no two
thousand miles. *And back.* Doesn't make sense.'

'Michael Wilson,' said Sidney softly. 'You the oldest. You
supposed to lead this crew. If you can't handle this trip, tell me, so
I can shoot you and find someone that can.'

Michael Wilson held his hands up, shifting gears smoothly.
'Right, man,' he sang. 'Just running the numbers, man.'

East breathed out and let his eyes adjust to the map, the thick
red and black and blue cords inching state to state. Dense and
jumpy. Every road had a number and joined up a hundred times
with other roads. He saw how they would go. This was like the
mazes they used to do in school while the teacher slept. What
they said in school was: don't worry. Keep looking at it. You can
always get there.

After Sidney lectured them on the route and the job, Johnny
handed each boy a wallet. East examined his. Inside, in a plastic
window, was a California state driver's license with his face
looking up at him. Dimly he remembered this, his picture taken
in front of a blue cloth. Somebody he'd never seen, in some room
the winter before. Some of the boys came in for it. Never asked
why.

The work was good – the two photos, the watermarked top
coat. Some kind of bar code on the back.

'Shit looks real,' Michael Wilson said.

'It is real,' Walter said.

'*Antoine Harris.* Sixteen years old,' read East. 'How you say it's
real?'

'It ain't my name either,' agreed Michael Wilson.

'Listen,' said Sidney. 'What is real? It's in the system. It's legit. Police pulls you over and looks you up, it's real. License like that cost a man on the street ten thousand dollars. So don't lose it. Read what it says and remember it in case some police asks you who you are.'

'Kwame Harris,' said Walter. 'What, him and me supposed to be brothers?'

'You the one sat closer to the table,' giggled Michael Wilson.

'Cousins,' said Sidney. 'Cousins. Know each other a little. Not too much.'

'Here is one for you, Michael,' Johnny said. 'Give me yours. I'll keep it for you.'

'If someone asks you where you're going,' said Sidney, 'you're going to a family reunion. If someone asks you where, you say Milwaukee, Wisconsin. If someone asks you where in Milwaukee, you don't know. That's three questions.'

Johnny said, 'Don't let nobody ask you more than three questions.'

'We just some lying motherfuckers all across America,' said Michael Wilson.

'You're getting it.' Sidney snapped out a thick stack of money, and the air between the boys grew quiet and warm. All the eyes watched as he dealt twenties from his left hand into his right.

'Three hundred,' he said to Walter. 'Three hundred,' he said to East. He passed the two piles. The rest, a bigger stack, went to Michael Wilson.

'Wait,' Walter said. 'I'm going out five days, *killing someone*, and all I get is three hundred dollars?'

Johnny moved in. 'Boy, this ain't compensation.'

'This is expenses,' bristled Sidney. 'You pay cash. There is no credit card. There is no gas card. You dig? Ain't staying in motels.

You go in and wash up in a rest stop, in a McDonald's. You ain't wasting time. You ain't making records of where you are. You the one supposed to *understand* this.'

'Walter, you're very smart,' said Johnny. 'But smarter people than you puzzled this out. So pretty please, shut the fuck up.'

Walter nodded, swallowing it down.

'Michael Wilson, you got a thousand dollars. If there's a problem? You fix it. This money ain't for clothes or having a good time. This money ain't yours. The oldest one gets to hold. He gets to solve problems.'

'All right,' said Michael Wilson. He looked around at the younger boys significantly as he tucked the money away.

'So that's your ride today. Right there,' said Johnny.

They all followed Johnny's eyes around the lot. The blue minivan was what he was looking at.

'What?' said Michael.

'Let me show you,' Johnny said.

'Show me what? You chose the sorriest car you could find?' Johnny took a handful of Michael Wilson and shoved him along ahead. 'This a *job* car, boys. This is my gift to you.' He railed at them quietly. 'Reliable. Invisible. Rebuilt. New six-cylinder, three-point-eight. New transmission. New suspension. New tires, brakes, battery. Doesn't look new, but it drives new. You can sleep in it. Most important, you ain't gonna look like ignorant gang boys, which is what, in fact, you *are*. Wisconsin plates. In this car you look like four mama's boys going to a family reunion, which is what you *want* to look like. *Please don't give me a ticket, officer.*' He popped the back gate. Three cases of bottled water sat behind the rearmost seat. 'You ain't got to love it. You ain't even got to bring it back. But this is the right car for the job.'

'And what the fuck do we have here,' Sidney said, looking up.

It was East's little brother. Shambling and grinning. He was small and two years younger than East. Lighter-skinned and already beginning to bald. But he had a sharp easiness. There was already something chiseled into him: Ty didn't care. He didn't want to be loved or trusted. He was capable and unafraid and undisturbed by anything he'd seen or done so far.

'Ty-monster, sneaking little thirty-six chambers motherfucker,' said Johnny. They touched hands.

'Ty,' said Sidney warily.

The other two boys stared. Ty ignored them, ignored East, completely. He sat down on the bumper of Johnny's black car and matter-of-factly drew a gun and reloaded the clip with bullets loose in the pocket of his blue T-shirt.

'This boy here,' Johnny laughed.

Ty finished and put the gun straight down under his waistband. When he stood up from the bumper, the barrel stood out cock-straight in his pants.

'Which reminds me,' Sidney said. 'Give it up. Phones. Guns. Any ID you got. I need it right now.'

'*Fuck* that,' Ty snorted.

'Whatever you got,' said Sidney, unflinching. 'Weapons. Knife or stick. Any digital other than a watch. If you got a bottle of something. Whatever you don't want the sheriff of White Town to find on you. Give it up right now.'

East had come with just his phone, but the others all had something. Michael Wilson gave up a small bag and papers. Walter gave up a knife – a Korean type for street fights. So light and springy it would shiver inside you.

Sidney beckoned. 'East? What else?'

'Nothing, man.'

'Don't make me fuck you up.'

He sniffed. 'Fin told me, don't bring nothing.'

'All right,' said Johnny, and he and Sidney glanced at each other. They didn't ask Ty, just closed in. He twisted and swore while they held his hands. Johnny hung him up, and Sidney patted him down. They took just the one gun from his pants. Sidney examined it.

'Man, *fuck* you,' said Ty, wrenching his wrists free and rubbing them.

'Thank you for checking your weaponry at the door,' Johnny said, taking it over.

'You best keep that for me.'

'I'm keeping it already.'

'Ridiculous,' Ty snorted, shaking his clothes back right. 'Sent to shoot a man with no guns.'

East studied his brother. So content in his fury. Still little and raw but ready, happy to strike. So he had known about the job too. They hadn't had to tell him what to do – only the where and who.

'Get close to where you're headed, you'll get guns,' Sidney said. 'Until then, we need you clean. We need you to be angels.' He wiped his mouth with his bare forearm – his tattoos glistened wet. 'You think it's the same out there? But you don't know. It ain't. Them police don't budget on you. That's their country. They love a little Negro boy. They pat your ass down and you go to jail. You go to jail, the job ain't done. And if the job ain't done, Fin goes away.' Suddenly, full-muscled, he lunged at Michael Wilson and bashed him back into the side of the van. East looked up, surprised.

'You listening to me, smiley-face motherfucker?' Sidney spat. He bared his teeth and raised his forehead to Michael's chin like a gouge.

'Sidney, man. We got it,' East said. Straight bullying the lead man, he thought. Setting up the whole thing.

Sidney was wound way past tight. 'The *job*. Do it the way we tell you. Got something funny to say now?'

'No,' said Michael Wilson, clutching his sunglasses.

'Anyone?'

'No,' said East. 'We're good to go.'

Johnny flexed the black rails of his arms. 'See, we're being polite to you today, the better for your educational purpose. But do exactly what the fuck we say.'

'We got it,' said East again. *Patient,* he reminded himself. A moment passed, the six of them wary and bareheaded in the sun.

'All right.' Sidney wiped his mouth, then settled a little at last. 'When you get into Iowa, look at the map. You gonna call for directions. Call this number.' He opened the road atlas to the map of Iowa. A pink phone-sex street flyer was taped over its eastern half.

'This number here?' said Michael Wilson.

'This number here. When the operator asks what you want, you say, "I want to talk to Abraham Lincoln."'

'You what?' Michael Wilson broke up first.

Sidney waited bitterly. 'Laugh all you want. But remember.'

'Abraham Lincoln gonna say, "Hi, Michael. Me so horny."'

Even East bent over laughing.

Sidney waited, jaw hard like a fist. 'Make that call,' he said at last. 'You'll get guns.'

'Paid-for guns. Guns we selected for you,' Johnny said. 'Use them and lose them.'

'The gun man is a white man. So be cool.'

The van. East slipped away from the rest to examine it. Dingy outside – a few dents and scrapes untouched, dirty hubs, no polish for years. The upholstery showed wear. But the tires were brand-new, the tread still prickling. The windows were clean. Definitely submarine.

In his mind he was boiling it down: drive the roads. Meet up for guns. *The job.* He tried to follow it in his mind, see where the problems were. But there was nothing to see. Only these boys. Kill a man? More like keep them from killing each other, these three boys, for two thousand miles in this ugly van. That was what they'd brought him in for. That was what he had to do to get back home.

Relieved of their things, armed with their new names and wallets full of twenties, they followed Johnny around the strip to the sporting goods store.

Above the clothes high banks of sick white lights spilled down. 'Dodgers cap. Dodgers shirts. Get you one,' Sidney was repeating.

Walter squeezed between the triple-XL ends of the racks.

'Dodgers are faggots,' said Ty.

'I don't disagree,' sighed Johnny. 'What can I say? White people love baseball. White people love the Dodgers.'

'What I care what white people like?'

'Boy,' Johnny said, 'the world is made of white people. So you just pick out a nice hat.'

All the clothes smelled of the chemicals that made them stiff and clean. The boys' hands sorted through the new and bright. East drifted back, found a rack marked CLEARANCE where the clothes didn't stink, grabbed two plain gray T-shirts with Dodgers script. Michael Wilson paid cash for it all at the register.

'Thank you for shopping with us today,' the girl in her braids gushed. 'Go Dodgers!'

'Thank *you*,' Michael Wilson said over his sunglasses. 'Okay, let's *vamos*, kids.'

Johnny reached for the receipt and crumpled it, then tore it to tiny bits.

Outside the damp, irrigated morning smell of Los Angeles flowers and fruit in the trees and small things rotting.

'Any problems? Any questions?' Sidney said. 'Any last requests?'

East shrugged. Michael Wilson looked down into the white bag from the store.

'I don't think so,' said Walter.

'Get going, then,' Sidney said, already reaching for the door of Johnny's car. Like he couldn't be gone soon enough.

Michael Wilson had a key. East did too. Michael went for the driver's door. East ushered Walter up front. He tried the sliding door on the right side and popped it open.

In the dark of the van sat Fin, alone. Waiting in the middle seats, head bent low under the headliner, arms wrapped around his shoulders like pythons.

'Come on in,' he said.

They exchanged glances and climbed in – Michael and Walter in the front, Ty sliding into the back. East sat on the middle bench next to Fin.

'You boys know how to lock a car?'

'Yeah,' said Walter. 'But we ain't gone anywhere yet.'

'You got keys, though. Lock the doors. Or someone like me will be sitting in here when you boys return. Got it?'

They all nodded assent.

Fin's voice was deep, but his face was pinched, unhappy. 'If I could,' he said, 'I'd do this myself. But I gotta trust you. You know the job?'

Four heads nodded yes.

'Michael Wilson, these the right boys?'

Michael Wilson found his voice, tried to steady it. 'Yep.'

'Anyone can't do it, walk away now.'

Quietly they waited, reverent and impatient both.

From the center of the van came a black flash: Fin had drawn a fat pistol and cocked it, barrel at East's temple. East felt the cold metal burr scratching at his skin.

'You know East is my blood. Now I am sending you all out as my blood.'

East's eyes kept a flat stare. Practiced. Like he didn't care. 'This gonna go all right?' said Fin.

'It's gonna go all right,' Michael Wilson repeated.

Walter nodded, eyes large.

'I need you boys,' said Fin. 'And I don't like to need.' Slowly he drew the gun back, then slipped it away somewhere. 'Michael Wilson, you're in charge. You're the oldest. East and Walter, you keep him honest. Keep him straight. And, Ty, you make sure it gets done.'

He slid the side door open.

'Any questions?'

Four boys shook their heads.

Fin lowered himself to the ground dryly, tenderly. 'Don't make no friends.'

Michael Wilson fired the engine. They watched Fin walk away down the row of loading docks, just a large, slow-moving man in the sun.

II

THE VAN

4

A LITTLE COMPASS ON the ceiling glowed E. Only once did East turn to look back. Everything he recognized was already past: The Boxes. His gang. His mother. The abandoned, bullet-pecked house. The jimmied window and his crawl-space den. Fin and the gun he'd put to East's forehead. Now it was just these boys he had left, this van. Nothing.

Behind him lay his brother, a video game squeaking under his thumbs. Uninterested. East tried to remember the last time he'd seen Ty. Maybe late summer. A couple of months at least. He hadn't known where or how Ty was living. Not that Ty would tell. Talking to Ty, you ended up knowing less than you started with. He took a pleasure in sharing nothing, enjoying nothing, a scrawny boy who'd almost starved as a baby, didn't eat, didn't play – *failure to thrive*, the relief doctor said. Smart but didn't like school, fast but didn't like running. Never cried as a baby, never asked questions. Never loved anything but guns.

Hadn't even said hi to East yet, his brother. Hadn't acknowledged that he'd noticed East there. East wasn't going to be the one to break the chill. He touched his forehead, the invisible scrape there, the gun's kiss that said, *This is important.* He stared away sideways through the curved, tinted glass: the traffic crawled and the streets changed, a scroll of places. East had never seen these streets or the ones beyond. Fifteen years old, he had never left Los Angeles before.

In the center seat he had an overview – he could watch the streets, watch these boys. Michael Wilson's head bobbed as he drove, talking, talking. Talking all the time, to everyone, even himself, a flow: he made music of it, he breathed through it. His sunglasses rode up top, and his head swung side to side, his white eyes dancing this way and that. So busy, thought East, working so hard. Walter, his head was lower down, bushier. He bulged off the seat into the middle and against the door. East had known some fat kids before, smart ones, worth something. But you couldn't work them in the yard. Not outside, a standing-up job.

But Walter was getting tight with Michael Wilson. Giggling at him. 'Never thought you'd be driving a fuckin florist's van,' he proposed.

Michael Wilson lifted his hands from the wheel. 'It don't *smell* like flowers.'

East didn't mind the van. He liked the seat, the middle view, the drab shade. The carpet was blue. The seats were blue. The ceiling was a long faded grayish-blue, little pills of lint in the nap. Where he sat, the smoky windows were an arm's length away. They wouldn't roll down; they only popped out on a buckle hinge. That would do. Everything was an arm's length away.

He tucked his pillowcase under his seat and scouted in the knapsack hung on the back of Walter's. Pens, a notepad. Soaps and towels, toothbrushes and paste. The sort of kit somebody's mother would pack. And under the seat, a first-aid kit: gauze, ice packs, a flimsy red blanket that felt like wood splinters. CALL FOR HELP – AMBULANCE/POLICE was spelled out on one side. And four pairs of thin black nylon gloves.

Then the fat boy, Walter, cleared his throat and turned. He locked in on East. 'Man, what you think when Fin held that barrel on you?'

'What'd I think?' East sniffed and looked off out the window. 'Nothing.' He didn't say: that is the second gun I've looked down in a day.

'Would stress me, man,' Walter said. Still staring at East. Finally East looked back, and Walter gave a little nod and turned forward.

'Nigger, for blood, Fin must not like you all that much,' said Michael Wilson.

'Fin says don't say *nigger*,' East said flatly.

'Nigger, that's unrealistic.' Silently Michael Wilson laughed at the windshield and bobbed his head to music, to a rocking horse in his mind. 'In the man's personal presence, I defer. But be for real.'

Walter said, 'Michael. That word don't mean nothing to you?'

'Not like it means to Easy.'

East shrugged. It was just a thing, a rule. Everyone broke it. But this trip was supposed to run tight. Rules were what they were. He supposed it would get wild at the end. That was later. Ty would see to that.

Out of habit, he studied them. Already bickering. 'You got to get to I-15, man,' Walter was saying. 'You gotta hit Artesia Freeway before you get to 605.'

'But you don't even say it right. Ar-tess-ya.'

'It says it right here. Ar-tee-sia.'

'You ever been there, man? Cause I had a girl that way, and she said Ar-tess-ya.'

'You ain't never had no girl except off a corner in the ghetto,' said Walter. 'Just get us moving out this shit.'

'Play some music, then, Walt,' Michael Wilson ordered up.

For a minute, crouched over his stomach, Walter reached and fiddled with the radio. Nothing.

'Doesn't work.'

'We supposed to have a genius,' mourned Michael Wilson. 'Can't even switch on a radio.'

'It don't *work*.'

Ty's game buzzed triumphantly. The screen for a moment turned his hands bright white.

'What you thinking back there, Easy?' said Michael Wilson, shimmying his head a few degrees over.

'He don't talk much,' Walter opined. 'He and his brother.'

'No, he don't.' Michael Wilson stopped at a light. 'He don't like you.'

Walter giggled. 'He don't like *you*.'

East kept his mouth shut. Now they'd be teasing him. You just listened. You let it go, you came in when it was done, you kept your hands clean. Otherwise never built anything.

He didn't see how he'd ever get any sleep in this van.

'You know, we might want to get some food before we hit the road,' Walter suggested.

'Oh, *we*,' retorted Michael. 'I didn't hear you taking no vote.' Walter too let it slide off, East noted. You didn't get to him by calling him fat boy. He'd heard it before. 'Good chicken coming up on the right. What kind you want? They got both.'

'Both what?'

'Both kinds. Black chicken and Spanish.'

'If black chicken what made you fat, I'll take Spanish.'

A noisy drive-through lane threaded between hedges and the little building. The loudspeaker squawked like a fire truck's horn.

Michael Wilson paid and fetched out king-size drinks and a bucket. Walter passed the big drinks back, member VIP cups – you could refill them if you ever came back. Napkins. Hundreds of them.

They crawled onto the Artesia Freeway.

Ty finished a drumstick and twisted his fingers clean in a napkin before he picked up his game. The boy still barely ate. Barely moved sometimes. Unnatural.

They crawled past big yellow lights saying something was happening up ahead. East tried to see over the people in the other cars racked around the van. White man in an Acura to the right, phone pinned to the top of the wheel. Line of little Latin boys in the cab of a pickup, sullen and sleepy. Walter was fishing out a third piece of chicken. 'Gonna be Christmas before we get out of LA,' he mumbled.

East tried to look ahead at the brown mountains, to think about the way ahead. He tried not to watch. But it wasn't in him. A career of watching – a few years was a career in The Boxes – had made him the way he was. He spent his days watching, keeping things from happening. And sometimes he could see things coming. Sometimes he looked through a pair of eyes and saw what a U was deciding, what a neighbor feared.

Sometimes this watching wound East up. It was never finished. There would always be another thing, another thread, another pair of eyes. Days began sharp and tuned themselves sharper, until by the time it was over, the world made a quivering sound, like a black string humming. He could barely stand to be near things.

He slept in his box at night just to dampen the sound of the string. To blind him, deafen him, gratefully. Sometimes in the night beneath the box he woke up gasping.

Cars merged fitfully: they'd reached the obstruction. A vast brown Pontiac lay beached in the right lane, broken down and proud of it. Two women, bleached hair shining and loose, awaited the tow like parade queens. They sat up on the back, perched, putting lotion on. After them, the speed picked up.

The air conditioner was killing him. East weighed a hundred ten pounds, give or take. He reached into the first-aid kit and wrapped himself in the flimsy red blanket. The boys in the front seat laughed.

The traffic thinned out, and as the van climbed toward the mountains, they darkened, the solid brown breaking into purples and grays. All East's life the mountains had been a jagged base for the northern sky. It was the first time he'd been this far toward them, in them. He'd never seen them broken into what they were, single peaks dotted with plant scrub and rock litter, and the open distances between.

He couldn't stop looking – the slopes and tops and valleys that slowly revealed themselves. Like a new U moving in slowly, taking a look at the house, at the boys, maybe going away, maybe hanging around, deciding he'd just go up for a look, deciding he'd go inside. They all went inside sooner or later. He wanted those U's to decide, to go in or go away, come again another day, so he could stop watching them. In the same way he willed Michael Wilson to drive faster, to pell-mell it down the highway past the Pathfinders and Broncos and Subarus heading up into the hills for the afternoon. He wanted into the mountains. Almost wanted them over with.

Light poured between them, careened around them.

The purple and brown details opened, resolved themselves, then whipped away as they were passed. Shattered pieces of things. At length the van passed through a canyon where an entire hillside was on fire, white smoke fanning low in the wind.

The boys made no comment on this apparently normal disaster. East studied it, not breathing. Then it too was past.

Green signs flared by. Cajon Junction. Hesperia. Victorville. Thousands of windows punched into the valley, cars sliding on and off, streets littered with people. His eyes sought them out and registered. Hard to stop.

When he closed them, let his eyes rest, he felt, as he always did, that someone or something had turned its gaze on him.

'Go on and sleep if you like, Easy. I got it,' Michael Wilson murmured. 'Fat boy already checked out.'

'All right,' East said quietly. Walter had gone facedown on the tray of his breast.

Ty's video game behind him trumpeted happily. A new level.

In the afternoon darkness, they stopped for gas.

The ground had flattened – hills and fences, scrub and arroyo. But mostly empty. Sometimes East found his eyes had gone blurry, the miles spinning past like bus-window reflections. Normal afternoons, he'd sleep seven hours and get up for a while before heading to the house. Last night's sleep had been full but fruitless: his head was dried up, his lips stiff. The sun lay way over on the mountains, behind a shelf of cloud.

'Where are we?' said Walter, blinking too.

'This the desert, son,' declared Michael Wilson.

Shimmering heat. The low sun wasn't sending it, but the pavement below them glowed white. East stepped quickly across.

The bathroom outside was locked, so he pissed in the back between two sun-cooked cars. Around him, the ground made a cracking sound, fine dry things touching in the breeze. Part of the moon was up, a white tab.

Inside the gas station, different oils, girl magazines. One ice cream cooler and one for drinks. Next to the counter where you paid for the gas was a grill.

'I can make you something, hon,' said a woman, white, sun-scraped.

There was nothing in the place that he needed. He wandered outside. Michael Wilson stood squeegeeing the windshield.

'Boy, did you just piss out in the field?'

East glanced down. 'Yeah. I just pissed out in the field.'

The older boy laughed. 'Country already.'

East didn't answer. The jokes, the small laughs. He recognized Michael Wilson working, trying to do his job. The light talk of the leader. He dawdled past the van and stood on the apron of concrete and loose stones, looking around at the unbuilt land. Something moved in the distance, a ghost or tumbleweed. He'd seen a tumbleweed once, in a cartoon. This looked like that, a cartoon tumbleweed in cartoon land, hills and rubble, nothing with a name. Nothing real.

'Get in, Country,' called Michael Wilson. 'We got to find something for y'all to eat.' And East turned back to the van, pale blue and dusty, like the sky.

5

ONLY ONCE DID MICHAEL Wilson try talking to Ty. They were riding out what was left of California. Or maybe it was Nevada. The land was dark, and sometimes the spread of headlights showed them low, brushy hills. Michael Wilson leaned away from the wheel.

'What's your story back there, young'un? Fighting them aliens still?'

A long, intent wait, and then the voice floated back, quavery, almost a little girl's: 'Are you talking to me?'

'Yeah.' Michael Wilson, for once, was not laughing.

'Tired of riding, man,' Ty said. 'Tired of bullshit. Why we ain't flying?' He switched back on the game with a musical flourish, as if the conversation were over.

This pushed Walter's button. 'Oh, no. Really, man? Impossible. No way.'

Michael Wilson: 'We trying to keep low, young'un. You gotta use a credit card to buy a plane ticket. ID to buy, ID to get on. It don't matter if the ID ain't real; they still gonna track you.'

Their song changed quick, thought East. Bitching about it themselves an hour ago.

'We'd be so fucked,' said Walter. 'They would know where we get off, where we catch a ride.'

'So there's some trouble? Four little black boys done shot a man? A man who's a witness in LA next week? Look, I see where we got these four little Negroes just flown in from LA.'

'I wonder when they flying back.'

'Let's get a picture of them off the video.'

'Let's call up the SWAT team.'

Michael Wilson laughed. 'Airborne Negro Detection System activated.'

To all of this Ty snarled, 'So what if they do?'

Michael Wilson and Walter glanced across at each other, holding their merriment.

'Fuck you,' said Ty. 'The both of you.'

East sat with hands folded inside the red blanket. Pinning it shut. So this would be it. The funny faces in front tangling with Ty. For days.

'Oh, maybe you could fly,' said Walter. 'But you a wanted man then. This way, we're sneaking in, sneaking out. You remember that astronaut lady who wanted to kill her boyfriend's new girl? Drove all the way from Texas to Florida to get away with it? She had gas cans in the back, never stopped. She wore diapers, man, trying to keep off the cameras.'

'You remember that *astronaut* lady?' Ty sneered, and in the back he muttered softly to himself like an old injured dog. Again his thumbs worked the buttons of his game. And that was the end of Michael Wilson talking to Ty.

They were awake, but softly. Then Michael Wilson spoke. 'You want to take a little drive into Vegas? See the sights?' The instrument panel lit the curve of his cheek like a moon.

'No,' said East.

'Let's keep moving,' said Walter.

But then the hollow dark of the desert was pierced, and colored light caught the undersides of the clouds. The boys stared ahead, rapt.

The van crept smoothly toward the emerging city's glow. It was like the orange flare of a cigarette – crawling, twinkling, growing bright. Buildings rose out of it like a great lighted forest. Vehicles of all descriptions visible on the road again in the spilled light. Then they were flashing through it, and everyone was watching, even Ty.

'Listen. We got to get off for gas anyway,' Michael Wilson suggested, and *Yeah, yeah,* they all agreed.

So much light. Crossing, crossfiring, leaving nothing empty, no shadows. Barely had the van cleared the ramp before a pyramid appeared. A grand white pyramid, razor-edged, spotlit. Everything dressed up: even the parking ramp had a fairy on it, or a genie.

'City of sin, my niggers,' drawled Michael Wilson, steering now with one hand.

He and Walter leaned out their windows, ogling, here and there letting out a holler. Evening, desert air. East sounded out the names as they passed: MGM. Aladdin. Bellagio. Flamingo. Treasure Island. Stardust. Riviera.

'Just like Disneyland, man,' Michael Wilson added.

Couples. Women in pairs or threes. Men in vast teams. Families fitted out with prizes and bags. Wandering blind, their shadows spilling out in eight directions, walking like nobody walked in The Boxes.

'"Biggest payouts on the strip,"' Michael Wilson read with a growl.

'But every sign's saying that,' replied Walter.

Abruptly Michael Wilson sat up and swung the van into a parking lot. Wasn't any gas station here, East noted, but he let Michael snake the van back where low glaring lights caromed off tall buses and campers. A colonnaded canopy shone ahead, dancing in neon light. Michael aimed them that way.

'Michael,' East prodded. 'Just getting gas, right?'

'Sure,' Michael Wilson said. They swooped in under the overhang to find one yellow rectangle outlined on the pavement just down from the door, a car just pulling out of it. Michael eased the van in there and parked it. Lights dancing in the wet of his eyes.

'You boys want to take a look?'

'*Hell* yes,' Walter said, already rolling out.

'*Hey,*' East insisted.

'Don't worry, E,' Michael Wilson said. 'I know you're on tight. But you basic street Negroes don't get to Vegas every day. We got to *see* this, man. Half a minute.'

A tall lady in a silver cocktail dress and heels wafted by, shiny. Then it was Ty, brushing past without a word. East reached in vain, but his brother was already out the sliding door. *Damn.*

So this is how Michael Wilson was going to do it. Sudden turns and promises.

To his left, a line of columns and potted palms. Lights moving on everything. They riled East, set his mind jumping. To the right, Ty wandered on the pavement, skinny, behind him a long row of golden doors. East clutched at his red blanket unhappily.

'Come on, Easy. It can't be that bad,' Michael Wilson crooned. 'If you scared, later I'll have fat boy read you a story.'

The black carpet seemed limitless. Patterned neon curlicues forever, up steps, down ramps, no ceiling above, just the blinking lights on a thousand machines with their nonstop ringing jangle. The din was aggravating. East had seen a casino on TV – that gave no hint of how it would be, like a factory, a city, clanging, clanging, bells that weren't real, that couldn't be stilled, from distances that weren't real either. Clanging that didn't matter, signaled nothing, just made up the air of the place. Everything clanging.

Just the banks and banks of lighted boxes, and placed before each one, a person, rapturously lit.

Signs on the pillars warned, NO PERSONS UNDER THE AGE OF 18! But nobody was stepping after them: the doormen, the head-nodding security with ear coils, the waitresses with drinks in monogrammed glasses, the burly Mexican women wheelchairing old folks with oxygen tanks. Nobody accused Ty. No one watched with a purpose.

These people looked drugged, East thought, *or lost.*

He straightened his shirt and made to catch up. Michael Wilson was monologuing: *yeah, yeah, I'm a show you what's tight.* Headed for something. Then at the end of a long, littered aisle, they came upon a clearing and a low, carpeted mesa – three shallow steps up. Glowing green tables in formation, ringed by white people. Michael Wilson took the steps at a trot, and the boys flocked along.

East hung back, parked himself on a column. Tried to see, not to be seen. He watched people eyeing the boys as Walter and Ty milled behind Michael's shoulder, peering down at the green felt.

Michael wedged himself in between two white women in dresses that noted the bones of their backs. 'Deal me in, man,' he demanded, fanning a handful of twenties. Sidney's money, East thought. Fin's money.

The dealer was the second black man at the table. Tall and prim with a silver clef on his tie. Neat. 'Hey, brother,' Michael Wilson addressed him, more directly. 'Deal me in.'

Now everyone looked up at this university Negro with his money hanging out.

The dealer pursed his lips; his politeness was contempt. 'Please, sir. First you put value on a card. Then at the table you buy chips.'

The money levitated in Michael Wilson's hand. His answer. 'This is not a cash game, sir.'

'Oh. It isn't.' Not a question, a challenge. No one else spoke. 'Okay, my brother,' Michael Wilson purred. 'I see you in a minute.' He broke away, pushing between Walter and Ty, and East caught his look: humiliated. An acted-out sweetness, packed with rage.

Now East fell in beside Michael, got up shoulder-close as they walked.

'Mike. We got to get. You said a half minute. We ain't supposed to be here.'

'Ten minutes, E,' Michael Wilson muttered, bulling high gear through the crowd. East glanced back at Walter and Ty, and they tried to keep up. Michael veered toward a spill of light jutting up: musical notes, blazing in turn, stepping up the wall into the dark. He found a service window, jailhouse bars over the counter, polished to a scream, and no one in line. Not a real window; like a window in a movie. Like *The Wizard of Oz*.

East caught up just as Michael put his hands on the white marble counter, the stack of twenties flat under his left. 'We ain't got time for this,' he argued.

'Sir?' came the voice behind the bars.

The cashier was not a young woman, but her cheeks and eyes were dolled up with glitter. She eyed them each in turn: Michael, East, and then Ty and Walter as they jostled in.

Michael Wilson faced the woman and lit his face up just like hers.

'I want one hundred dollars' poker chips, ma'am,' he announced.

'Sir.' She inclined her head, as if reciting a rule in school. 'You must be eighteen to enter, sir.'

Michael's smile. 'I'm twenty, ma'am.'

'Yes, but, sir,' the woman said. Patient, undeterred. 'Are these gentlemen with you? Do they have ID?'

East watched Michael's eyes: one flash. Then his smile hooked itself back on. 'They aren't *gambling*,' he said. 'So, what? They can't even watch? Can't see me?' He laughed. 'How I'm gonna leave my babies in the car?'

The woman took a step back out of Michael's breathing room. She had decided. Michael saw it too.

Walter spoke first. 'Mike. Let's step out, man. We don't want any trouble down here.'

East caught a movement from the direction of the card tables. A big blue suit with a headset was bearing down. A security guard, the size of a football player. 'Now look out,' he warned.

At last something made Michael quit smiling. Now his strut became a hurry as he herded the three boys back. They skittered between the ringing machines, dodging players who careened, drugged, from stool to stool. But where had the door gone? Ty broke off ahead, scouting; East had lost his sense of direction entirely. Walter was lagging behind, and East waited up.

'*Go*, man,' he snapped.

'I'm going. I'm going.'

Something made him cruel, made him jab at Walter. 'This is your fault,' he said. '*First* one out the van.'

'I said I'm going,' Walter panted.

The players saw them coming now, and they got out of Walter's way, tokens rattling like chains in their plastic cups. East glanced back: the security man was cutting them room. But still he trailed, talking into a cupped hand.

A short whistle from ahead. They'd located the exits.

Past the first set of doors, they spilled out into the vestibule, piano music raining down. But now Michael Wilson had stopped, knelt to tie his shoe. East fished his keys out and slipped them to Walter: 'Start the van.' The doors sucked air as the seals broke, and East caught a slice of the night outside, the heat and sound of motors. The guard trailing them had stopped near the doors. They'd done what he wanted them to do.

Except Michael switched feet, began reknotting his second shoe. East couldn't watch. 'Quit stalling, man.'

'Ain't the most family-friendly establishment you could ask for, is it, E?' Michael finished the knot and admired it before he stood. Cheery now.

'Mike, I'm gonna tell you something,' East began.

'East, man.'

The grin on him. It didn't matter what you said. It just came back.

East faced Michael Wilson up. 'How long you gonna take in there? And how much money you gonna spend?'

'East,' Michael Wilson purred. 'Just a *taste*.' He sized his thumb and finger a half inch apart. Like a U in the yard – he wasn't even seeing East. He was staring back through the inner doors. 'Slots, man – you put twenty dollars on a card, you can play it in a minute. Might even win. I'll let you play, man. You gonna like it.'

'Fin's twenty dollars?'

'Fin ain't here. I'm in charge. Like Fin said.'

'Then *be* in charge.'

'I am,' grinned Michael Wilson. 'All that's holding me up is one whiny little bitch.'

The seal of the golden doors broke again as a pair of ancient women staggered in from outside, gasping, '*Oh, my goodness. Oh, my goodness!*' Then the revolving lights outside found their way in too, announcing it, some new, bright kind of trouble.

Outside, under the canopy three cars wide, things were sudden and sharp. Every sound, every fidget of the lights was back in focus; every sound had a maker. An engine whined. A woman was shrieking. The palm leaves shivering in an invisible breeze.

The yellow light was spinning off a big white tow truck, and somewhere East heard Walter's hollering, a muffled squawk.

Michael Wilson: 'Where's the *van*?'

East pointed; then he ran.

The tow truck was bulky, a wide silver bed tipped back like a scoop, and a steel cable ran taut down under the little van's nose, reeling it in. East's stomach slid. High on the wall he glimpsed the sign now: RESERVED PARKING/TOW ZONE. Of course.

East headed to Walter's window. Walter was pop-eyed and frantic in the driver's seat. Nobody was paying him any mind.

'What are you *doing*?'

'I'm in the car,' Walter ranted. 'They can't tow it. It's a rule. Tell him!'

'Tell who *what*?'

'Him!'

East saw then. Down low on the wrecker's left flank, a burly guy with a beard was working the levers, making the winch squeal and spool the thick line. But it was running the wrong way: he was turning them loose.

'He's letting us go?'

'Uh-huh,' Walter hyperventilated.

'How come?'

A quiver passed down Walter's face. 'Your brother.'

Again East looked. Ty was poised high on the running board, staring down like a wildcat. Below him, the tow truck guy hurried, one-armed, shielding his head.

Michael Wilson stepped right up to the tow guy, bellowing: 'Man, get my car the fuck off this thing.'

Pushing a lever, the wrecker man stopped the winch. He stood and winced and spat something red on the pavement. 'I *am*,' he said, and East saw it: something had made a mess of his mouth. Beard full of blood. Plainly afraid, the wrecker man nodded quickly at Michael Wilson and got away, rolling himself under the van's front bumper, out of sight.

Everything seemed to sizzle in the battling, shifting lights. Like they were caught in a camera flash that went on and on. Off to the left, by a concrete pillar, two security guys were watching everything.

East still could not comprehend. 'Letting us go, right?' he asked Walter, and the fat boy said, 'I *think*.'

'Fuck it, then.' East stepped off and whistled, beckoned Michael and Ty. *Back in the van.* Because the security twins, they were getting ready. Bow ties, shiny patent leather shoes, but he could tell by the necks – all muscle. 'Come *on*,' East warned.

Michael Wilson cursed down at the wrecker man's legs as he scampered by. Ty hopped down off the tow truck. 'Oh, God,' said the shrieking woman, 'look what you done!'

Only a minute, East thought. A minute ago they were making time. Rolling. He knelt and watched the wrecker man work. He'd watched tows before, broken-down cars or repossessions. But never like this, peering up under the fender and counting seconds. The grips and chains came off the left wheel, and the guy shimmied over to work the right.

'Start it up,' East barked to Walter.

'It *is* started,' Walter replied over the noise. A third security man arrived, triplet to the other two.

East tasted bile, spun around the back of the van, and climbed in shotgun. Michael and Ty huddled wide-eyed in the back. 'You gotta wait for him,' he instructed Walter, 'but when he comes up, get us the fuck out.'

They listened to the sounds, the wrestling going on below. Then the tow driver's legs flailed out and spun, and he was lifting himself upright. He uttered something inaudible, his mouth wet again with blood. What was it? Did it matter? Walter was already crawling the van back. Two more bow ties came bursting out the golden doors. Walter was clear: he found Drive, and swung the van out around the big wrecker.

'Steady,' East urged. The tow guy stood on the now-empty flatbed, cursing them. 'Don't give them a reason.'

'They *got* a motherfuckin reason,' moaned Walter. 'They got one.'

'Just be cool,' East said. 'Just get us out of here.'

Walter muttered and steered. East glanced back at the security crew spreading out across the pavement where they'd been. 'They're deciding do they want a piece of us.'

'Got our plates. Got our pictures. Everything,' mourned Walter.

'Drive, man,' East said wearily. To nobody in particular he added, 'Who was the girl?'

'What girl?'

'The girl that kept screaming.'

'I don't know,' Michael Wilson put in. 'I didn't hear no girl.'

'There was a girl,' Walter sighed. 'But that ain't had nothing to do with us.'

Past the buses, toward the street, the white blaze where each light now seemed aimed straight at them. A sign by the curb read: PLAY IT AGAIN, SAM!

The shining monuments slid away, but all the boys were watching was the road behind them. Walter ran yellows to get them back on the interstate. Cars and trucks flashed by on the left, roaring;

Walter was too tense to speak. After three miles he took them off at an exit, picked out a gas station, and stopped at the pump. He closed his eyes for a long minute.

At last East remarked politely, 'I'm beginning to feel you. About the cameras.'

'Got them here too,' sighed Walter. 'Why we need to keep from doing stupid shit.'

East turned and shot a look at Michael Wilson. Michael saw East glaring and paused. 'Mighty weird casino back there,' he began.

'You shut the fuck up.'

Walter bit his lips, looked sideways.

'Don't freak out, Easy,' Michael Wilson said.

'Shit,' East said. 'Lucky we ain't facedown on a police car right now. You can't even *park* without fucking up.'

Meticulously Michael Wilson wiped something from his brow. 'What do you want?' he said. 'You want a little note, I'm sorry? I'm a get you flowers? *I'm sorry.* But don't say you didn't want to go in too.'

'I didn't want to go in.'

'But you went.' Michael Wilson opened the door and climbed out. He dabbed at his hairline. 'This is when I go pay for things. Who's pumping?'

East cursed. He climbed out and set the nozzle in, then stood waiting for the pump to click on. Just listening, the night sky starless, smeared pale by lights, by his pique. Unacceptable. He blamed Walter almost as much as Michael. But he was too mad to even begin with it.

At last the pump beeped and the orange numerals zeroed out. He began running the tank full of regular and banged on Walter's window. It rolled down.

'We got problems with that one.'

Walter moaned, ghost-faced. 'He's right, man. We all did go in.'

'You first,' East insisted. 'None of us would have gone if you didn't.'

'If I didn't,' Walter said, 'we'd still be there. Outside, waiting. Wondering was he gonna stop before all the money was gone. You think he was just gonna come back out in five minutes?'

East slid dead bug crisps around with his feet. 'All right. What happened outside, then? The tow guy?'

Walter's face pinched shut. He shook his head.

'You best tell me. I need to know.'

The pump kicked off, and East hung up the nozzle. Inside the bright station he saw Michael Wilson waiting in line, his head bobbing to a song inside it.

Walter squeezed himself out of the van. He glanced at East and stepped to the other side of the pump, furtively. East glanced back at the van where Ty was and followed Walter.

'It said *No Parking*. Right? We didn't see it. When I walked back out, the van was already hooked up. They probably keep that truck in the lot all the time. So. The law says you can't tow when somebody's in it.'

'Don't give me law. This ain't California.'

'It ain't just California.'

'Stop with the truck,' East sighed. 'What happened with the guy?'

'So I'm yelling at the guy,' Walter continued, 'telling him stop. Then whoop, here comes your brother.'

Walter swung his arm once.

'What'd he do? Hit him?' East scoffed. 'Boy weighs a hundred pounds.'

'Hit him with a gun,' Walter whispered. 'That's what I believe.'

East frowned. 'But Johnny searched him. He's clean. You saw.'

'I know,' said Walter. 'Whatever it was, that guy changed his mind quick. And security, standing back watching like they did – explain that.'

East looked up and tried to swallow the bad taste in his mouth. Above them, a big plastic dinosaur spun on a wire. Cars rushed by out on the highway, and East had to keep himself from staring down each one. Things moving. At first, the ride had felt like getting out, like being set free. Into nothing. But since Vegas, this felt like being stuck back in it. Like every headlight that rolled past was pointed at him.

'That boy is trouble,' Walter said, looking away into nowhere.

'Which one?'

'Your brother.'

East's back went up in spite of himself. 'My brother is on the job. College boy is the problem.'

'You talk like you're sure,' said Walter, 'but you best *be* sure.'

East was not sure. What East didn't know about his brother would fill the van. You heard stories. Things he'd done, scenes he'd been on, that he could get in anywhere, was too little to catch, too young for the police to bother with. Only stories, and nobody, least of all Ty, would say what was true.

Gloomily East glanced at the closed, smoky window where Ty lay listening to them talk. Or not. Then across the pavement came Michael Wilson, white shirt glowing, white teeth grinning, paid up and ready, his hands clean.

6

THEN IT WAS LATE and dark, the scenery switched off, somewhere in the flat, empty Nevada that lay past Las Vegas. 'So this the Wild West, huh?' Michael Wilson said. 'Like, if the sun was up, they'd be riding horses and shit.'

Walter rode beside Michael Wilson, who drove, and Ty slept, his video game switched off, across the back bench of the van. East sat tired and worried on his middle seat, crouched forward, hands uselessly figuring atop his knees, listening to the two boys in front telling lies.

'One time when I was at UCLA, man,' Michael Wilson remarked, 'we had a horse.'

Walter said, 'Horses don't like black people.'

'Why don't horses like black people?'

'Why you think?' Walter said. 'Who owns them?'

'But black dudes train horses. That one horse, what's his name, in the movie. Secretariat. Old nigger trained that horse.'

'Train him to what?'

'He was a racehorse, man.'

'Huh. He any good?'

'He won the Kentucky Derby.'

'*Course* he did,' said Walter. 'All right, that's one.'

'Anyways,' said Michael Wilson. 'This horse liked me fine. He was a stolen horse.'

'What do you mean, a stolen horse?'

'Some dude stole the horse,' said Michael Wilson. 'And he kept it on campus. The horse grazed the yard and shit on the sidewalk. Everybody giving it ice cream and pizza all the time.'

'Horses don't eat ice cream.'

'This one did,' Michael Wilson said.

'Could you ride the horse?'

'Wasn't that kind of horse.'

'What kind of horse was it?'

'I don't know what kind of horse it was, fat boy. Just stayed put and made a mess.'

'What's interesting about that?'

Michael Wilson exploded. 'You ain't supposed to have no horse in college, man. Simple.'

'Why not?'

'Because you ain't. You got to follow the rules, or they kick you out.'

'Why they kick you out?'

'They didn't,' said Michael Wilson. 'I left.'

'You told Diamonds you got kicked out. I heard you.'

'Oh, you were there for that?' Michael Wilson laughed. 'Don't nobody tell Diamonds the truth, man.'

'Who is Diamonds?' East put in.

'Eastside runner,' singsonged Michael. 'Sorry-ass Covina wannabe with one gun and a Nissan, trying to muscle in. Didn't know what he was doing. Fin involved him in a little business for about three weeks.'

'Why they call him Diamonds?'

Walter said, 'I think that's cause it's his name.'

'Diamonds Wooten.' Michael Wilson nodded. 'Nice name. Back in Covina now.'

'I don't like horses,' Walter said. 'They big and they bite and they mess you up. You like horses, East?'

'I never seen a horse,' East said, 'except with a cop on it.'

'You a professional street nigger, East. I like you,' Michael Wilson said. He laughed delightedly at himself.

Walter told a story about the U who'd walked into his house one day a few years ago with a Food 4 Less bag with two rattlesnakes in it, trying to scare his way into a fix. It might have worked, except the rattlesnakes went into a hole in the wall, and when the word spread, nobody wanted to use that house till Walter announced he'd gotten them out – though he never had. The snakes might still be in there.

Michael Wilson told about the research he'd done for Fin at UCLA. Michael Wilson said Fin wanted to know how much weed he could run at UCLA, thinking the college kids had to be underserved. What Michael Wilson found out was that there was more weed at UCLA than you could keep track of. More supply, more lines you never saw on the street, varieties, hybrids, designer weed, organic weed, heirloom weed, weed that was vanilla and weed that was chocolate, weed cut up this way and that, kindergarten weed all the way to cop grade. Selling for nothing. Giving it away. What happened rather than Fin trying to move in, said Michael Wilson, is that Fin started bringing weed out. UCLA was like Fin's docks. What UCLA did not have was cocaine. They didn't have it, didn't know how to get it, didn't know how much to pay for it. So that was a great couple of years, said Michael Wilson.

Walter said he thought Michael Wilson went to college one

year. Michael Wilson said that for one year at college he studied; the second year was business.

Michael told about the day when he was sixteen and started working for Fin: his first job was secret shopper, just walking around buying drugs off everyone to see were they doing it right, were they straight, did they treat him right, what did they charge? Every hit he bought, he had to report. At the end of the day he had so much cocaine on him, he'd have gone inside, ten years mandatory, if he'd been hooked. His first day.

A motorcycle flashed by them in the left lane, doing ninety, a hundred, maybe more, a chainsaw roar in the dark. They watched the single red light shrink in the darkness.

'Never catch that,' Michael Wilson said with conviction. 'Those dudes got it made. Cops don't even try.'

Then Michael Wilson asked East what it had been like, who was on his crew again, how long had he been on, when his house got policed. East stirred. Maybe he'd been dozing. His sleep was messed up.

'How was that, when it all came down?' asked Michael Wilson. And Walter, yawning, echoed, 'Yeah, how was that?'

East didn't answer. It had been a weird day, all day a weird feeling, the fire trucks lost on the street, the old guy lying down to sleep in the backyard. For the first time he remembered that guy, the one who said he owned the house. For the first time since they'd pulled out of Los Angeles, he thought about his crew, thought about the police coming down.

He wished he'd gotten in touch with them, Dap and Needle, the ends who hadn't called in when the police cars had gone by them. He wished he'd found out why.

When he'd run, it had felt like he'd ditched everything. He'd been ready to accept whatever came – whatever Fin or one of his guns dished out. He was no different than the U's scrambling out, on a fix or wishing they were, trying not to get caught. From the castle of their getting some into the cold should-have-known.

In the darkness inside the van he remembered the whole yard – the porch, the walk, the beaten grass the color of dirt. The fingers of morning light spilling onto the street, the houses across. The helicopter and fire trucks.

And the girl who'd been shot there. He wasn't ready to think about that.

Walter snored once loudly and jerked. 'Damn,' he wheezed. 'Fell asleep.'

'You can move back,' East offered. 'I'll ride up front.'

Michael Wilson stopped along the highway so Walter could maneuver out and climb back in. East tried to make out Walter's face as they traded places. But the night was unreasonably black.

He buckled in as Michael set the van rolling. It was just them and the white lines, one car fading away a mile ahead, a pair of red eyes.

' *"My crew is mad deep, I hope you niggas sleep",'* recited Michael Wilson.

'Oh, now you gonna rap for us?' East said. He lowered his seat belt and brought the seat forward a notch. 'So, at the casino, man.'

He watched in the dashboard lights as Michael Wilson reset his lips, then ducked low under the visor to read the road sign. 'Make sure I get east on I-70, man.'

East set his feet. Ignore the ignoring. 'What was that, man? That mad-dog shit?'

Michael just rode his hands up on the wheel and bit his lips again. East stopped staring at him after a while, watched the reflectors pass instead. Little blots of light. A million of them already. His eyes were tired.

'Mad-dog shit?' Michael Wilson said at last. 'You make that up last night standing yard in The Boxes?'

Now East stayed quiet. He'd cast his line.

'Listen,' Michael Wilson came up with eventually. 'You ain't gonna hear it. But when I stopped, I did it for you.'

East snorted. 'For me.'

'For y'all. All of us. All right? It didn't work out. But I was trying, you know, to fire y'all up. I thought you'd *like* it. I thought we might win or lose, man, but go in and look, play a bit. Come out as a team.' Michael Wilson muttered as if the world were lined up against him. 'Every good coach don't win every game.'

'You ain't a coach is why.'

'East, honey,' Michael Wilson said. 'You want to fuck with me? Do it straight. Not sideways.'

'All right, then,' said East. He took a pleasure in letting it out. Let everyone wake up. 'You *ain't* a coach. This ain't a team. This is a job. Keep on the job.'

Michael Wilson nodded. 'You done? Is that all?'

'If you can. If you can keep on the job,' he taunted.

'You all, "The boy stood on the burning deck."'

'Well, I don't know what that is,' East sniffed.

'I know you don't, my brother,' said Michael Wilson. 'I know. It's okay. Be a pal. Don't let me miss east I-70.'

East let it rest. He didn't trust Michael Wilson.

'I went skiing up here one time,' Michael said. 'I went on this, like, black-diamond motherfucker. Dudes barreling past me on snowboards, I thought I was gonna die. I figured, okay, watch out for them two motherfuckers, then here comes another –'

'There it is.' The sign. The wide green banner across the road. They were already under it. 'Go that way, man.'

Neither of them had been watching.

'You sure?'

'East I-70. Go right.'

'Whoa, whoa, whoa, whoa!' Michael Wilson hollered, checking

his flank and then banking the van right, sharp but smooth, across lines and the apron strewn with gravel bits. 'Whoa. Thanks. See? We gonna help each other out!'

If I'd never said, East wondered, *what would happen? Where would we be going to?* Slowly the compass on the ceiling returned to *E.*

Michael went straight back to the story: 'Anyway, these dudes on snowboards, they be zipping in there. And I think, and I'm, like, man, these dudes *gotta* be getting high.'

'You skiing?'

'Yeah. So I –'

'No,' said East. 'I mean, what? Skiing? You, man.'

'Went up with my dad,' said Michael insouciantly. 'He had business.'

'Huh.' A dad. So that was another thing Michael Wilson had. 'What he do?'

'Salesman. Pharmaceuticals. He sells medicine.'

'Yeah? Why you do this, then? Why don't you do that?'

'He don't like his job.'

'Yeah,' East said.

'So I figure,' Michael Wilson explained, 'you could sell a lot up here. Same kind of deal like UCLA. But you got to find the right people. Local.'

'So Fin lets you check things out,' East said. 'On the ground.'

'Right,' said Michael Wilson. 'Market research, you call it. But the mountains – not for us, E. You can't be standing yard up here. It's different. You're alone. Black boys can't hide in the snow.' He laughed at himself.

He rattled on. It didn't matter. Michael Wilson didn't hear him not answering. Right from the top East had known why Michael Wilson was along: to talk. To front them through. To bore any cop with his shiny record and UCLA smile.

But there was a problem. Michael Wilson was a fool. A rich boy and a gambler. Maybe that was all. You could bring worse problems. And if Fin had picked him, then Fin knew already what he was. What Michael *did*, that was East's to handle. But carefully. Because Michael *was* a pretty face, a storyteller; because Michael did pull Walter along. Even Ty. Even his brother, the real mad dog. He wasn't following East. He was following the tall boy with the year of college and the wad of cash out of the van.

East did not have those things, so he was pinned down. For now. He breathed and watched the dark go past, the cold, relaxing nothing. White lines measuring it. There would be so much time just like this, waiting.

The road dipped, into a valley where no lights showed. Space like you never saw except in commercials. Strange dark land without people in it, miles of space between. For as long as he remembered, his business had been keeping people at arm's length. Keep the U's quiet and orderly, moving on. Keep his crew watchful, not too familiar. Keep people who didn't have business from even passing the yard. Keep his mother from worrying.

Standing yard.

Out here, everything kept at a distance. You could go an hour on the freeway without seeing a person walking, standing. One red ghost eye of a car a mile up. Maybe the same car. Maybe different. You'd never know.

He reached back onto the floor for the thin red first-aid blanket and doubled it up between his head and the window. After a minute he closed his eyes. But they would not obey; his lids would not soften. Every rise, every little tick in the inertia: they were hard. He checked Michael, checked the road ahead, the black nothing in the side mirror.

They were to trust each other, Fin had said. But East trusted nothing.

East stirred. Michael Wilson was slowing the van – a long parking lot, lights hung high, angled spaces. He pulled in and killed the engine.

'Gotta sleep,' he murmured.

East sat up. Weird, sculpted land with no trees. Signs everywhere. 'What is this place?'

'Rest stop, dummy.' Michael Wilson breathed, his eyes shutting. 'I miss my motherfucking phone.'

East flexed his legs. He looked around outside. Nothing moving. Walter and Ty lay sleeping in back, and Michael was passing out against the window.

East took Michael's keys from the ignition and stepped out. The pavement seemed to clutch at him like pond mud. A whole day riding, his legs and ass had gone numb.

Half a dozen cars and trucks slumbered. A back lot over the rise showed the lights of big trucks, their box tops white under the high lights. At his feet, sprinklers fed a few planters, bright yellow flowers alert in the night. A pair of small buildings. Fiercely he looked around for whatever.

Restrooms. Cautiously he approached. THIS FACILITY BUILT AND MAINTAINED BY THE STATE OF UTAH. Utah, then. He pissed sleepily into a urinal in Utah. Green light. Moths stumbled drunkenly around the walls. The strange white soap gobbed automatically onto his hands when he reached. A man came in and looked at him with interest. He ducked his head and left.

The second building had Coke machines. East bought two cans. A dollar apiece. A clock said two-something in the morning.

Near the van, atop the weedy rise, sat a picnic table with a view of everything: front lot, back lot, all there was. East sat and drank. The van was dusty. He watched a truck, tipped with light like a fantastic ship, fly past.

There were no trees.

When he awoke with a start, the can was tipped over, dry to the touch. Grainy light. Flat clouds smudged the eastern horizon where the light was beginning. He cursed himself for falling asleep in the open.

Some of the parked cars had changed. A man combing his hair outside a Maxima was the same man who'd eyed him a few hours earlier. One of those. Dark birds hung like kites.

East descended the slope to the van, tapped Michael Wilson, and thumbed him over. Michael nodded, ashen, and squirmed across to the other seat. As soon as he'd fastened his belt, he was asleep again. East split open the warm can of Coke. He shortened the seat up and cranked the mirrors down.

Driving. He'd driven a few times for Fin, or dropped someone off, someone too gone to drive. He knew how.

On the other hand, he'd never been north of forty miles an hour. For some miles he ran slowly, feeling the van track on the road, letting traffic funnel past. More cars now than in the evening. He could see them.

Then he picked it up to seventy-five.

The scene of the night before troubled East still: the flashing light under the canopy, the blood on the pavement, the chance that Ty was carrying a gun out here where they were supposed to run clean. And before that: the four of them bolting the van, leaving the job behind for – for what? *Just a taste.* It was all on camera – they'd made trouble. Maybe running down the road would let them leave it behind.

Only option he had.

The land changed – orange sky, light, the white of the flats giving rise to orange stone, crumpled and ridged, and dirt. The windshield filled with sunrise working its way up to blue.

He could glimpse the people in cars, the pickup-and-toolbox men, hidden behind wraparounds, heading to some job. The sleeping families, drivers with their coffee cups. The lone rangers, a man or a woman, sometimes intent on the road ahead, sometimes on the phone yammering. White people. Maybe some of them outrunning something too.

A half hour, an hour maybe, before everyone would wake up. That much alone, that much peace. The tires hummed, and he felt what Johnny had said about the van now: sorry-looking, yeah, but solid. He liked being up high, liked the firm seat. He could see the land, the flash movements in the brush, an animal, too fast to spot. Dog, maybe, or coyote. They had coyotes in LA, but they were skulking creatures, big rats. They ran down alleys and stayed in shadows, and before long somebody would shoot them dead. No law against doing it. Just another gunshot in the night.

When the other boys stirred and began cursing, East was sad. They rolled their limbs, spewed their night breath. They would be back with him soon. A chimneyed orange mountain loomed beside him, and East studied it closely as he passed it, its worn layers, saying goodbye. A secret. The last thing that was his alone.

Bright morning. East stopped at a shiny new gas station, TV screens humming at the pump. All the boys jumped out: East pumped the gas in the dry air. Los Angeles had dry air, but it smelled like something – always something. The air here smelled like nothing, or nothing that had a name.

Inside the store loomed hanging race cars and inflatable superheroes. A massive grill counter stretched across the back: no one there, yet people were taking food from a window. Walter studied it: you touched a screen till you had pointed out everything you wanted. Every item on every shelf had a price lit up in LEDs. Every little thing made a noise.

'This joint is fucking cool,' said Ty.

Finished pumping, East headed for the bathroom and its cherry-cake smell. Some things never changed. A white boy pulled up at the next urinal. Hat on backwards.

'Sup, homes,' he said.

East raised his eyebrows. This boy right up on him.

'Sup,' he pronounced ironically.

The white boy finger-stabbed. 'Manny Ramirez. My man.' East wasn't sure. He tightened his eyes, rushed his hands below a faucet, then rushed out. What was it with some people?

This was white boy's turf – he recognized that.

Outside the bathroom, Michael Wilson stood in line. Prepaid with twenties, so he had to wait for change every time – the price of doing business in cash. Blankly he stared, just a customer, and East watched him from behind. The cashier was an older lady with a huge amber stone caught in a fold of her throat.

'Seven dollars and thirty cents from sixty, sir,' she said.

'Ma'am, you got scratch-offs?'

'There's no lottery in Utah, sir.' The same note in her voice. Michael Wilson bobbed his head agreeably, and East let him walk away. What was it? Buying lottery tickets. Stealing a little. How much?

What did Michael Wilson expect to do if he won?

Something hit him on the shoulder. It was the same bathroom white boy on his way back out. 'Be cool, bro,' he said, jabbing his finger. 'Fly's open.'

East looked down. Bro was right.

Just ten minutes here, but his morning calm was plucked. The dark string inside blurred and buzzed. He followed Michael to the van, every bit of air a puzzle, every person a future event. He climbed into the back and slid the door shut.

'Awesome station, man,' said Walter, a fragrant family box of chicken biscuits steaming up his lap. 'They all need to be like that.'

East buckled his belt. 'Who is Manny Ramirez?'

Both boys in the front let go a snort.

'Ninety-nine, Easy,' said Michael Wilson.

'You ever check your shirt?'

East looked down. *Dodgers*. 'What?'

'On the back. His name is on the back of your shirt, man.'

'Yard boy don't get out much,' Michael Wilson crowed.

After an hour, they crossed into Colorado. East felt the ground rising. He rode up front as Walter drove, Michael dozing, soft-eyed, in the middle. The hot food had upset East's stomach.

Mountains stood before them, above them, like in LA. But in The Boxes, the mountains were only a thing, like a wall or a tree: a sun-baked ridge above the valley full of everything. Here the ground was nearly empty of buildings and the mountains were like people, huddled figures, blue and gray and white, so high.

They were unmoving stone, but they tore East's eyes from the boys in the van and the unidentifiable people motoring up the same road. East gave up watching the people so much. They didn't stare back as much as they had in Utah. The people seemed younger, fitter. Some gazed at the mountains too. Some rode hollow-eyed. Families with kids drowned in their movie players; mountain boys with their racks of bikes and skis and packs; thin, straight-haired white women in their Subarus. They didn't stare back. Unsurprised by him.

Only one black man they saw, driving a moving truck.

Come noon they bought a tank of gas and two pizzas at an exit called Glenwood Springs. A bathroom stop, a round of sodas, little wooden buffalo roaming the counter near the gray cash register. Boxes so hot they singed East's fingers; they steamed on the van's floor till the windows ran wet.

They drove on until a sign announced a turnoff: SCENIC OVERLOOK. 'Let's hit that,' Walter said. 'We can eat there.'

'Oh, *we*?' laughed Michael Wilson, but Walter took it well. The view, framed between two immense, square boulders, revealed just how far up they'd come. A gorge opened below, green, vertiginous. Two little kids from the gigantic white Navigator next to them hollered, 'Wow! Wow!' East started, expecting them to be staring at him.

But they were just teetering on the edge, gaping down into the gorge below.

He slid out of the van. Again he had to find his legs, find his stance. Behind the handrail the ground was slippery pebbles. He approached the edge and looked down gingerly.

It took a moment for East's eyes to read the scene. He could see the valley's depth, feel the real wind dipping down it. But he could not convince himself that it was real. Space both vast and unattainable, opening up between the blue walls of stone. The air below was cold, he could feel it, a reservoir, and he could sense something about the chasm, all the time piled up there. Close to forever. More time than he had in a hundred lives like his.

Birds wheeled in midair, far below.

'Mommy, Daddy!' the kids cheered again. 'Look! It's amazing!' East stood there too, the cold air streaming up his face, full of the smell of snow and stone.

For hours they worked in and out through the passes: town-size shadows sliding over the mountainsides, dark mossy valleys, clouds on the road that blinded their way. How blank it had looked on the map, this space, this state. How different to have to cross it. The road sank in and swelled out, like intestines. East asked for a turn at the wheel, but his stomach made him give it up right away. Sitting shotgun, next to the guardrail, was worse.

Their next stop was so that he could throw up. He was awake, dripping sweat; he had been dreaming of a terrible yellow goldfish. 'Stop the van,' he gasped.

Michael Wilson skidded off along the guardrail.

East fell out, a first taste like cement; then his backbone arched and his lunch rained over the rail.

Pizza, Coke, the rest. *Jesus.* He looked away, at the miles between him and the next solid ground. Same birds, flecks beneath him. The air smelled wet, like the rock.

He felt better – for a moment, he knew. But he breathed in wetly, the air of that moment.

'Who's next?' Michael Wilson said. Nobody in the van was even laughing.

'Never been up in the mountains before, huh, Easy?'

'I don't know,' East grunted. 'It's different than I thought.'

'Never been nowhere, huh?'

It wasn't in him to argue.

Stickers covering the Jeeps and Subarus: THE EARTH DOES NOT BELONG TO US, WE BELONG TO THE EARTH. IT'S NOT A CHOICE, IT'S A LIFE. CRISTO SALVA. Bicycles on the back, in the bed, on the roof, wherever they could strap on. '*Crazy* motherfuckers riding bicycles up here,' said Walter. 'You know there's no air? Go out and see if you can run a hundred yards.'

'*You* can't run no hundred yards,' said Michael Wilson, '*any*where.'

Somewhere in the afternoon they topped out finally and started coasting downhill toward the city of Denver. East eyed the silver Colorado State Trooper cars, Chargers and Expeditions and the long, flat Fords. They scattered everywhere on the downhill, working the speeders like sharks tracking prey. Once a trooper dogged their back bumper for miles. 'I'm going fifty-five, motherfucker,' Michael Wilson protested. 'Fifty-five minus two.'

The trooper hit the lights, jumped out from behind them, and bit on a Jeep. Everyone started breathing again.

Ty's gun, thought East. *Ty's gun, Ty's gun, Ty's gun.*

The van knifed past the city, the buildings low and shiny and suddenly too colorful below the cold blue sky long-grained with clouds. As they merged from one highway onto another, East turned back to look. The mountains stood in line behind them, still close but collapsed now, pressed together. No hint of what they were, what they held. Just another line, a little brighter and sharper than the brown line of home.

And they could see what was coming. Flatland, an endless sea of it.

'Someone else drive,' said Michael Wilson. 'I'm tired of seeing shit.'

Walter took the wheel. Michael reclined in the shotgun seat, rubbing his face with a pair of fingers. East sat back on the middle bench and watched him fuss and prod. 'You learned that where? Tokyo Spa?'

'East, baby, no,' Michael said. 'I learned this from your mother.'

East smiled and watched the road, the eastbound trucks. After a while he shut his eyes too. Let himself fall off to sleep.

Except for the chirping. He peeked around at Ty. Ty did not look back. The muscles in his fingers twitched around the gray plastic tablet of his game. Something with aliens and bombs. Ty could lie around playing forever.

'Don't that thing run out of batteries?' East protested at last. Ty's eyes zeroed in. 'Run out all the time,' he murmured. 'But I don't.'

'You go see your mother?'

'No,' snorted Ty. 'Did you?'

'Yes. I took her some money,' said East. 'Night before we left.'

'Well,' said Ty, more quietly, 'ain't you nice.'

East said, matching Ty's quiet, 'Somebody said you might have a gun on you.'

His brother's eyes ticked up and down, following something minuscule along an inch-long track. Then at last the game flashed in his face, and he relaxed.

'That's my business.'

'You know you got no need to be holding,' East pressed. 'Fin said stay clean till we get the guns.'

'*Fin* said.'

'I ain't trying to take it. But you should let me know.'

Ty dialed madly with his thumbs, and his game trilled. 'Shit be crazy, ain't it?' he murmured.

Shit be crazy. Between the two of them, it was a refrain, an old one. It meant nothing and everything at the same time, unreadable and obvious. Like a glance, like a wave in the street. It stood in lieu of ever being in their mother's house at the same time or knowing where the other slept. It stood in lieu of East having the slightest control over his little brother, or of his owning up to losing Ty. For Ty belonged to nobody now, an unknowable child, indolent as bees in autumn, until he rose up and moved in a spasm of energy and force.

Where Ty had come from, where Ty was now: these things East knew. What had made Ty what he'd become: that was the unseeable, the midair coil the whip made between handle and crack. That was anybody's guess.

Big brother taking the little, they called it babysitting. But it was not that. Nothing like it.

Deep in his game, Ty smiled. His thumbs drummed out a sprint. Then he relaxed his gaze. 'You made me lose,' he said.

7

EAST LIKED DRIVING HERE – the flat, unruffled fields with no one in sight, blind stubble mown down into splinters, maybe a tractor, maybe an irrigation rig like a long line of silver stitches across the fabric of earth. The flatness. There was more in the flatness than he'd expected. The van's shadow lay long, and the fields traded colors. The boys slept in intervals or complained. Riding in a car for more than a few hours, he thought, was like suspended animation – somewhere under the layers of frost, your heart beat. To the left, a thunderstorm hovered, prowling its own road.

They crossed under the front end of a line of storms, everything wet and alight in the slanting sun, and then they were out the other side but in the cloud's dark. The tank was low again, and East angled in for gas and stepped out. Little park of pumps under long white storm shelters and a steak-and-eggs place with a shop under a bright yellow plastic roof. Pickup trucks moved in the low, narrow roads on either side and climbed onto the highway, high and chromed or capped and rattling or stuffed with tools or crops or white bags of dirt. Men and women in their windows looked at him, eyed him with interest.

'You boys the only niggers they ever seen in real life,' drawled Michael Wilson, 'except Kobe.'

'That was Colorado,' said Walter. 'We're in Nebraska now.'

'Don't tell me Kobe ain't got some girls in Nebraska too.'

East waited while Michael Wilson paid. Then he filled the tank and parked the van. Ty was sleeping, a reptile: East locked the doors around him and went in to sit in a bathroom stall. The farther east they got, the dirtier the toilets. Like every toilet in the country had been cleaned the moment they left LA and none of them since.

East shook his head. Sleepless. The person in the next stall wore his music through headphones and moaned along under his breath. Straining, suffering, only one word audible, at the end of the lines: *You. You.* He smelled like rotten eggs, like rot inside, and then he was gone. East grimaced and stopped breathing. Trying to press his gut out like a toothpaste tube. His thinking was frayed, sleepless: he had to think straight. They were close to getting there. He had to make sure everyone slept tonight. And walked around, cleaned out their heads.

He zipped up and left, no lighter.

Outside, the storm was about to catch them. It rose flat-faced, a gray curtain, sweeping loose trash along. Walter had taken the wheel and was idling at the curb. East swung himself up and in on the shotgun side. Then he noticed the smell. Like the mall, the kiosks where Arab girls tried to spray you: *Sample, sample? You like it.* That fruit-sweet smell.

The second thing he noticed was the shoe. A golden shoe, like a wedge of foil, with a girl's foot in it. It hovered brightly between the front seats.

The rest of the girl sat in the center of the van. Michael Wilson was beside her, all sideways and charming. In the back, Ty sat straight in his seat like an exclamation point. For once aroused but not sure what to do. Walter, steering the van away, was trying not to even look.

She was white. Sixteen, seventeen, red hair in curls and loop-the-loops. Bravely she looked at East, or curiously, as if she were nervous. But she was used to courage seeing her through.

No one else was saying anything, so East said it: 'Girl, who the fuck are you?'

Michael Wilson made a crackling with his tongue. 'E, this is Maggie. She just might ride for a while, over to Omaha. We can drop her off at the airport.'

East said, 'No. She ain't.'

Michael let out a grin and a sigh.

'E,' he began. 'This girl needs help. She was just lost up in this rest stop.' He had a hand snaked across the girl's belt, which, East saw, matched the golden shoes. 'Wasn't nobody going her way. But we *are* going her way. Right?'

The girl put her hand down on Michael Wilson's black track pants. Put it right on his dick.

A cold wave rolled up East's spine. The yellow-outlined parking space in Vegas. He made dead eyes at the girl.

'No she ain't. *Stop*, man.' He whacked Walter. 'Drive back in there. Back where you were.' Walter exhaled a shaky breath and swung the van back around the apron.

The girl kept her hand on Michael Wilson, and he rolled underneath it.

'E,' Michael Wilson drawled. 'Girl needs a ride. That's factual. Maybe something in it for all of us. Something in it for me, I *know*. So why don't we drive now so I don't have to fuck you up.' The girl blushed uneasily and Michael laughed his little, trailing laugh. Something had happened to his face. His mouth crooked open

103

as if dangling an invisible cigar. 'Drive, Walt,' Michael Wilson added. 'Don't listen to this boy.'

Walter rubbed his cheek, wasn't sure. 'Right there,' East insisted. He pointed out a space. 'Right by the door.'

'East, I'm gonna hurt you, man,' Michael Wilson warned.

East dimmed his eyes, stared a cold hole through the girl. Her green eyes bright, but she stared back; she was used to sizing people up. For an instant he was looking at the black girl outside the house, the Jackson girl. The same: defiant. And curious.

'Get out, girl,' East said. 'It's nothing good for you here.'

She did a little hitch with her lips, a smile. Then she leaned forward, her hair swinging like a fragrant bough. Her fingers climbed his left hip.

East uttered a strangled cry and slapped her hand, like a snake lunging. The girl drew her fingers back. He tried to go dead-faced again, but he was shaking.

'I'm sorry,' said the girl, Maggie. Her voice was higher than East had imagined. 'Maybe I shouldn't –'

'Aw, Maggie,' Michael Wilson begged. 'This boy, this little boy – Maggie, don't be listening.'

He put his hands on her and she squirmed. 'I better go.'

East reset himself. He knew: the way she glanced back at the station. Like now it held things she'd forgotten: people, stuffed animals. She longed for it. Her nerve had fled.

'Maggie, aw,' moaned Michael Wilson, sticky with desire.

Girls had sense. You could back them down. Girls saw bluster, knew its purpose. Boys, they just flew into the air over nothing, rose up with their dicks all hard, and then people got killed. Like at the house.

Michael Wilson was going to fly up now. Had to.

He pled with her first, grabbed at her. 'But I *can't*,' she said, and then the gold shoes were on the pavement. The glass door –

WELCOME, THESE CARDS ACCEPTED HERE – opened for her.

Michael Wilson made a little click in his mouth. 'Damn,' he said. 'There she goes.'

He clenched the hand he'd been grabbing at Maggie with and fired it at East's head.

East ducked and sheltered down. 'Drive,' he muttered, and Walter did. Michael rose up under the low blue ceiling, but he couldn't throw a right, not with East balled down in the shotgun seat. Between the seats, he came with two lefts, the second hard enough to light East's eyes with salt.

'Go!' East gasped. 'Drive!'

The sliding door rattled open, cool air rushing in. Again East ducked and the turn around the lot rocked Michael Wilson. He recovered and swung again, and East deflected it – another hard turn made Michael brace.

Walter sped the van up the ramp hard, as if he could stop this fight with gas. 'Careful, Mike,' he complained. 'You gonna make me crash.'

'Pull off, then,' Michael steamed. 'Because I'm gonna whup this bitch.' He sat back, fists clenched. 'Fuck you up,' he promised East.

As soon as an EXIT 1 MILE sign came up, Walter hit the turn signal. East touched his face. His blood was in his ears and head now, the black string yawning, almost audible. He knew he had to play his cards now.

'What's up with you, Walt?' he appealed. 'You just, "Cool, we with this girl now"?'

Walter whined something indistinct. Hunkered down with his steering wheel. Behind him Michael Wilson sat and laughed, stretching his shoulders, limbering.

East turned on him. 'Oh, now you're a muscleman. Just do your job.'

In a high, public voice Michael Wilson declaimed: 'Easy. I know where you're at. You just a little street faggot, ain't ever seen a girl. But I *have*. That girl was pussy for *everyone*.'

Trying to line the boys up.

Walter braked the van down from eighty, seventy, fifty-five. The exit was a dead one, disused fields, one cracked concrete lot where someone had built once to make money. Across the highway, one lone gas station still hoisted its sign.

Nobody in sight. Here is where it was going to happen.

'Boy, you do not do to fuck with me,' Michael Wilson boomed, 'and now you will know.'

Walter put the van in Park, and East just held on. *This is it,* he thought. Didn't know when it would come, but he knew that it would.

If all there was was a fistfight, he was going to get beat. Maybe worse than beat. But if there was a vote, maybe he'd win it. East had Walter. Walter had wanted that girl, but he'd dropped her off too. Walter wanted what was right. Maybe he would help.

Ty? East didn't know what he had.

Michael Wilson was getting up. East hollered, 'Everybody out!' and jumped out first. Sweating already.

He made two fists, weighed them. His arms had never seemed skinnier.

This is it.

Then Michael Wilson was rushing across the cracked pavement. They said that sometimes when you got your ass kicked, your mind sold out your body, stopped taking it personally, only crept back when the whupping was done. East's mind went nowhere. Calculating. Michael Wilson wasn't gonna kill him, not over this girl. But what did a fool do when he'd shown himself? He built up. He went pro on it. Became the hardest fool he could.

Michael Wilson stopped then, to strip off his meshy white

Dodgers shirt and drape it on the van's side mirror. Gym muscles
down his belly like puppies in a litter. The muscles were what
broke the bottle of fear inside East.

'Listen, man,' he pleaded. 'I'll spell it out for you.'

'Shut up,' said Michael Wilson. 'Should have done this a
thousand miles ago.' Some Chinese tattoo in the meat of his arm.
He locked his fist and drove.

East ducked. But Michael was quick. He got an arm around and
slugged East's kidneys: East felt that bitter spurt inside. 'Come on,
Easy,' Michael grunted, wrapping East with his long arms. East
grappled for footing. Stay up, you had to: the pavement was not
your friend.

Michael Wilson tried harder. He wrenched sideways, lifted East
around the ribs, trying to slam him. East spread his feet wide to
catch himself. Michael sucked air, swore, and spun again. Again
East got a foot down, fought to stay upright. Walter bounced by,
shouting wildly. Michael's arms cinched, and East smelled his
lotion. One fist peeled off and shot up, off his eye this time. At
once he felt it throb and swell. With hard nails, Michael probed
East's head; he took the ear and started to twist, to tear at it, until
East let go a shriek. Then everything stopped.

Silent: the silence of hard, wet breathing. Something black and
cold teased East's face, like a dog's nose. Ty had a small gun leveled
at him, lazy and straight.

'Quit it,' Ty said. Aiming the gun as if it didn't even hold his
attention.

Michael Wilson cursed. He popped East free, right into Ty and
the cold black barrel.

A big truck with a cartoon milkman on its side flew by.

'So, you got a gun,' Michael Wilson said.

Ty didn't answer. East tried to clear his eyes, get his voice back.
He'd bitten himself inside his mouth. But now was his best chance.

'Give Ty the money,' he slurred, his mouth swelling around his teeth.

Ty kept the gun on *him*, though.

'Fuck no,' Michael Wilson said. He caressed one fist with the other. 'Your boy gonna shoot? Don't look like he's decided who. So what you gonna do? Put me *out*?'

'Yes,' said East. He'd thought it before. But now that Michael had said it, it was the only way.

Michael Wilson surged from his toes and hooked East once more, side of the gut. Sucker punch. It crumpled East, and he heaved with the pain. 'See?' Michael Wilson smirked. 'You ain't shit.' He stepped and loaded up for another, when a hard crack like thunder hit them all, and East was untouched, backpedaling in the light.

Ty held the gun in the sky. Its hard gray pop echoed back from nothing.

Michael Wilson spat. 'Oh, nigger, please.'

Ty aimed the gun at Michael for the first time.

'I'll take that money now,' he said.

Michael Wilson scowled a terrible scowl at Ty. From his hip pocket he threw a curve of twenties to the ground. They fluttered, and Ty put a foot on them.

'There you go.'

Walter spoke up. 'That ain't all the money.'

Michael Wilson glanced across, measured the overpass to the station.

'Give up the rest of the money, Mike,' said Walter.

'Let him keep the rest. He'll need it,' East said. 'Now you go.' Michael Wilson chuckled. 'Just right out here on the farm?'

'That's right,' East said. He grabbed the white mesh shirt off the mirror and tossed it at Michael Wilson. Michael shook it out and put it on. 'Let me get my bag, then,' he said. East nodded, and Michael fetched it out of the back.

'Pretty bag,' East couldn't resist remarking.

'Let me tell you something,' Michael Wilson announced. 'I ain't sorry to leave you. I'm glad. I get home with one phone call. And you are lost. You can't get guns without me. You can't find the man without me. Don't none of you even look old enough to drive a car.'

'We don't need you,' East said.

'Ain't talking to you,' Michael Wilson said. 'I'm only talking to the youngster with the gun.' He turned his back on East. 'You a neighborhood boy. You ain't in no neighborhood now. There is plenty you don't know, gangster. You don't know you can't go back, because when you fail, there's no place for you. Johnny and Sidney will kill you just for knowing what you know. Or somebody will – it don't matter.'

'Say what you got to say,' said Ty.

'Just understand the picture.' Michael Wilson chewed off the words. 'You ain't even grown.'

'I hear you,' said Ty. 'Goodbye.'

With his immaculate sneakers, Michael Wilson tested the ground. Here, after the fight, in the middle of a cornfield, he looked as polished and bright as he always had: black track suit pants, glossy gym bag, white nylon shirt with his skin dark in the mesh. Stray raindrops blew at him and disappeared.

'Just remember,' he said. 'You will die. And fuck you.' Michael Wilson nodded – at the gun, not at East – and turned and took the first step away. Then he jogged. He ran, and Ty pocketed the gun. For a moment East couldn't believe it, that Ty had jumped in like that, and then he was letting Michael Wilson go. The Ty he'd expected, the Ty he wanted in the red, bruised part of his brain, would shoot Michael Wilson and leave him off the road for the birds. Not this. Not Michael Wilson on the country road, white shirt billowing under the roiling clouds, his necklace glinting. In a minute he had crossed the bridge and was descending. He did not look back.

8

EAST'S FINGERS KNEW MORE than the mirror did. His eye looked all right but felt fat and hot, liquid beneath. The napkin full of ice from Walter's drink just made him wet.

'How bad he get you?' Walter asked again. Checking the mirrors every second. As if Michael Wilson could some way be gaining on them.

Ty sat dully in the back seat, staring out.

East remembered the last time he'd been beaten up. He was eight or nine. Yes, nine – it was in third grade, a week before summer. Third graders were going up to the next school. But four who were being held back would catch a boy each day and whup him, just to say goodbye. The principal wouldn't suspend them – to be suspended was what they wanted. One of them was being held back for the third time. He was eleven already.

They'd bruised East's face and shoulders, blacked his eyes, loosened a tooth. His mother screamed how she'd go to the school and there'd be hell. But she'd never gone. That was worse. But this hurt more.

That was the year Fin started taking East under his wing. Started showing an interest, making sure East had what he needed. Ty, he didn't take much notice of. Ty was not his blood.

When East took the napkin off his eye, something was coming out of his skin. Walter took a look and bugged out.

'Telling you, man. Let's get to a pharmacy. Get you some ointment. You need medicine on that. And bandages.'

East's voice came small and faraway. 'How does it look?' Walter stifled a giggle. 'Like you got your *ass* kicked.'

East put the napkin back.

'You all right?'

East nodded. He didn't want to talk about it.

The high battling wall of cloud cut off the sun. Cars switched on headlights along the road. With stiff, trembling fingers, East opened his wallet and counted, one-eyed. He had two-sixty. He checked it again.

'How much money you got?' he asked Walter with his little hollow voice.

'Three hundred twenty-two dollars,' Walter replied without looking.

'How you get three-twenty-two if we started with three hundred?'

'Man, I *had* money. What, you don't carry any?'

'They said no wallet,' East said. 'What's two-sixty and three-twenty?'

'Five-eighty. And whatever Ty has.'

'Ty. How much money you got?'

They waited, Ty looking mutely out the window.

'Ty,' East said again. 'We trying to find out what we got.' Nothing.

'Here's a town,' Walter announced. 'Let's get off. I'll find you a store.'

East surrendered. 'All right. How's this gonna work, five hundred eighty dollars?'

'Minus gas,' said Walter.

'Minus guns,' said East.

Ty coughed. 'They said you ain't have to pay for guns.'

East said, 'Oh? Did I hear a noise?'

'You heard me,' said his brother.

Now East turned, showing his brother his swollen eye. It hurt, hot, like a wound that's poisoned, like a snakebite. 'You want to tell me more?'

Ty stared mutely at the sunken median running by.

'You two, man.' Walter shook his head. 'I need to be getting combat pay.'

East stayed in the van outside the drugstore. Ty didn't budge. They watched the doorway glowing blue and white, a plastic city. White people teemed in and out, carrying chips bags, cases of drinks. Everyone seemed to know each other, talking or at least waving.

'Ty,' East called back. *Here goes nothing.* 'What do you know about the guns?'

'This don't seem like a drugstore,' Ty said.

'Says right there. *Drugs.*'

'Oh,' Ty pronounced ironically. 'Guess it is, then.'

'You going to answer my question?'

'No,' said Ty.

'Did you set it up? Do you know the people?'

Ty just snorted low, like an old man.

It was like that, talking to Ty. He'd been a willful baby, a stubborn child. Now he was a wall. Every conversation, he made East feel like the police. Sometimes he thought Ty must have been learned from being brought in once or twice, spending time in questioning, stone-facing it across a police desk. But you couldn't ask Ty. You would never find out.

Ty's inscrutability refused the mother's blood they shared. East could rally a gang of boys his age, shepherd junkies in and out safely. He could stare down a gun. But Ty had found a way to negate their childhood together, the two years of age East had on him. There was nothing East could do with him.

Walter brought antiseptic and a bandage as wide as a credit card. 'I ain't wearing that,' East said.

'You're welcome,' Walter warned. 'See how you feel by tonight. Might wish you had.'

'We'll be at that gun house tonight?'

'You better hope Michael Wilson didn't tell that girl where we're headed.'

East thought about it. 'Too stupid. Even for Michael.'

'Even to say Wisconsin, though. Even to say east. She *knew* we were going east.'

'He didn't say nothing.' Here he was, defending Michael Wilson's good sense. 'Man, everything's going to be all right.'

'The reason we are out here is,' Walter said, 'everything is not going to be all right.'

The ointment stung, but East made a slick of it, along his brow, under the eye. He rubbed with his fingertip as they regained the road. Now the van with only three in it seemed too long, voluminous, a dark burrow from front to back. East rolled the window half open, taking air and the afternoon light. The same storm was behind them now, piled up and coming. Across a fence East saw a new little neighborhood already policed by streetlights, rows of houses in a knot. Two white girls shot hoops in a lighted driveway.

His face had stopped hurting after the first hour. Now it was the drawn-out, scraped feeling inside, where Michael Wilson had slugged him in the back and then followed up, sucker-punched him, in the side. Hot mixed with cold. Like purple bruises going all the way, meeting in the middle: he pictured a rotten pear. His breath had a hitch, like a child trying not to cry. The pain angered him, and the anger made him quiet.

He took the road atlas up from between the seats, flipping through listlessly. State by state. Arizona. Arkansas. California. He stopped and studied the full-page city map of Los Angeles. He recognized names in the sprawl of towns. But could not find The Boxes on there. Nobody had ever taught him maps. It took faith in them, believing they were going the right way. Faith in the road, the book, the plan. That whatever they were following made it to somewhere.

He came to Iowa with its plastered pink flyer. Black woman with long tits like footballs. The phone number beamed out beneath her like a black seesaw.

Traced the number with his finger. 'When you want to make this call?'

Walter sipped a drink. 'When do you?'

'Next stop is good.'

'All right. I'm a need to stop again anyway. That drugstore didn't have a bathroom.'

'Piss out back.'

'*You* piss out back,' said Walter. 'With your ghetto ass. I was brought up with some dignity.'

East let himself laugh.

'How you feeling?'

'Tell me how much money again.'

'Five hundred eighty-two dollars. Minus five for your Band-Aid.'

'All right,' said East. 'Don't ask me how I'm feeling no more.'

'You got quarters?'

In back of a gas station, air hissing from the fill hoses, East and Walter huddled together at the phone, road atlas in East's hand. 'It ain't a cell phone. It don't dial free,' Walter said.

'I know it,' East said, but he gaped at the dial, the instructions. Resenting.

Walter read the number out: 213. Then 262. Then 8083. The buttons were sticky.

'Ask for Abraham Lincoln, then?'

'Abraham Lincoln.' They kept straight faces.

'Shit. Get this done before it rains.' East rechecked the pink flyer. A voice in his ear asked for the money then. 'Give it up,' he said spitefully, till Walter held out the silver coins, shining, warm.

Something in him was tired of Walter too, the chirpy voice, the can-do all the time. Something in him was not content yet.

At first came some slow jam and a woman's recorded voice: *Hi, baby. Glad you called me.* Half a minute. The live operator was quieter, just wanted payment information. East had to cough up his voice again. 'Let me talk to Abraham Lincoln,' he managed to say.

Walter giggled this time.

'I will connect you,' agreed the woman.

Who was it? A cool voice, anonymous. The slit-mouthed woman at Fin's house? No, but he thought of her again, the net of shiny beads in her hair. Her hands, bringing the tea.

A man's voice came next.

'How you boys doing?'

Automatically East said, 'All right.' A new strangeness took the next moment to get over. For two days they'd been riding, mouths zipped, their mission buried deep. All the worries of the van. Now it was back on the table.

'Abraham Lincoln,' he said warily.

'Right,' said the man. Deep. Not Fin, but some of his gravity. Walter hissed, 'Who is it?'

'We're in Nebraska,' East reported.

'Where at in Nebraska?'

'Gas station.'

'Listen to me,' the man said. 'Where's the station at?'

'Oh. I don't know,' East admitted.

'You don't know? You don't know what town you're in?'

'We been in Nebraska awhile,' East stammered.

'All right,' said the voice, grudging. 'You made good time. Good work. Call me back in an hour. Make sure you got a pen or pencil. I'll have directions for you.'

'Got it,' said East.

'I'm a confirm it,' the man said. 'Make sure you know where you're at. Exactly.'

'Sorry.'

'Call me.'

The line went dead. East stared at the hot plastic receiver. He touched his face again where it still held the mouthpiece's warmth.

Walter was twitchy. 'Who was it?'

'I don't know,' East had to say.

'What's the deal?'

'Call back in an hour. Next time, know what town we're in.' Walter slapped the side of the phone box. 'I know what town we're in.'

'You should have said.'

'You should have asked.'

A little pout. Fat boy missed his chance, East thought, chance to ace the test. He curled the atlas under his arm.

'I'm going to piss then,' Walter said.

East went inside briefly, to buy a cup of lemonade, mostly ice. He took off his socks and shoes and shirt in the middle seat and bathed himself with melting ice. The cold bit clean through his tired skin, but the gray illness throughout his left side still dragged at him. He pulled fresh underwear out of his bag, and the second gray Dodgers shirt, and changed. He put his pants back on and iced his face.

It was beginning to be cold outside. Not night cold but winter cold. Big trucks pounded past both ways, their high exhaust pipes hammering.

Walter returned and they got rolling, the storm behind them again, looming high, boiling. East held the ripe, ripped Dodgers shirt outside his window and let it flap, tattered like a flag. The moment he let go his pinch, it was gone.

East dreamed interstate dreams, dreams he'd never had before, choppy, worrying. Running the wrong way, or driving against oncoming traffic, or impossible land: a highway emptying into a river, a bridge wobbling, a prairie breaking up. Or ahead of them in the east, LA, with its smog and brown mountain scrim, where it shouldn't be. All the land – people talked about America, someday you should see it, you should drive across it all. They didn't say how it got into your head.

He awoke. Walter was intent in the driver's seat, his lips mumbling something, repeating, like a song. He glanced at the rearview mirrors.

'How far we come?'

'I don't know. Fifteen hundred miles. Shh.' Walter gestured back with two fingers.

East blinked, wriggled upright. 'What?'

'Shh,' Walter said again.

Out the back window he saw the dying light of the day below the shelf of the storm, a layer of smoky blue. One pair of headlights nosing behind them in the lane.

'That's state patrol,' Walter said.

East looked again at the silhouette behind the headlights. 'How you know?'

'Wasn't so dark out when he picked us up,' Walter said. 'He's on my ass this whole time.'

'You speeding?'

'No. Right at sixty-five,' Walter said. 'I wish this van had cruise control.'

'So maybe we're okay? If he wanted, he'd light you up.'

'Maybe,' Walter said. 'Maybe. Maybe he's just taking his time? Maybe he's checking us out in the database.'

'Database?' East yawned.

'Every plate,' Walter said. 'I forget what it's called now. Cops run a check. Find out are you wanted, are you missing, is the car stolen, do you owe money. Find out whatever they want.'

'But Johnny said the van was straight.'

'The van is registered in Johnny's family. Someone named Harris who can't be found. Insured. Licenses are straight. I know; I had them made. Everything was straight until Vegas.'

'Stopping at that casino?'

'It wasn't the stopping,' said Walter. 'Wasn't even getting up on the tow. You can always pay the guy, give him a hundred dollars, the problem goes away. It was you two, jacking it up. Slugging the guy.'

'That wasn't me.'

'All right. Your brother did.'

'That ain't on me,' East insisted.

He glanced back. Nothing from Ty. No way to know if he was even alive.

'All right. Anyway. So what you gotta ask is: did they call it in, those guys? Is there some bulletin out on us? Or did they keep it in house, make themselves a promise they'd kick our ass next time?' said Walter. 'Wisconsin plates. So they knew there probably wasn't gonna be a next time.'

East said, 'How'd you learn all this?'

'That's what I do,' Walter said. 'Projects.'

'Projects?'

'I know people,' said Walter. 'I got jobs. I watched a house for a bit like you. But I moved up.'

'You made the licenses,' said East. 'What's that mean? That license ain't real, that's what it means.'

'East. Fin has a whole setup. People in the DMV. People at the state. I got a part-time job there; they think I'm twenty-two. So we can float records. We can make people up. Some sit in the system for years, man, before we use them. When we need them, I take care of it. I make it happen.'

'You make what happen?'

'I make a license,' Walter said.

'You an artist? You print it?'

'No, state does that. I used to, but it wasn't good enough. Get you past a bouncer. But a cop would spot it. Now they're real.'

'But they ain't real.'

Walter said, 'What is real? These got everything a California license has. There's backup in the statehouse says there is an Antoine Harris. State trooper calls it in, it checks out. That real enough for you?'

'I don't believe it,' said East.

'Well,' Walter sniffed. 'Best hope you don't have to prove it. Antoine is clean, man. Keep him that way.'

'I'm clean,' said East. 'I never been picked up. My name's good.'

'Ain't you lucky,' Walter said. 'Shh, here comes the man.'

The trooper had hit his light, blue and white pulsing off everything. Walter cut speed and shifted his path right.

But the cop sped on by.

'See?' East said. 'Nothing to worry about.'

Walter exhaled a long, tense breath. He smelled like fried food, sweat, and oil. 'Oh, yeah,' he said. 'I should have woken you up earlier. Talking to you, it's sure to make me feel better.'

Walter was floating before the headlights, big 4XL Dodgers jersey lit to boiling. Another dream East was having about the road – or so he thought. Then he saw the chain-link, that they were in a rest stop, not in a lane. Behind Walter's body was a pay phone.

Walter was making the second call. East bolted up in his seat. But Walter was already hanging up, the pink flyer in one hand, atlas in the other. He turned, spotted East behind the windshield, and nodded.

'Got it,' he grunted, opening his door. 'You want to drive, or should I?'

'You must have crept out smooth,' East accused him.

'You were sleeping.'

'You got no business making the call without me.'

'I'll drive, then.' Walter tugged the seat belt around himself uncomfortably. There was no good fit. 'Yeah, I got business.'

Bitterly East said, 'I need to be on there when we call.'

'East,' Walter began, 'I ain't your boy. I made the call. Like you did before. Do I feel better, since now I know? Yes. Who got directions? The one who can read did. Read a sign. Read a map.'

'I can read,' said East.

'Ain't you lucky,' Walter said. 'You ready?'

East snatched the flyer from Walter. Handwriting covered the back side now – terrible writing, scratches, loops slanting downhill.

'I can't read this,' East said at last. 'No one can read this.'

'That's right, son,' Walter said. 'Nobody but me. I can read every word.'

It was night now, thickening. A bread truck sat disabled two spaces down, the doors gaping. Like a foreclosed house.

'What they say about Michael Wilson?'

'We didn't talk about Michael Wilson. Why we want to talk about him?'

'Don't sneak around on me,' East snapped.

'You're so angry,' Walter said. 'Put me out too. Go on. It was always gonna come down to you. You and your little brother. I knew it. You headstrong street Negroes. You were always gonna win. So do it now.'

'Come on,' East said, steaming.

'I mean it,' Walter said. 'Here the keys, then. Put me out.' Schoolgirl drama. But Walter had him beat.

'Come on,' East groaned again.

Walter spat out the door and palmed the keys back. He started up the van and checked the mirrors. 'About an hour,' he said. 'Then we get off the road.'

Finally East relented. 'What did they tell you? About the stop?'

'Easy. Grocery store about twenty miles off the road. We meet up with a truck. Follow them. Everything's paid for. They don't know us. We just get and go.'

'What kind of people?'

Walter picked up speed. A strange field of lighted wire deer glowed in the distance. 'They didn't tell me that.'

9

'WHAT STATE ARE WE in again?'

'Iowa.'

Walter was still frosty at East. He'd dropped off the interstate without an announcement. When East had asked, after some driving, 'You headed where the guns are?' Walter nodded once. Merely.

'This the way the directions said?'

'Uh-huh.'

It was their first real stretch off the interstate. First time East had seen country like this. All East thought of *Iowa* was a map and outlines of products: corn, a tractor, the smiling head of a dairy cow. That was Iowa to his mind.

This road had none of those. Houses thrown up like milk cartons in lonely space – dingy, flat, unpainted cinder-block foundations. Strips of siding hanging off the corners like bandages. In front of each waited a little collection of beat-up vehicles like a boy would arrange in a sandbox. Cheap LED Christmas lights glowed from behind the windows, and sometimes, behind the drainage ditches, a Baby Jesus was standing yard.

Their backyards stood empty, a darkness forever.

The boys rode quiet and tense, East feeling the shifting road through his seat. A little town arose with its dull light reflected on the bottoms of clouds. Signs, steeples, a little grocery store closed for the evening, red still glowing in the plastic letters along the roofline.

'This is it,' Walter said. He coasted into the lot, splashed through the puddles. Out here it had already rained, or been hosed down, one or the other.

'This is it?'

'Ain't it enough for you?'

'Walt, man,' East said. 'Just, you don't run guns at the food store.'

'They do.' Walter pulled the van around once and then sat idling, lights on. 'You feeling better?'

'Fine.'

'You look a little less green than you did,' said Walter. 'Thought you'd be puking again.'

East snapped, 'It don't hurt so much if you don't talk about it.' A light drizzle speckled the windshield.

'How *you* doing, Ty?' Walter called.

The reply came, 'Fabulous.'

'You psyched, man? Getting your hands on more guns?'

'Yeah. All I ever think about,' said Ty drolly. 'Guns. Guns. Guns.'

Something, East thought. Something Walter knew about talking to his brother that he didn't. Even jiving him. As if they knew each other, when they didn't.

He and Ty, they *didn't* know each other, when they did.

Then, from behind the grocery store, a small black pickup

tiptoed out near them, not a glance from the driver, no signal, almost indifferent.

'Is that it?' said East.

Walter's eyes were buzzing. The truck's turn signal pulsed once. Toward the road.

Walter pulsed the light back, and the pickup revved and began to crawl out. 'We're in business.'

Walter crouched over the wheel, maintaining the distance between the van and the little black truck. Back down the highway the van unwound them, past the houses and signs and fields they'd already seen, then onto an eastbound route. Here, fewer houses and no maintenance – the pavement was lined by dropouts, potholes the size of dinner plates chipping off onto the shoulder. Both vehicles nosed along the center line.

'You set this up too, Walt?' said East.

'No. They did,' said Walter. 'I mean, there's a guy. A broker. Guy they call Frederick. He does it all by phone. He never handles a gun.'

'Is he here? Or in LA.?'

'This ain't my bailiwick.'

'It ain't what?'

'I don't know where the man is. I didn't set this up,' Walter said through gritted teeth. 'Ask me a few more questions, why don't you?'

'All right,' said East. 'All right.'

Another road, wider, ran straight between two fields dressed in stubble. The headlights touched the white, embarrassed carcass of a deer. Then the pickup slewed diagonally and stopped astride the center line. It surprised Walter: he chirped the tires stopping.

A passenger leapt out. Blue sweatshirt, hood knotted tight around his face. Just a nose, a white nose, a pair of eyes like coal-black holes. Walter grabbed the shift lever. But there was no time to do anything, nowhere to go.

'Be cool,' East cautioned.

The passenger strode past them into the field, up the beginning of a beaten two-track. He popped a bolt on a metal gate. Then, turning, he beckoned.

'This freaks me out,' said Walter. 'They could lock us in.'

'Well, that fence ain't much,' East murmured.

Walter swung the van toward the track. The hooded passenger motioned to roll down the window.

'Grim reaper-looking motherfucker,' Walter said under his breath, and cranked the window down.

The air pushed in, starry-cold. They saw the ball of the boy's head turning but not the face, heard his words but nothing in his voice. He *could* have been the grim reaper. He could have been anyone. 'You're going to go till you hit a barn that's got two Harvestores. Tall blue silos,' the voice came. 'It's about a mile up over the hill.'

Courteously Walter said, 'What hill?'

The passenger gave no sign Walter had spoken. 'Follow that trail. On the other side, you will find it, down the hollow. You can't miss. Understand?'

Walter and East both nodded in a daze.

The boy's nod back was a single chop of his nose.

'You can get back out this way,' the nose said. 'Or there's a drive out the other side if you can find it.' He pushed the long gate and it creaked open before them.

The boys sat stricken. Not sure of the etiquette. Like being little at Halloween, at the weird house, when somebody's dad answers the door in a costume and offers you a pull off his whiskey – what you do then.

'Go,' the nose said. 'It ain't no good out here waiting.' He scented something up the road and tossed his head: *In.*

Walter touched the accelerator and the van lurched through. In the taillights the boy swung the gate shut and departed. His small taillights moved away like tiny stamps.

Walter stopped, distracted, the van idling, working his chin with his fingertips.

'I don't know, man.'

'What?'

'Do you like the feel of it?'

'The feel of it?' East sized up Walter. Got this far before he decided it was scary? 'Like you said, it's set. It's all ready. No time to change our mind.' More gently he said, 'Go on, man.'

Walter strapped his fingers around the wheel again.

But the van pitched this way and that, as if carried by hand. The track was a rough bargain between tires and ground – polished in places but muscled and bushy with weeds in others. The headlights danced ahead in the mangled fields. After a short time they made a shallow climb on a long, triangular bulge in the earth.

'This must be the hill,' Walter said.

'Was that a mile?'

'I got no idea. I could use some coffee,' he admitted.

On the other side, only dark fields.

Two more such ridges, and then they saw it: twin silos, strange and quiet, nearly invisible below their galvanized caps. A farmhouse two stories high, unlit, paintless, or left unpainted so long that its paint had darkened to match the wood. On the far side, a barn. They rattled their way past the farmhouse and descended to a large bald spot beaten flat by tires, not by treads or hooves. The barn was large, corrugated aluminum. One large low window suggested a light somewhere behind it. A little grass fared poorly.

Walter eased the van in, peering up at the alien silos.

Ty drew his breath loudly. 'And here come the wolves,' he announced.

East caught his door again. Two dogs came galloping – the footsteps sounded through Walter's window, and he rolled it up at once – loosed from somewhere, dull teeth flashing as they rounded and reared in the headlights, snarling. They knifed in and spurred back. Vicious and giddy, gang animals doing simple math, two of them, one truck, therefore with an edge. Was something wrong with them? East wondered. They reared and howled at the van, throats open, but made no sound – nothing but the scuffling of their paws on the beaten ground. East cracked his window: not a thing. Dogs without voices. Like in a movie.

'Bet y'all don't need no coffee now,' cawed Ty from the back. Then a whistle came from somewhere back in the shadow of the barn, and the dogs pointed and stopped. Their noses came down, ears spread out. Automatically. Someone hailed them again, and away they went.

'Jesus,' Walter said. 'That wigged me out.'

'I hate dogs,' Ty said.

'You do?' said East.

'Yes,' Ty said. 'Always making noise, drooling. Trying to be your friend.'

East sat stunned and leery. He did not like dogs either. A dog changed the situation, always.

The bit of light their van threw had not given him any sense of the space around them. And nobody was coming out.

'Everything was right,' Walter said. 'Black truck. Short drive. Pickup at a farm. All this I got told by ol' Abe. All checks out.'

'Let's wait then.'

'You supposed to get out and go,' Ty said.

For a flash of a moment, East felt everything he'd ever felt for his brother: righteousness and rage, exhaustion at the impudence.

'Take a look,' Ty said. 'That window. It's like a drive-through window off a bank.'

East turned. The window was indeed the right shape, low and wide. A single metal drawer perched along the metal sill, a loudspeaker mounted there.

'I'll be damned,' said Walter. 'I never saw anything like that.'

'They stole a drive-through window?'

'Likely bought it. At some auction for five dollars,' Walter said. 'Business ain't so good out here, if you hadn't noticed.'

East said, 'Maybe you can drive up?'

'They don't want you to,' said Ty. 'Ground isn't flat. Tip the van over.'

'Shit.' Walter clicked his belt open and unwrapped it.

East looked around again. 'Ty? What you think?'

'Here's what we're gonna do,' Ty said. 'You two go out the front. Unlock the back gate for me, but don't open it. I'm a stay in here and watch.'

'Oh?' said East. 'You ain't gonna come?'

'I think that makes sense,' Walter said. 'Come out hard if we need you?'

'Right. Keep me a surprise.'

East sighed. 'All right,' he said. 'Stay in the van if you like.'

'I like,' Ty said.

East opened his door. The cold startled him – his breath became visible and lit in the stray light from the van. East headed around the back and unlatched the gate without opening it. Walter joined him in the exhaust and frosty red light.

'How cold is it, you think?' East asked.

'Not so bad,' Walter said. 'It's the wind that makes it feel cold.'

'Not so bad?' said East. 'It's cold as hell, son.'

'You skinny boys,' said Walter ruefully. 'Well. Here goes nothin.'

They approached the window – loose scraps of concrete and chunks of sod made a pile at its foot, as if they did indeed mean to keep cars away. East looked for a way to step up to the little call button colored an unlikely red. A two-way speaker. It crackled now.

'You the boys?' said a voice from inside. 'From out west?'

'That's us.' East glanced at Walter.

The voice came high but quaky, an old man's voice. 'First off, you boys is covered,' it said. 'So let's do like we said.'

East wondered whether to believe this. Another gun sighted on him – how many was that? He kept himself from looking around.

'Where's the other two?'

'Other two what?'

The voice said, 'The other two boys you got?'

'Oh,' said Walter, taking over. 'In the van.'

The speaker crackled. 'We got to see them. For safety's sake. Nothing funny. That's the deal we made.'

'That's a problem,' Walter said. 'They're asleep.'

'No matter about that,' the voice said. 'You come back when they wake up. Or you can even wake them up, can't you?'

'We don't want to wake them up.'

'Seems strange, you'd drive out here,' the voice said. 'And then you aren't willing to wake them up.'

'Well,' Walter said. He bugged his eyes at East.

East had nothing.

'The deal is one, two, three, four. We done our part of the deal. I got a package here for you, exactly what you asked. And I'll be here when your boys wake up,' the voice said.

'Hold on.' East stepped back from the dark-tinted window and studied the barn. The wind-blasted house, the two anonymous silos. Every window and shadow too dark to read. There may have been half a dozen gunners covering them. Or no one at all.

The cold prickled on his bare arms.

Walter retreated with him and leaned in close.

'Like he's trying to trap us,' said Walter. 'Bank robbery: you put all the people together so you can cover them.'

'Why'd you make it so we have to have four?' East hissed.

'I didn't make it, I told you,' said Walter. 'Be different if I did. I would have been happy doing the deal back there at the grocery store.'

East rubbed his cold palms together and cursed.

'Old people,' Walter said. 'Country-ass religious people. Somebody told them four, now that's the scripture. I dealt with people like this before.'

'You dealt with everyone.'

'Tell you a story sometime. You want to fetch your brother out?'

East said, 'He ain't gonna make four.'

Shivering now, again they approached the window. The speaker shot a burst of static as they neared it, then cleared.

'Hello again.'

Walter cleared his throat. A burst of mist rolling out. 'We put one out on the road,' he said. 'So we're down to three. That's all we have.'

'I seen you talking it over,' came the voice. 'I just do what I'm told.'

'Come out and look. Ain't no fourth to see.'

'I ain't stupid,' said the voice. 'And I cain't change on the plan. We agreed it was four. You show me four and I place your order in the drawer.'

'The plan changed,' Walter said. 'Let me make a phone call.'

The static came thick, like fry grease. 'Go ahead.'

Crestfallen, Walter said: 'I mean, if we can use your phone.'

'No phone,' said the voice of the man.

East eyed the hard glass, the reflected blur of the van, the frost-lit world. His lips and skin were shrinking, emptying of blood. Black sky, taunting stars.

'Search us,' Walter was saying. 'We got three. That's all. Tell me what you need. But don't waste the whole day.'

'I do what I'm told,' the voice came back, unruffled.

'This is a whole organization we're here for,' Walter tried. 'You are stopping it up. I don't know how or why you got put in the way. But you got to understand that you are now a problem.'

The old man coughed into the microphone. 'That's why I sit in here, where it's safe.'

'Can I make a new arrangement somehow?'

'Yes,' said the voice. 'You made an arrangement before. Follow it again.'

'Can't you call your boss, whoever that is?'

The crackle insisted, without annoyance: 'No phone.'

In his shirt in the cold air, East had detached from the moment, detached from responsibility for it. Their strangeness in this wind-whipped Iowa farm field was plain – three black boys, deal gone bad, needing guns and knowing nobody. He watched Walter, watched the fat boy solving problems, inventing. Walter was an option man. He played around a thought, discarded it, played around another. That was what a furnace-size body afforded him, the time to try every key.

You could see what people liked about him.

East himself, he had been cold before. Never this cold. Back in the van there were sweaters. But he didn't want to break off from this old man. To credit the cold that the old man seemed the soldier of.

He wasn't sure he cared to stay. He wasn't sure he cared to win this. Guns, after all. Never had he cared for them. The noise, the mess. He'd held a gun before but never felt safer for it.

All the same, he was no fool. He knew guns made his world go round.

He shivered, and the air inside his mouth was no warmer than the outside. The bite inside his cheek stood out like a wound.

This black man, this judge they had come all these roads to shoot, the mission he had defended: he couldn't see it. Couldn't imagine. The bullets, the body. *Not* shooting him, he saw that now. Not going on, not succeeding: that was real. *That* was a bone in his freezing body now. There was no getting it out.

This old man saying no made that bone hurt. Made it harden. But there was no sharing this with his brother, ever. No having that discussion. His brother, his blood, had different bones.

East breathed in the icy air. His eyes were caked with something, starting to freeze. Walter stood lit pink, making his arguments to the tinted window. East couldn't even hear beyond the blood churning in his ears. The problem was beyond discussing.

'Walter,' East said. 'Fuck it. I'm too cold.'

Walter broke off and looked sideways. Surprised. Sometimes you could read him like a book. 'All right,' he said.

But as they turned away, a scraping sound at the window made them jump. An old, rusty machine sound. The drawer waggled open, like a silver tongue.

'Go to them boys,' the amplified voice said.

Walter stepped back up the mound of rubble to the metal tray and pulled something out.

'Them boys will sell you what you need.'

'Wait a minute,' said Walter. 'They'll set us up? How do you know that if you don't have a phone? If you didn't *call* them?'

'I know. They'll sell to you,' the old man said. 'They'll sell to anyone.'

East opened the back of the van, behind Ty's bench, and found the sweaters. There were four – woolen, all dark, the kinky weave, cold already, prickly on his skin. Two were small – one he left for Ty. One was a large – Michael Wilson's. He put it on over his own. The 4XL he handed across to Walter.

'What's this?'

His face was so cold, he couldn't make a word.

Walter looked amused, then sympathetic. 'Easy,' he said, 'I ain't even cold yet.'

East was half-deranged with cold and lack of sleep. The dark of the night started flaking away. *Bugs,* East's mind said, and then: *Something is wrong with me. Something wrong with my mind.* Then he saw it: the lightest snow. The most helpless bits, riding instead of falling on an imperceptible wind. Unseen, unstoppable, brushing past them like strangers.

By the time he had put words to it, it was gone.

Walter made the heater blow its hottest. East bent to it, but it did not warm him. He shook like a machine spinning off center, like a clothes dryer walking and breaking apart. He quaked. Slapped his arms, his palms, his sides, his thighs. 'Ty, man,' he began, and he lost it. Walter touched him: 'East, man? East?'

Could not hold his jaw still on his face. Cold drool dripped. 'East? East?'

At last it lifted, the palsy, the shivering, and East's mind came back into his body, the touch came back to his fingers, he could hold his mouth closed. Embarrassed but surprised too, to feel himself together again.

With some effort he talked. 'Ty, man. The gun you have. Is that enough? Will it do?'

Ty drew out the silence. As if, even after his brother's suffering, it cost him dignity to make an answer. At last he conceded: 'Not this little gun. We gonna need more guns.'

East nodded. At least he'd gotten an answer.

The soundless dogs poured forth to chase them out.

'Lord. Get us the fuck out of here,' Walter said, though he was the one driving.

They regained the pavement, leaving the way they had come. East deciphered the old man's note. They made away north, to the same town with the glowing grocery sign: HY-VEE FOOD STORE. Three skateboarders in parkas traced the lot. One cop watched them from his Impala.

East was quiet. The cold had mortified him.

'I see three options,' Walter said. 'We can go on to this other house. I don't know. We could call ol' Abe and ask what he can do. Or we can drive around until we spot some black dude and ask if we can borrow him.'

'You ain't finding nobody black out here,' East said. 'So let's call Abe.'

A pair of phones waited in front of the Hy-Vee. But Walter didn't like the cop being there. So they searched until they hit a gas station: brushed steel box, quiet radius. Walter pulled the van up close.

'You want to do it this time?'

'You can,' East said. But he got out and stood with Walter at the receiver – somehow the predawn neon buzz of the gas station made it seem less cold – and he made the call. Cold buttons, still sticky. The same quiet operator: 'I will connect you.' But then the phone went quiet.

Walter fished out more change, and East dialed again. The sexy girl blared, welcoming – East dreaded her now. She went on forever before the operator picked up.

'Abraham Lincoln, God damn it,' East said. 'It cut us off.'

'No, sir. I tried to connect you, sir,' protested the operator. 'Please, sir. He isn't answering.'

'All right,' fumed East.

'Please, sir. I'll try again. It's a relay line: someone will always pick up.'

East grunted. The operator was afraid of him. He put his

elbow up to lean, but the steel box bit through the sweater, too cold. A truck splashed into the lot, and a woman with wet hair and a bright, glowing cigarette hurried in under the lights. One bicyclist wobbled up the road in the dark, dun jacket, gray hat, the reflectors on the bike the only concession to visibility.

'Look!' hollered Walter.

'Yeah.'

'He's black.'

'No he ain't,' East answered automatically, and then the operator was in his ear.

'Sir? Sir? There is no one answering.'

A dark buzz of alarm spread down East's back. 'Did you try everybody? The relay, like you said?'

'I relayed to three numbers. Each number rang and rang. I tried each twice,' the operator explained. 'I'm sorry. It's late here. It's three in the morning. They're supposed to pick up, sir, but I can try again.'

Her politeness infuriated East, moved him to fury. 'Yes! Ring them again.' He faced Walter, and Walter clutched at him.

'Let me go get that dude. He could be number four!'

'Let me finish.'

'He's gonna get away!'

'On a kid's bike. On a highway,' East said dubiously.

Walter said, 'I'll circle back. Pick you up.'

Like a ram East lowered his brow. 'Not leaving me in the cold, man. Not for ten seconds.'

The biker receded into the gloom.

The operator: 'Sir. I rang them again. All three. No one is answering, sir . . . Sir?'

East thanked the operator and hung up the phone. 'What do you think that means? Nobody answering the line?'

'No idea,' Walter said. 'Let's chase that damn bike while we can.'

'Okay,' said East. 'We'll chase your damn bike.'

The bicyclist was still weaving along the north-south road into town, advancing crazily. His knees chopped sideways like wings. Twice as large as his tiny bike. Walter backed into a driveway fifty yards ahead of the wobbling bike and rolled down his window.

'Hey, my man,' he called. 'Hey.'

The black bicyclist stopped and stood astride his bike like a gray scarecrow. His gray hat was tied down over his cheeks with flaps. His coat was grime-streaked – this wasn't the first ride he'd had on the highway. In Los Angeles, East thought, this was a crazy man. Here and now, he envied the man's outerwear.

'Where you headed?' said Walter, friendly.

The man gave a minimal shrug, more a pinch, and pointed ahead. 'Going down here, boy.'

'Listen, man, we need somebody,' said Walter. 'We need somebody black. We got to pick something up, man, and we need another man for it.'

'Somebody black?' the man said. 'What you picking up? Like a sofa? At five in the morning?'

'We can pay you for your time,' Walter said. He showed a split of twenties out the window.

The man's eyes dropped to the money, then came back up. 'Good luck.' Flat.

'It's nothing heavy. Just fifteen minutes. Take a ride with us.'

'Oh, no,' said the man on the bike. 'No, no.' He dropped his weight back onto the seat.

East leaned over and showed his face out Walter's window. 'Hey. Check us out. We ain't bad boys. We'll give you a lift where you going.'

'I'm just going down *here*, son,' the man said, and he put feet to the pedals. As he passed the van, he spat.

Ty laughed. 'He's sure he's gonna die in this van.'

Walter fished out the crumpled paper with the address. Now it was all they had.

Plain little bungalow the color of butter. East wanted no part of it. A street they'd never seen, a town they knew nothing about, a deal they didn't even know if they could make. But now this house seemed locked around their necks. They sidled the van down the street, squared around a few blocks, tried to feel things out. Regular. Chain-link sectioning off almost every yard. Small boats rusting on trailers, a few lawns with newspapers waiting in blue plastic bags. A few dogs out early, testing the air. Trees unlike the trees in LA: these rooted hard, grew up tall, muscular, their bare limbs grabbing all the air in the world.

Nothing moving. For East it was strange, this looking, this studying a neighborhood again. The way he had at the old house. The dogs, the doors, the windows. Scanning the surroundings for eyes.

Walter stopped down the block, and they watched the yellow house. The whitish farmhouse next door to it had security bars on every window.

They'll sell to anyone.

Improvising now. What choice did they have?

He turned around. 'Ty. You see what we're doing?'

'Do I see?' Ty said. 'Am I stupid?'

Ever did anything like this again, he was getting his brother a secretary.

'Seems pretty straight,' Ty said. Surprising East.

'Two go in, one stays out?'

'Right.'

'So you got one gun,' Walter said. 'What do we need?'

'Walt. You know anything about guns?'

'A little.'

'A better gun, then,' said Ty. 'I got this little popgun I can hide behind my dick. We get something real. Two guns. One of you can hold this. East can. Plus points.'

Walter asked, 'How much is that gonna cost?'

'Depends what the man charge,' said Ty. 'Begging your pardon, but we got a seller's market out here. Take all the money you got, try to bring some back.'

'So who's going in?' Walter said.

East rubbed his eyes. Exhausted, he wanted no part of it. Fin had people who would work this, go in cool, shake hands like businessmen. Or there was Circo, who would go in with a gun in each hand and all the burners hot. He himself was a watchman. He could run a crew, keep them working all night. But walking in where people were ready to kill you was not his thing.

The feeling in his fingers had come back, and he rubbed them together, letting the skin heat.

'Well, Walt, my man,' said Ty drolly. 'Who you want on the outside, if you have a problem, coming to save your ass? Me or him?'

'It's you and me, man,' Walter said across the front seats.

East nodded and closed his eyes. Plan was broke, gang was broke, Ty trying him at every chance. Might as well go.

Ty kept on. 'Glock or a Tec. Glock or a Tec be nice. If they got real guns. If it ain't all duck-hunting shit. You got five hundred and some dollars. If you can't get two guns that work, fuck it, we driving back to LA.' He laughed. 'Now pull this up and park close. Right across the street. We doing business.'

The cold air braced East. He decided not to waste words. The yellow house's door opened on a thick chain.

'We're here to buy some guns.'

In the crack was a white face, beard, wire-rimmed glasses. 'Show me money,' it said.

Walter made a motion at his hip. Same handful of twenties he'd offered the black man on the bike.

'You packing?' said the bearded man. 'Because if you are, hand me what you have now. Change and keys too. And Phillip will come around and wand you.'

'We're clean,' said East. 'All right. But it's cold out here.'

Around the corner of the house appeared a shamefaced man as skinny as a dog. He had a metal-detector paddle semi-concealed beneath his arm. It squelched as he jostled it. The man nodded uncomfortably before he climbed the stairs.

'You ready?' he said.

'That a metal detector?' said Walter.

'Yep.'

'I know you ain't gonna scan us standing out here on your porch,' said Walter.

'Yep.'

They submitted to the nosing and grazing of the paddle. East wasn't sure the skinny man was using it right. Skinny enough that his shoulder joints bulged at the seams of his shirt; his knuckles stood out like knots. Hard to say how old he was.

'All right,' the man Phillip said. 'Now you may go in. But let me give you some advice. Okay? Don't be arguing. The nice man wants to sell you what you need. But everyone else in the house wants you dead.'

Again the country manners, East thought. As if they'd come from a planet a million miles away.

'We just doing business,' Walter soothed him.

Phillip stared with the same red-bitten face. 'Remember what I told you.' He nodded at the door, and they heard the chain come off. It opened, and Phillip led them in. Out of his collar curled the beginning of a tattoo, some ancient declaration.

They entered a parlor set with antique, dark furniture that

was upholstered in pale peach. 'Sit together there,' Phillip said, indicating a sofa, and he slipped through a doorway at the back of the room. The bearded man with glasses split off and crept up the stairway running up behind the front door. To its railing was lashed a thick, transparent slab two inches thick – just roped on haphazardly with yellow nylon cord.

'Bulletproof glass, that is,' Walter murmured.

East nodded.

Walter sat obediently, and East moved that way, but something over the sofa caught his eye. On the wall hung portraits, rectangular and oval, of tall, gaunt men with beards and white women with their hair in curls, or grandmothers with their last wisps. White faces, stolid expressions, their postures rigid in these antique frames. To East they were mesmerizing – the oldest pictures he'd ever seen. These strangers stood in poses that didn't fit them, that family lined up unhappily in front of a house. Pioneer faces, dead now, but their eyes still blazing, vigilant, even in sepia. He felt drawn, felt them watching.

Reluctantly he sat when Walter tugged at his arm.

Across a low, formal table sat the sofa's love-seat cousin, also peach. Not far away on the floorboards sat a bassinet in dull gray plastic. A large orange stuffed crab waited there – clutched in the hand, East saw now, of a damp, sleeping baby.

'Make yourself comfortable.' Phillip's voice floated from the back.

Through the door frame East saw the antique dining room – long table and chairs, a tablecloth of lace, littered with plastic plates and mail. Cheerios had spilled across the floor.

Another creaking, and presently the doorway filled with a man in gray sweats. East almost whistled. The man was gigantic: Walter was 4XL fat, but this man made him seem a youngster. He was bald and he moved tenderly, shifting from foot to foot, sizing them up. His blond lashes made his blue eyes seem peculiar and dark.

'Hi,' he said softly. 'I'm Matt.' He perched on the second sofa. 'Pleased to meet you two. Maybe today is the day that the floor caves in.'

Walter said, 'You okay if I get right to it?'

'Be my guest,' said Matt.

'We came to buy two pistols. One should be semiauto. Second one, anything that's straight. And bullets for both.'

'Bullets for both,' the man repeated dreamily. Almost a sigh. 'How you boys this early morning? Come far?'

'A long way,' reported Walter.

'You staying here? Or just passing through?'

'Passing through,' Walter said concisely.

Walter was straight. It pleased East, reassured him – the straightest line between now and getting out. Made sense. He looked up at the other man, Matt, whose politeness felt effortlessly derogatory. Eyeing the two boys, Matt worked his mouth on something.

'Passing through. You sure? Ain't much here to steal.'

'Leaving as soon,' Walter said, 'as we get what we need.'

'Welp.' Matt leaned slightly forward, a pivot somewhere in the base of his neck. 'You seem like you're serious business. Let's see what I can show you. Phillip. Phillip. Bring out that bunch you'll find above the refrigerator.'

The skinny man's footsteps scraped onto linoleum. East eyed the third man, the bearded one with wire glasses, lying in wait behind his barrier on the stairs. Was he armed? Figure he was. Figure Phillip too was just listening with the safety off. Small-town manners.

Phillip returned with a metal tray, tarnished, like it once was precious. The man named Matt accepted the tray with soft fingers. His blue eyes grew round, and he peered at the guns like a pawnbroker doubting jewelry. Then he placed the tray down before the boys.

Three guns. Two magazines.

'These are nice guns,' sighed Matt as if the boys had given him heartburn.

East stared. Guns were not his thing. He'd carried a few, even fired a few to learn. But these guns were not for boasting or learning.

'This is yours to choose, man,' he murmured to Walter.

Walter wiped his hands together and picked up the first gun. Checked the chamber first, then the action. Sighted it against a ceiling corner. *Click.* Quietly replaced it on the tray and tried the next.

'We good?' Matt said agreeably.

Walter said, 'Not these.'

'Oh?' Comically the fat man cleared his throat. His eyes went round again. 'Not these? You want what, exactly?' Over his shoulder he said, 'Phillip. He says not these.'

'These guns are fine,' said Walter, 'but not these.'

'These ain't the low-end Saturday-night specials city niggers use,' said the man, licking his lips. 'No offense.'

There it was. East saw it fly out and watched it sink. Just a stone in the water.

Walter made a plain, thin line with his lips and let it go. 'Why don't you show us what else you got?'

'Tell me what road you came in on,' said the fat man Matt.

'From the south,' said Walter. 'From the interstate.'

'Didn't you go visit somewhere else first? Before you came here?'

Now Walter elbowed East. 'This motherfucker,' he scoffed. But East saw the cubes of windowpane light curving in Walter's eyes, the cock of his eyebrow: *Where we going with this?* Improvising was wearing thin.

They'd done some things right. But nobody would tell you how many things were left.

East intervened. 'We went somewhere else. Come on. Ask us what you got to ask. Then let's see some more guns.' His voice came harder than he meant it to. Maybe that was all right.

Matt chewed on something, encouraged. 'Did you go to a barn? A big-ass barn in a field?'

'Maybe.'

'Why didn't they sell you?'

'Who knows?' said East. 'I guess they didn't like us.'

'Did they not like you because a lot of little African Americans steal? Or because a lot of little African Americans actually turn out to be cops?'

'A lot of little African Americans trying to be polite here,' East said. 'Whyn't you bring another bunch of guns if you got any? Or we can just go buy them in the next town.'

'Oh?' said Matt. 'What town?'

Walter cut in: 'Dubuque.'

'Well, I don't know nobody who sells guns in Dubuque.'

'We'll find someone,' said Walter. 'But we here doing business with you, or trying.'

At this statement the baby stirred. It stretched one hand out, then emitted a loud complaint. Inside East, the black string sang murder. He hated the baby; he hated the men for using the baby, leaving the baby in the main room for show. Like the antique photographs, the upholstered furniture. As if it all meant respectability, as if you couldn't be touched.

Somewhere its mother was probably still asleep.

Matt moaned and shifted himself on the love seat. 'Phillip,' he crooned, 'why don't you see what you can find in that drawer?'

'Which drawer, Matt?'

'Second one,' said Matt. 'Below the toaster.'

'Second one below the toaster,' Phillip repeated, retreating to the kitchen once again.

The big man Matt smiled, and in his sickly whine he said, 'How about you, string bean? You know where you're headed next?'

East squinted. He'd been called String Bean sometimes as a kid. That Matt had put his finger right on it annoyed him, like someone had screamed his name inside a house. But he couldn't mean anything by it. He meant that East was long and skinny. That was all.

As much as East hated these men, he wanted to make the deal. He wanted it to be over. And he wanted to have done it.

'I'm going with him,' he affirmed.

'Mmm,' mused Matt. 'That's good. Okay, here he comes.'

The second tray: two guns, one extra clip. 'Be my guest,' Matt said again.

Walter picked up the first, a gray semi, jimmied the magazine out, checked it over. 'Seventeen,' he murmured tunefully.

'Good gun,' said Matt. 'Not Glock's best.'

'Why ain't you bring this out first time?'

Matt smiled and said nothing.

'Do I get to fire it? You got room in the basement?'

'In the basement is my wife,' Matt said. 'Asleep, we both should hope. No, you don't get to fire it. If we go out in the fields, you can shoot it. But you're in my house, first thing in the morning. You're lucky we're even awake.'

'You have a wife?' said Walter.

Again Matt smiled. 'Big boys get it done, junior. You're on your way yourself.'

'Not that big,' Walter said. He pointed out the second gun. 'Not much of a toss-in. Can't you sell me a better one?'

'That little Ruger in the last round,' said Matt. 'But it costs. Or you can have that Taurus.'

BILL BEVERLY

'How much, these two?'

'Five-twenty-five.'

'Four hundred.'

'Oh, I'll say four-fifty,' Matt said. 'But I will also say: I came down. I come down one time only. Take it or leave it.'

'Four-eighty,' said Walter, 'and you take back this cracker box and give me that Taurus.'

'Five hundred and you can have all three.'

'I don't want three,' said Walter. 'I don't want this leaky thing anywhere near me.'

'A man who thinks he can spot shit,' said Matt, 'will still end up wondering why his shoes stink.'

Walter said straight, 'Four-fifty for the Glock and Taurus.'

'Mostly now what I want, actually, is you to get out, actually,' said Matt. 'I care less and less if I get your money or not.'

'Well,' Walter said, 'right now you get to decide.'

East's stomach rolled. He watched Walter with a low, grudging admiration. Trading was all it was, maybe. But not everybody could trade.

'All right,' said Matt with resignation. 'Four-fifty for the Glock and Taurus.'

East could not stop the little leap his hands made in his lap. 'Deal,' said Walter. 'And we stop outside town and see do they shoot. If they don't, we come back.'

'You can *look* at them and see they *shoot*. A child can see they *shoot*. The question is, can you aim?' Matt made to stand up but winced instead. 'Phillip, get that little Taurus gun off the top of the fridge.'

Walter counted out twenty-three twenties. 'Got change?'

'Not if you want bullets. I got about a box and a half fits those both.'

'Oh, shit,' said Walter. 'Yeah. Here's another twenty. Gimme it all.'

Phillip opened a door in the dining room sideboard, near enough that East could watch. Red and black boxes were stacked beside vases. Phillip placed two in a bag that said Dollar General and walked them to the front door.

Walter said, 'Where's he going?'

'Putting it outside for you,' said Matt. 'You think we invite boys into my house and hand them loaded guns?' He counted the twenties. 'Four hundred eighty dollars. My handshake is my receipt.'

They stood, but none of them shook hands.

Outside, behind the steering wheel, Ty waited, quiet-eyed. He slid back in the van as they approached. East peered down into the plastic bag. New bullets, a sealed box and a half one – nice.

'Those guys had guns in every drawer in the house,' East said. Walter snorted. 'I know. A thousand guns. We could have been there all day.'

'What you get?' said Ty the moment they opened the doors. 'Now we'll get schooled,' said Walter. He unpocketed his gun and passed it back. East fished the Taurus out too. Walter set the van moving as Ty examined them.

'This Glock, nice,' said Ty. 'Other one, a piece of shit. You could smack somebody with it, I guess.'

Walter smiled. 'See?'

'What you pay?'

'Four-eighty for all of it and bullets.'

Ty gaped. 'Four-eighty? These guns? Four *hundred* eighty?'

Walter turned a corner. 'That a good price?'

'I get Glocks like this in The Boxes, two hundred,' Ty said. 'How many dudes were there?'

'Three,' said Walter. 'And a little baby.'

Ty said, 'Stop the truck.'

'No!' said East. But Ty didn't wait. He threw back the side door and took the street at a leap. East popped his door too, but the seat belt caught, and then the van bounced as Walter pulled it over, and he cursed and fumbled with stinging fingers. Ty darted between houses and was gone.

Back on the seat he'd left two guns. He had the Glock. There was no chasing him.

East slammed his door. 'Are you stupid? Never do what Ty says.'

'What's he doing?'

'We'll find out,' East said grimly. 'Take us back. *Go.*'

Lights were waking now in the kitchens, behind the porches with their hollow Christmas lights. Walter downed the windows: no dogs barking. Nothing. No sign of Ty. Silently they rolled toward the gun house.

'You want me to stop here?'

'Not right in front,' East said. 'Don't want them noticing us and wondering.' He scanned the block, eyes burning.

'Do we go look for him?'

'No. Not yet.'

Walter said, 'What's he gonna do? Walk in and ask for a refund?'

'Walt,' East steamed. 'Nobody knows what Ty's gonna do. He don't plan things. It's always *pow* with him.'

'Ty saved our ass,' Walter reasoned. 'Got us out of Vegas all right – and when Michael was latched on to you? Ty improvises.'

'Listen to you, man. *Last night* you were saying he was trouble. He's an animal.'

'Maybe he's lucky,' said Walter. He pulled a three-point turn at a cross street. Jubilant accordion music spilled from a parked car there, all four doors open. A short Latin man was shining his dashboard in the cold.

They made one more flyby. East's stomach burned cold. He wished he'd marked the time. Walter pulled the truck up fifty yards from the house, and they quieted and watched.

Six-eleven on the clock. Six-thirteen. How long did they give? The pink of the morning clambered across the ceiling of the sky.

East knew this hour from years standing yard – in minutes, light would ooze down the treetops, color the chimneys, charge through the yards. The shabby street dawn tightened East in the way he had tightened for years – the standing there, regardless; the watching everything that moved. The not blinking.

The molding a group of boys you'd maybe met yesterday into the people your life depended on. And never to know whether you'd succeeded. Only to await the moments of test. Like this one.

Six-sixteen. A work truck with a big white Reading box mounted in the bed rumbled by slowly like a cart drawn by invisible horses.

Walter said, 'How long you think we can wait?'

'I know,' said East. 'I *know*.'

'Time is gonna come we have to decide.'

East kept his eyes on the gun house.

'He's your brother.'

'Not that I'd die for,' said East curtly.

Six-eighteen.

He'd always been bigger than Ty, stronger. Always been older, and also the good son, such as it was. Always the one who tried to put a good face on it for their mother. Always the one she could count on, even if Ty was her baby. He remembered the first time he'd tried to celebrate his mother's birthday with a cake he'd bought with his own money. Brought it home and hid it, but Ty found out. He slipped out before dinner and stayed out, unaccountable, until three o'clock in the morning and her birthday was through. Just daring East to go ahead and serve it. Without him. And he didn't. That night he cried bitterly at his defeat. Nine years old and just trying to be the man of the family.

That unaccountability was the trick Ty had. The way he'd found of taking those two years East had on him and shattering them.

At nine he'd begun tomcatting out in the street for nights at a time. Had left the house entirely at eleven. His mother's baby.

'You decide,' said Walter. 'He's your brother. You want to gun up and go, I'm good. You want to drive away – either way. Who knows when one of these town ladies calls up the police – could be already. And then we're in some shit.' He stopped and rolled his chin around on his knuckles. 'Like, if he's still there at seven? At eight?'

'I should have followed him,' East murmured.

'Let me ask you a question,' Walter said. 'We're supposed to have four guys. Without him, we got two. You and I, we're the same type. We're watchers. We manage. We ain't gunners, particularly. If we went, two of us, who does it? Who shoots?'

'You mean the guy?' East was annoyed, distracted, keeping his eyes peeled. 'I can shoot.'

'Yeah,' said Walter, 'but are you gonna shoot? You ain't that crazy about guns.'

'I can shoot,' said East blankly. 'He'll be back.'

'Not if he isn't.'

Then dogs exploded, barking, and Walter started; East sat bolt upright. A dark slash between the houses. Ty was sprinting out, footing it down the street toward where he'd jumped out of the van. 'Catch him,' East said, and Walter put the van in Drive and veered it. Ty held the gun out plain as he ran: *Do not fuck with me.* Sprinting down the street as if he didn't even see them, didn't even care.

At the last moment he cut to the van and popped the door. 'What?' East demanded. 'What did you do?'

Ty slid onto the middle seat. Panting and laughing both. 'I told you, man, you paid too much.'

Walter ran the stop sign heading them out to the county road. 'What did you do?'

'I told you.' Ty threw down the fold of twenties. 'Four hundred eighty dollars. Now who's your daddy?' Regally he surveyed the world through the windows, the morning coming down.

10

IT WAS NATURAL, Ty said, the way into the yellow house. A window up high was cracked open to the cold. He'd stolen a stepladder off a garage. If he could make the back-porch roof, he could get inside.

But he hadn't had to. He was crossing the backyard with the aluminum stepladder when someone came out of the house. 'Crippled dude. Bad spine.'

'Phillip,' said Walter.

'Skinny. Look like he hurt to walk.'

'Yeah. That's him.'

'Phillip. First thing Phillip sees, black boy stealing a ladder. He came for me, man, gonna whup me with his car keys. You know, *crime stopper*? So I take my ladder and I knock Phillip on his ass, thinking, this will work: I'll just walk him back in with a gun in his ass. But guess what's in Phillip's hand with the keys?'

East said, 'Four hundred eighty dollars.' So crazy, he marveled, this charging on, with no idea what lay ahead.

'So beautiful,' Walter cheered.

Ty grinned, angelic, contemptuous. 'Thinks he got mugged by some kid from the block!'

Twenty miles east, they picked out a pancake house for the first sit-down meal in two days. Pancakes like no pancakes East had ever seen. Fluffy, meaty, thick as steaks.

'We'll make it today,' Walter was saying, 'just a few hours.' Euphoria had chased off the morning chill. It was easy to explain: new guns. Plenty of bullets. Money back. Ty smirking, all his dice landing sweet. That afternoon they could find a place, get some rest. But that wasn't everything on East's chest. The other thing that had warmed him that morning, even in that horrible house with the men and their pioneer ancestors standing guard together, and the baby on the gunpowder floor like a business card – even there, East had found himself hungry to make it work. To make the deal, straight, shake hands with the bastards. They had almost closed it, businesslike. Then Ty made his raid, and they all had that to hoot about, even if it was cheap and hard, even if it marked them, set them apart.

So that's it, he thought, working on his stack of pancakes, which he never should have ordered; he could never eat all that. So that's us. Just some thieving hoodlums, all across America.

Back outside, the cold was a jolt.

East drove. He nudged Walter: could they afford to stop somewhere, anywhere, get a room, shower, and a good sleep? 'Don't want to do that,' Walter replied. 'Don't want to have to register. Not now, not this close to, you know. Where we're going.'

So they would go until they got there, they decided. Arrive, circle, spot out the land. Make a plan and follow it.

Walter took the wheel back after a couple of hours. He exited onto a smaller highway, a Wisconsin state road, two-lane, rich black pavement, deep flood ditches dug on either side. The trees grew higher – and closer to the road. Pines, not thin and fire-hungry like California's, but tight-knit, impassable, winter-coated trees, their cones as thick as cats on the branches, green so deep it was blackish. Passing so close, they ripped East's eyes with their tiny, intimate spaces, tree to tree, branch to branch, too quick to see. They flashed by like the opposite of mountains, the grand spaces, the eons of time. Here, too many things to see and zero time to see anything. Around the back of every trunk, something could be hiding. East closed his eyes, but he didn't feel comfortable not watching either – Walter, the van, the narrow road. The deep, unforgiving ditches, the reaching trees. His eyes saw faces in them, every frightened bird an attacker, every mailbox a blaze of threatening color.

He was exhausted and could only watch. Walter was exhausted and could only drive. Like neither of them knew how to stop. And then they were there.

WILSON LAKE, read a tall green sign posted on redwood beams, surrounded by the emblems of clubs and lodges and churches of the town. Then another mile of jacketed pines.

Then a hill and a dip and the lake showed itself: just patches between the trees, a blur, the blue a murmur below the noon-white glare. The houses that appeared were not the bins of siding they'd seen for the last day, but triangles of stone and brown wood, frames of wood, walls of wood, jutting up like cabins, or in A shapes, from clearings in the pines. Names on signs out front by the driveways: WEE SLEEP, GREASY LAKE. And the mailboxes were fancy too: not just plain black U.S. Mail, but barns or jolly men with mail holes in their stomachs or monster animals whose heads hid the box.

'What the fuck is that one?' said East.

'It's a badger,' said Walter.

Ty said, 'A what?'

'A badger. It's the state animal. You ain't heard of badgers?'

They zigzagged quietly, getting the layout. There wasn't much. Big old houses. The lake was mostly round – half a mile across, maybe. Two beaches, three ramps, and a little strip of quiet stores. Three streets running parallel, a handful of connectors, and one road that looped around the far side of the lake. The address, Walter figured out off his page of scratchings, was 445 Lake Shore Drive. That turned out to be the road that circled the lake.

There on the far side, the houses were new, cabins and party houses, with skylights and roof decks thrust high like helipads, gas grills left out in their weather shrouds, flags East had never seen flying everywhere, in driveways, over doorways. He wondered at them as they drove by. People here were gonna know each other. Wedges of pines curtained the lots off, but next door could be a yard of noisy dogs, or a single nosy lady. It was a neighborhood. You never knew.

Some squirrel or small creature zipped in front, and Walter pumped the brakes. East looked up. Nobody watching them.

They were so tired.

'This is it,' Walter announced.

The driveway forked. Two mailboxes at the foot, 435 and 445. Quietly the van crawled past: no other cars on the road right then. No one near, no one to mark the van cruising slowly. The house was an A-frame with bedrooms popped out on either side of the base. Two stories. Jagged corners with log-cabin beams, a grayish mortar holding them together.

Big windows cut either side of the door, and no flag.

'Big house,' East said. One little sport truck out in front, black. 'These are vacation homes,' said Walter. 'Big and empty. By the way, shouldn't you wake your brother up? He might want to see it.'

East peered back, tried to see Ty. 'Naw. Let him sleep.'

Two women approached, jogging down the road. In their fifties, wearing thin fleeces and mittens with reflectors. They raised hands at the crawling van, and Walter raised two fingers back. A natural.

No yards full of dogs. No high decks nearby with neighbors looking out over the trees. East's eyes ran a check automatically.

'Phone wires come in there,' said Walter. 'Pole behind the house, lines in on the back to both houses. We could take them out.'

'Why? They got cells.'

'But do they get a signal out here? Negative bars,' Walter giggled. East grunted, eyes on the woods. A tire-track path led back into the woods behind the row of houses that included 445. 'You could park the van and walk up on that, get in from the back.'

'Watch out for badgers,' Walter said.

They looped back around the lake and headed into town. Found the police station, small, tucked behind the firehouse. Two black-and-whites in the lot and one unmarked, a little white SUV with good cop tires and a winch. Good to know.

'I got to sleep, man,' said Walter. 'I keep thinking I'm gonna throw up.'

'All right,' East said. His exhaustion had begun crashing down. Walter put them back on the highway, the pines ever closer and closer around them, and cruised up until they found the next little village with its lake. It was smaller, this lake, the banks rough and muddy, the public lot an old reach of concrete leading down to some crumbling boat ramps. The homes along the shore had once been vacation homes, but the people living in them were no longer vacation people. Broken chairs and propane tanks in the yard, small sedans turning the color of dirt.

'We found the ghetto lake,' East remarked.

'The *people's* lake,' insisted Walter. 'You think it's safe?'

'We got guns.'

Walter laughed and set the parking brake. The whole lot banked downward to the shallow, dark beach.

'Your brother,' said Walter, 'that boy can sleep through anything.'

'I'm full awake, son,' Ty spoke up.

'Better sleep,' admonished East. 'We gonna need to be awake and available later on.'

'Oh, I will be.'

They closed their eyes on the bright, final day.

11

EAST SLEPT LIKE A drowned man. One time a pair of kids ran by with fishing lines, disturbing him. Their footsteps and yelling: his tongue in his mouth felt hard and lost. He remembered something people said: *never eat a fish so sick you could catch it.*

That was The Boxes. Who knew what kids caught out here? Walter had moved back to the middle bench. East curled up in the shotgun seat. He closed his eyes again. Sleeping without cover wasn't as hard as he feared. Maybe there was something different here, out of the city.

Or maybe he'd just given up on peaceful sleep.

Later the sun crossed behind the pines, and now their jagged shadows lay on the icy water. Three metallic knocks sounded nearby.

East raised his head. It was a red-haired kid outside, seventeen or eighteen, maybe, his face as flat and empty as a dinner plate, a young moustache that looked just combed. And he was rapping on the window with a pistol.

'Open up.' A cop? East's mouth was sour. He cranked down the window partway and said, 'What?'

'Right now,' the red-haired kid said hurriedly, 'you're gonna need to give me your fucking money.'

East squeezed his face and yawned. 'Hello,' he said. 'You see we're *asleep*?'

'Wake up,' ordered the red-haired kid. He might have been a year or two older than East. His moustache was brave, hairs ranging from orange to fishy white. He tapped the window with the gun barrel once more. Punctuation. Like a schoolteacher, East thought.

'Man,' East yawned. 'I don't want to make you sad. But everyone up in this van got a bigger gun than you, dig? The more people I wake up, the more people gonna be shooting at you.'

From underneath the pale moustache came 'Bullshit.'

East considered this. A kid was gonna do what he wanted. It wasn't your job to change his mind.

'I'm gonna give you five dollars,' he offered, 'and you go away. Or else I'm gonna wake everyone in this van up, and then you in some shit.'

'*Fuck* that,' the moustache said.

'Whatever you decide,' said East. 'You woke me, man. Only reason I'm not shooting you right now is I need you to go tell all your friends to let me rest.'

The redheaded boy scratched his face with the barrel of his gun, then pointed it here and there, disheartened, as if picking out a substitute target.

'Here,' said East. He rummaged around in his pockets. Nope: most of his roll was with the gun money Ty had retrieved. He had a ten and three ones left.

'You got change for this?' he said, holding the ten up behind the window.

The redhead squinted. 'No, I ain't got change.'

'Then you can have these,' said East, offering the ones instead. 'I ain't trying to scant you, man, but I need this money worse than you do, so.'

This kid. East saw that bored excitement in his eyes. Every neighborhood had a few of these.

The redheaded boy put the gun away in the gut pocket of his sweatshirt. He reached up to take the ones. East held on tight to make a point.

'If I see you again,' he warned, 'I'm gonna shoot you in the stomach, man, first thing. Right in the stomach. Nine millimeter. You might live. It will hurt, though. It will change your life.'

'Okay,' said the boy, and East let the dollars go.

'Be cool, gunner,' he said, and rolled up the window.

East watched the boy pocket the three dollars and go, walking off past a playground, where he gave each empty swing a frustrated shove. Soon the pines swallowed him. East closed his eyes.

But he couldn't go back to sleep. It wasn't smart, staying here. It wasn't The Boxes. No home-field advantage. Chances were that Gunner wasn't coming back, coming with ten or fifteen friends, all packing. Chance was that Gunner had his three dollars and was done for the day. But you could be wrong about that.

You could be wrong about anything.

He moved over to the driver's seat and ran the van slowly, gently, another mile up the road, finding a place to park it in the back of a Lutheran church. A group of boys and girls were holding a mad-scramble basketball game fifty yards away. Four adults – parents, maybe, or ministers, whatever, it didn't matter – stood with coffee and watched the battle. East parked the van in among their Fords, their Hondas. He would accept their company gratefully for an hour or two.

Thicker clouds, dull sun. Since late morning they'd slept. Six hours. Not a whole night. But it would focus them, East thought, let them work in the dark. Tonight's dark. On the middle bench, Walter was still knocked out, whistling and wheezing.

Then he realized with a punch: no head in the backseat, no knees or feet propped. Ty was gone.

He sat up, damp with sleep sweat. The gray lot, yellow lines. The kids had left their basketball game, and the lot of cars had emptied. Nearly six on the clock.

Then he located Ty, sitting at a picnic table across the grayish lawn, looking out across the yard into the trees. His sweater was dark green, like army leftovers. However cold it was, he wasn't bothered. Skinnier than East, even, but he stretched his head back, eyes closed in the feeble light. Cracked his neck.

East sat still, listening to the saw-blade whine of Walter snoring, watching his brother through the grimy windshield. He stretched his legs and arms, but they were leaden.

Ty. East had let him sleep as they'd found the house and checked it out. No – decided not to wake him, to let him sleep. But even that wasn't it. Postponed it.

Cursing silently, he took a breath and popped the door, then climbed out. Ty saw him coming and rose. 'Wait a minute,' East said, and Ty, with a sour look, loitered a few paces off.

'Get any sleep?' East inquired. 'We rode past the guy's house. I didn't wake you up. Now thinking maybe I should have.'

A shrug. 'You thinking,' Ty grumbled.

East swung his legs in and sat down at the table Ty had just abandoned.

'Cold,' Ty said. 'I'm about to get in.'

'Talk a minute,' East urged. 'Walter's asleep. What do you need? Want to see the place while it's light?'

'Don't matter.' Ty's voice was quiet, almost watery. 'You two seen it.'

'It looks pretty straight.'

'Oh?' Ty said. 'What did you learn?'

East fidgeted with his key on the pale, weather-brittle planks of the picnic table. Scarred with initials and names of the kids in this town: BEAU. RH AND JM. I LOVE SIGRID. The older marks swamped with the honey brown of the last coat of weather sealer. The new ones raw.

'You want to talk it over, how it's gonna go?'

Ty: 'How?'

East blinked. 'We're gonna do it, right? The way you want to do, man.'

'You still want to do it?' Ty said softly.

'This is why we're here.' A gust of wind, suddenly a note blowing in the gray air. East glared at it over the trees until it subsided. 'But remember,' he said, 'be cool. We got a lot of getting away to do.'

'"Be cool," he says,' said Ty. 'I *get* away. The way I do it. Fact, if it was just me, it would be done, and I would *be* away.'

'Maybe,' said East. No: he did not doubt. He imagined Ty flying in and out under his own name: luck and will and a supreme indifference to anything else. 'But Fin sent us out like so. The four. So that is the way it has to go.'

'You got all the answers,' said Ty drily, 'like always.'

So Ty was making him call it. Making him, then scorning it. East let it go. He stared at his key scoring a line into the old table. 'Tell me something, Ty. How'd you start doing this?' he asked.

'Huh?' said his brother, hands in pockets now, edgy. 'Did you ask me something?'

'I asked you,' said East, 'what happened, man, that now you're a gunner?'

'Sure,' said Ty. 'What do you want to talk about? What I do? Or how I do it? Or you want to talk about why I left home?'

The constant difficulty. Like wrestling someone with three arms. East's key slipped, gouging a long splinter out of the table. A woody fiber. Exposing the light softwood below. With spit and his finger he patted it back.

'I don't know.'

'Oh. So you don't *know* what you wanna know.' Balefully Ty eyed the basketball hoop. Its soft-laced net.

'I mean, like…' East said. Another day he'd have scratched his whole name in this table. In another life. 'I don't see you, man. I don't know who you work for. Who taught you. Who you run with.'

'Nigger, no one,' Ty growled. 'I'm here. I'm ready. I got nothing else to say.'

East said, 'You want to be that way, go ahead.'

'I know what you think,' said Ty. 'I'm on the inside. Got a steady job, and when you lose it, you get another. That ain't me. I'm a contractor.'

'You're thirteen years old, boy,' East laughed. 'You can't be no contractor.'

'Tell Fin that,' Ty said. 'I live by my wits, man. Not like you.' A thin, hot line of anger split his clear, high brow.

East stared at his brother for a long moment, then down at his hands. Digging the key along the grain of the wood again, doing nothing.

'Anyway,' said Ty. 'It's cold.'

'So we'll go.' East stood. 'You want to plan it out, talk about it?'

'Ain't nothing to plan,' Ty said, 'and nothing to talk about.'

Midway back, they found a drive-through: chicken sandwiches, milkshakes in the car. East wanted fruit, something natural.

Somewhere in the van was the orange he'd picked up in LA. Couldn't find it now.

They made it back to the beach a quarter turn around the north side of Wilson Lake. The lot there was big and shaded, a couple of cars.

They idled the van while Ty checked guns and loaded. He took the Glock and handed the other to Walter. At East he flipped a glance.

'You want me to carry yours?'

An insult. East shrugged. 'Give me that little one.'

Ty handed over the little snub that he'd brought. 'The lady's pistol.'

Pushing it hard now that it was his time. East kept quiet. They spilled money out onto the seat and split it three ways – Ty put in the Michael Wilson money too. Most of three hundred dollars apiece. Then they pocketed it, because you didn't know.

'I don't have a key. So leave the van unlocked,' Ty said.

'You don't think we're all coming back together?' said East. 'You don't even drive.'

Ty just said, 'You don't know.'

'It can be unlocked.' Walter shrugged. 'People out in the woods don't even care.'

'They don't care. Ha-ha,' Ty said. 'All right, let's go for a walk.' A walk. East closed his door and stretched his arms inside the itchy sweater. The van's engine cooled, ticking. Walter bounced on his toes. Exercising. Ty went into motion without showing a thing. East tried to do the same. He didn't look at Walter. Walter would show back what East was feeling now, as surely as if they'd spoken it aloud. And as impossible to take back.

They walked the curve of Lake Shore Drive, the three of them in single file. But keeping close to Ty. Barely any light left in the day.

As the line of pine-rimmed houses drew near, they cut off on the track running through the trees and behind the cleared-out yards. The path led uphill from the lake. They found a loosening between trees and cut through to spot the houses.

'What's it? Fourth or fifth house?' said Walter. 'No numbers on the back.'

'Look for that black truck,' said East.

A swish and hard squawk, and the pine straw beneath seemed to flip up and give forth a black ghost, a risen, screaming thing. East grabbed on to a tree, and Walter fell down. Ty nearly somersaulted to get away. It was a bird, a turkey or pheasant or something awakened in the pine straw, awakened from darkness. East could see nothing of it fleeing, but he heard the legs scrambling, the wings chop the air as the bird beat away, crying harshly.

'Damn,' breathed Ty. 'Could have had that.'

'No shooting yet, junior,' said Walter.

'No shooting. I could have *tackled* that bitch.'

East brushed off pine needles. They looked around. Lights burning on half the houses. An old white swing set like a gallows in the dark. No people around that they could see.

Three houses they'd passed. A couple more to get there. They moved together under the pine boughs in dark, scented air. East's eyes were opening up to the dark, but still he could not see all the branches, had no feel for space. There wasn't really space. He listened to Ty creeping ahead, Walter trying to stay on his feet. A snap of branch, a muffled curse.

He breathed it. He could sleep in here. The dark, the soft ground. Not even cold. But he too made his way. Nothing to carry, just the hard little spigot of the gun at his hip.

The ground kept climbing slightly. They passed a fourth house, lights on upstairs but quiet. A ceiling fan turning above the light. The fifth house was dark.

East was separated by fifteen, twenty yards. The fat boy had gotten himself snagged, had to unhook himself, fell behind. His brother likely was already there. That was it. That was the right house; he was certain. He picked a way under pines toward the dim light in the clearing.

Ty was already there, waiting just outside its edge.

'The house?'

'The house,' Ty agreed.

Boxed in tight except for the drive – trees came to within ten or fifteen feet of the house. Not wide enough for a firebreak. The clearing was uncut field grasses, calf-high, still green.

Walter came creeping out, hands and knees. 'Easier to crawl,' he grunted. 'Not so branchy.'

One yellow light hung unlit over an empty deck, another over the back door.

For East, the house was stunning in its anonymity. They'd crossed all this land to an address: this was it. Just a brown house in the woods. Big *A* on each end made of windows running light from front to back.

'Seems empty,' Walter whispered.

'Nice to be sure,' said Ty.

East looked up and gauged the sky. Seemed dark as they'd walked up, but now silver, strangely luminous, in the gap between the pines.

'Easy as pie,' Ty whispered. 'Angles on every inch of the place. Big windows on the bedrooms. No basement.'

Walter said, 'Where is the guy?'

'Can't see,' said Ty. 'Could be in bed in the dark. Could be out to dinner. Could be sitting right there on the sofa in the dark with a gun, waiting.'

'You expect one or more than one?' East said.

Ty rolled his eyes. 'I don't expect. We take what we get.'

Walter said, 'So what do you want to do?'

'How about we spread out a little and get some angles on this.'

'All right,' Walter said. 'But stay back. It's no rush. Make sure we got the right guy.'

'Did you call your George Washington?' needled Ty. 'Is this the place?'

'It's the right house,' East hushed. 'Let's get the right guy.'

'I don't see any guy,' sniffed Ty. 'Why don't you two collaborate on that. I'm gonna go see what I see.' He began picking his way left along the seam of yard and woods, creeping along the flank of the house.

Walter stood breathing heavily beside East. They listened to the pine needles crackling under Ty's steps.

'Drive all that way thinking about it, man,' Walter said. 'And then here it is.'

'I was thinking that,' East said.

'Sure seems empty.' Walter stood stock-still. 'Seems nobody's home.'

'You don't want to wake somebody up, and then you got a now-or-never in the dark,' East reasoned.

'Yeah. Question is, how long you want to stand and wait?'

'I can wait awhile,' said East.

Nothing sounded or moved. They'd lost track of Ty.

Walter said, 'You gonna recognize him?'

'Who? The judge?'

East recalled the photos. The fierce, thick head on the man. The sides of gray. But it could have been sharper. The face swam with different faces in his mind: Fin's. Walter's. His own.

'I think so,' he said.

'I'll know him.'

'I will too,' East said. But he wanted to get away from Walter.

'How many times your brother done this?'

'Ask him,' East said. 'Good luck,' he added.

'How big was he when he started?'

'Who knows.' He took a step away.

'He knows what he's doing,' said Walter. 'I mean, he goes right at it.'

'He's got a reputation to protect,' East said. 'I'm a check the other side.' He started tracing the seam around to the right.

'Fine. Stay invisible,' Walter said uselessly.

The ground could be quiet if you slid your toe into each step. Like putting on slippers. East found a spot shaded by branches where he could see in the side windows and see the drive out front, the black truck and a glimpse of the road. He stood there, black face in a black hole. He could barely see his hands. He put one on his heart and tried to calm his blood down. Inside the black string was buzzing with irritation. Like he got sometimes at the crew at the house, when they ceased to watch, ceased to be in the moment. Became wild again. It annoyed East, made him bitter. And stubborn.

He made a smooth spot in the needles and tested it. Dry – but cold. He sat down anyway. Funny – a few days back, he was used to twelve-hour shifts on his feet, did six a week. Now he was eager to sit.

How many days had they been going again?

As if his mind was sand. The irregular sleep was one thing. But the road: as if he'd been brainwashed. As if he'd stared into a washing machine for days without closing his eyes. Even the lines and reflectors on the highway: like a code he couldn't read but couldn't stop, like a sound he'd wanted no longer to hear. His head felt out of shape, weak.

For years he'd guarded a place that mattered, looking out, seeing everything. Now he sat against a tree, staring in, seeing nothing at all. Nothing in the wooden house sounded or moved. It was wearing him out.

He thought he'd have time to think about it on the trip – killing a man. Or that in all the work of keeping things straight, the killing would become just another motion, another step. This was the address. They would find a man. He would be the man. Put it on the tab.

But he hadn't thought about it. What he hadn't seen was that in the rush across the country, the man would be forgotten. The face, the plan, inapparent. Only the miles and the goal remained. He'd declined the subject of the man until he was sitting outside his yard, waiting. Waiting on him to come home and die.

Darker. He heard something in the trees behind him – skitterings, like a bird. Something watching him. And then a heavier crunching. Walter coming like a freight train through the trees. East could not believe the noise he was making. He sat still until Walter had nearly blundered past him, then hissed, 'Hey.'

Walter stopped and peered around until he located East. He said, 'Ty says it's empty. He's gonna check it out.'

'What if somebody drives in?'

'Then we're loaded,' said Walter. 'We have the jump.'

'He might drive in alone or not,' East said. 'We don't know. We're not even gonna know if it's him.'

'You know what Ty said?'

'No,' East exhaled. 'I don't wanna know what Ty said. I know if there's anyone home on this road, they can hear your ass.' His veins clouded with annoyance. He got up, but the cold stuck on his butt, an unpleasant circle.

He sized up the yard. 'Tell you what. Go back. Take the back corner, left side. I'll get the front corner, right. We'll see all four sides. Then Ty can go close and look around.'

'He's already doing it,' Walter said.

'Still.'

'All right.' Walter turned and began again toward the back of the house. Making painful progress through the branches. Ty came out then. East watched his brother move. Casual, erect, no cat-stalking dramatics. He carried the gun in his hand but kept it shadowed. He crouched when he went against the house's frame. There he tested the ground and crept low along the window line. Popped up against a frame and peered inside. With one hand he tried the front doorknob. Didn't open.

East watched Ty working, recognized his careful pace. Taking time at each window, noting the rooms, the layout and angles. Shooters thought things through two ways. Where were people likely to be, before they knew about you? Then after, when they did, where were they likely to go? Where was shelter? Did they cover? Head for a closet where the guns were? If they shot back at you, from where? Or would they flush right out to the yard? A shooter understood a home just as well as the people who lived there. But to different ends.

Less cautious by the moment, Ty worked around the back. A car rolled by slowly on the stony road without slowing. East stood inside the clearing now, drawn to the house by impatience.

After four minutes Ty had made a full lap. No caution in how he stood now. Contempt for the house that had no people in it. Contempt for the time he'd spent working slowly. He spotted East along the face of the woods and approached, sticking the gun away with a swagger.

East felt almost apologetic. 'Any minute he could be home.'

'No.' Ty shook his head. 'No. No clothes, no suitcase. No dishes in the sink. No soap in the bathroom. Water's switched off. House is cold. Nobody's been here. Or if they were, they won't be back for a while.'

'You want me to look?' said East.

Ty laughed. 'Be my guest.'

East made his own circuit. His eyes were hungry in the dark.

He peered inside but nothing broke with Ty's account. Items to interest a thief – nice speakers, espresso maker, a flat TV up high. People with houses like this didn't skimp. Stealing wasn't his game but he knew enough from listening – most of the boys he'd led were thieves at some time. Once they stopped stealing, they stopped being quiet about it.

The back glass door was braced against sliding but not barred, like in the city. Probably an alarm, probably a glass-break sensor. No security badge on the windows, but he would have bet. It didn't matter much. If Ty saw his man, he'd be making noise.

Walter wandered up. 'What you want to do? Stay here and stake out?'

'Wish we could bring the van up,' said East. 'It's cold.'

'Scare him straight away too. Van full of black boys idling by the house?'

'I know.'

Now the chill penetrated him. But the heat of the van seemed a hundred miles away.

'You want to go?' Walter said.

East slit his eyes. 'No.'

'I'm even getting cold myself,' Walter said, undulating his bulk. East turned away, played the judge's features in his head again.

What he could remember.

'You want to go?' said Walter.

'Didn't you just say that?' said East viciously.

Ty came out around the corner, face pinched in, like he was chewing it up from the inside. 'Shit. Forget it,' he said. 'I'm done with this.'

East said, 'Let's give it another hour.'

'Oh?' said Ty. 'You in charge? Fine, stay here. I know you like standing by a house. Me, I'm finished.'

'I second that,' said Walter.

East rolled his eyes at the sky. Fading but still silver above the grave-black square the trees made.

'We can call Abe back up. Might be a plan B,' said Walter. 'Come on, East. Sitting out here ain't gonna be nothing but cold.'

'But what if they don't answer.'

'Then they *don't*. Let's warm up at least. Get some food.'

'I don't need to warm up.'

Ty snorted. 'Listen to him. Fucking cowboy, man. I seen you get cold last night.'

Darkly East glared.

'I don't know,' protested Walter. 'I don't know if they'll answer. But maybe he's at a hotel or buying gas or at an airport. But I do know if he's somewhere else, we can find that out.'

'How you gonna find that out?'

Walter pressed his lips together grimly. 'Stuff you don't know about, man.'

'You saying –'

'I'm saying I can't talk about it. But it's real.'

'Fuck it,' said Ty. 'Fuck you both. I'll be in the van.'

Walter glanced at Ty as he went. 'I gotta agree,' he said.

Quiet now. Even the birds stopped shifting in their trees.

'You coming?'

'Just trying to do my job,' East said.

'Okay. I hear you. But I'm ready to get out of this icebox, man. Come on.'

East hesitated, then followed Walter out to the road. Ty was a hundred yards ahead, out in plain view. At least it was dark. East hurried to catch up with Walter.

'Tell me one thing,' he said. 'The judge, could he have gone to LA already?'

'I guess,' Walter said. 'Possible. But I'm going to say no.'

'Because of what?'

Walter winced. 'Stuff you don't know about,' he repeated. 'More stuff. Shit.' East kicked a pine cone. 'Burn these woods up, man.'

Somehow they'd gotten low on gas. All tired. All angry. East took it personally. The empty house was another house lost. He had tried to keep it straight. But now everyone would kill one another at the first sideways look.

East fired the van through the little bubble of light that was the town and back into the dark, pine-jagged night. The big highway home lay to the south, so he took them north – toward the other lake, the ghetto lake, just by instinct. Just a glimpse of the big highway and it was over. The job would be over. If it weren't already.

All the miles, he thought. Nothing.

'Why we ain't got a cell?' grumbled Ty. 'So much time wasted finding these phones.'

'You know why,' Walter said.

'You know there's a way to do it. You just too scary of everything.'

'I'm Murder One scary,' Walter replied. Staring out at nothing.

'All right. All right,' East broke in. 'Look. Wasn't there a pay phone up at Welfare Lake?'

'Yep.'

'Do you know, while we were sleeping, some dude tried to rob us up there?'

Walter giggled. 'What do you mean, tried to?'

'White dude with a little gun in his hand. I gave him three.' Before it had seemed funny, a story he could save up and tell. Now it didn't have much in it.

'So he *did* rob us,' said Ty. 'Whyn't you wake me?'

'Think about it,' said Walter. 'Think for a minute why he didn't wake you.'

Yes: a phone booth, a fisherman's phone, at the second lake. It hung on a power pole beneath a light, the last few buzzing insects struggling through the cold air.

One woman, maybe thirty, forty, in dirty pink sandals, was on the line. Dolefully they watched her.

'What do you want to do?' asked East.

'Wait,' said Walter. 'What are we gonna do? Drive around? Go back and freeze? How long you think she can stand there in that housedress?'

'That housedress looks warm,' Ty put in from the back. 'I say she'll be there all night.'

East parked the van two rows of spaces out and killed the lights. Left the van to idle. He broke open a water bottle, but it only made him colder.

'Wonder what she's talking about,' Walter said, cracking his neck side to side.

Her feet were bare in the fuzzy sandals. She looked over her shoulder and winced at the sight of the van. Then turned back.

'When we get on there, talk if you want. But I got to ask a few questions,' Walter said.

'I don't even care. You talk,' East said. 'What is *stuff I don't know about*? That's what I want to know.'

'We see his credit cards. Okay?' Walter said. 'Don't ask who, don't ask where. I'll tell you two things, then you forget them. One, we got people watching his credit cards. Two, if something like an airline ticket came through, Abraham Lincoln would have told us. Told us when, told us where. That's why I don't think so.'

'But Abraham Lincoln ain't answering his phone.'

'Today he ain't,' said Walter gloomily. 'I'll concede that.'

The woman on the phone held out a hand and backhanded the air five, six times. Like she were reenacting the slapping of a child.

'Shit, I can't stand it,' said East, and he swung the door open and jumped out. Colder here, now. And quiet.

The woman bared her teeth at him before he was ten feet away. 'You get away from me!' she raged. 'You get back! I got here first!'

'Ma'am,' East said. 'Ma'am.'

'You git back!' she hissed. 'This is my call!' A yellow rubber bracelet on her wrist holding one key. Gripping the receiver jealously, ready to give up everything for it, her one treasure on Earth. 'There's this *boy* here,' she shouted into the phone. 'He wants the phone! Yes! And I told him, it's my call. I paid! I came first! And now he won't go away.'

East pushed the air down with his empty palms down, trying to settle. 'Ma'am,' he cajoled. 'Not hurrying you. Not hurrying you.'

'Yes, you are. Yes, you are!'

He had Ty's little squirt gun in his pocket. It gave him an odd, lopsided feeling.

'How long you gonna be on, though? Ma'am!'

'How do I know?' the woman protested. 'A minute, maybe? A few minutes? Damn!'

Blankly, East stared at the woman. Well, this sawed it. Ride for days, then crash up on this creature. Beggar-woman, they would have called her in The Boxes: steel-wool hair. Shoulder blades quivering under the housedress. His mother in white.

'A few minutes,' he conceded bitterly. He turned and walked to the van, where they'd be teasing him, he knew. Yes. Pealing laughter as soon as he opened the door.

'God damn,' wept Walter. 'You should have seen her eyes flash.' East slid in with what he could salvage of his dignity. 'A minute, she said.'

'All night. I was right,' Ty said. 'Do what you wanna do. That was funny.'

East tried to consider it funny.

'So, what did this robber look like, anyway?' Walter said. 'The one who was gonna take us?'

East shrugged. *Stuff you don't know about.* 'Big and white. Moustache. Red hair. Teenaged. Wore a green coat like the army.'

'Probably *was* the army,' Ty said. 'Oh! Look!'

The woman was scurrying off in her slippers. Wasn't taking a chance.

The operator was a new one. It took her forever to dial through. 'Are you still on?' Walter asked twice. 'Did we get disconnected?'

'I'm still here.'

Then the silence of a new connection on the line. 'Yeah,' a male voice said.

East put his head in so close to Walter's that they were breathing each other's breath.

'Man,' Walter said, 'we're there. We reached it. You guys been offline. And the man isn't at the house. Do you understand me?'

'Yes,' said the voice.

'You got any news for me? Anything I can use?'

'We got a different setup,' reported the voice. 'Police came down this morning. Arrested a few people.'

The curve of Walter's ear just past the dark receiver, pinkish-brown.

'A few people? Who?'

'You know,' the man said. 'I don't really want to say.'

'The big man?'

'Definitely got the big man.'

'*Fuck*,' said East. His body recoiled beneath him, wanted to smash something, to go running off. He bit down hard and listened.

Walter asked, 'The two dudes who sent us?'

'Definitely arrested them. Definitely cleaned out that whole area.'

'How many?'

'Maybe fifteen, twenty. Put it this way. Yesterday there was an organization. Tonight there ain't. We'll see what we can do tomorrow.'

Walter put the phone to his chest. 'You hear this?'

'Yeah,' East whispered.

'Things are changed,' the voice on the other end said. 'I mean, it might be cool, you making that stop. More important now. There's more people he can talk about now, you dig?'

Walter said, 'I dig.'

'But I got no instructions. You do what you got to do,' said the voice.

'You still got him flying out Sunday?'

'Flying Sunday,' confirmed the voice. 'Nonstop to LAX.'

'Remind me,' said Walter. 'What day is it now?'

'Thursday night,' the voice said tersely. 'You boys strong? In your pocket?'

'Yeah, we're strong,' said Walter.

'Okay,' said the voice. 'The next conversation should be like this conversation. Smart.'

'So you're telling me to make up my own mind,' Walter said. 'Yeah,' returned the voice. 'I guess you can do that.'

Walter cupped the phone. 'It's up to us,' he whispered. 'What you want to do?'

East looked long and hard at Walter's brown eyes. 'We go,' he said. 'We do what Fin told us.'

'All right,' said Walter, and drew a long breath, the van full of guns idling behind them, blind.

12

ONCE AT THE HOUSE in The Boxes a boy named Hosea was going to fight a boy they called Cancer. Everyone knew it would happen, and no one wanted it to, because Hosea was well liked while Cancer was not, and Cancer was going to whup Hosea's ass. None of that was a question. The boys knew, too, that it would happen, because Hosea had asked for it. He told Cancer that nobody liked him, then went on and explained it. He insulted Cancer and then insulted him again. Everyone knew Hosea was telling the truth. Hosea was a good kid.

But stronger than their feelings for Hosea or telling the truth was a principle: know when you're fucking with someone. Know who you're fucking with. Know that things have their cost. The boys knew the fight was on, because Hosea could not say what he'd said and not pay.

And then the fight didn't happen. It was a windy, blast-furnace day. First Cancer was there, waiting for Hosea. When he left, Hosea showed up. Then they were both there, and ready, but Sidney called out from inside with some work: a U had stopped breathing on the kitchen floor. He had to be taken out. He was all quaky and blue. You did not have people dying in the house. It was best to save their lives, or have them die somewhere else. Either way, you took them out. Cancer and Hosea were both called into that, and they helped carry the U out and put him in a car. In the car, the U went ahead and died, so the event became less a drop-off and more a dropping-the-body. You could not just drop a body anywhere or at any time. Bodies were complicated. And the dead body dissipated the charge between Cancer and Hosea.

But not the other boys. That tension had not been released. And the rest of the day, East had to settle them, to separate them, to keep the electricity that had stabbed the air like a knife from cutting into them, from sending them honed at each other. No matter that Hosea and Cancer stood together and let it drop; no matter that a dead man lay in temporary storage, waiting to be cast aside when darkness came. A knife had been thrown up into the air, and the boys would not settle to their work until they saw it land.

There was a gas station. The lights in the cold made the cars gleam like licked suckers. East pumped and paid, and Walter tried calling the number again. Nothing. Nothing had changed. Nobody knew anything more.

They bought hot dogs out of a steamer and drove off.

It seemed they were reaching the end of the world of people. No towns on this road to speak of, only points where the trees peeled away, the road bent, and suddenly there'd be a house on the land, a single light atop a garage; it blazed, filled the yard as they passed, then the trees snapped shut like a curtain behind them. Roads as dark as rivers, absorbent of everything, only the reflectors in their measured rhythm, *here, here, here*, on posts, and *here, here*, down the center stripe.

Scuttling eyes disappeared along the edges of the road.

But Walter, having warned East not to ask, was now conversing on how you tracked a man through his credit cards. 'Ain't hard to get someone's number,' he rambled. 'Any waiter can do it, any cashier at a store. If you don't mess with it, if you aren't trying to steal, then no one knows you're watching.'

'So you doing this?' Ty put in. 'On the judge?'

The judge. His name lay low in East's memory.

'I set the account up. I maintained it. Some people never check their shit online. Sometimes you gotta work at it. Sometimes you set it up once, and it works forever.'

'How you learn?'

'Just learned,' said Walter. 'Kids at school.'

East watched the inscrutable dark outside. Had to take this break, he reassured himself. It was necessary. Everyone needed to warm up. The night was even colder than the night before at the gun house, when it had snowed. This cold would freeze you. Everyone needed the heat. Everyone needed the food.

They ate the watery hot dogs and wadded the cartons up. No finding the trash bag anymore. East stuffed his into the crack of the seat.

Ty put his feet up on the back of Walter's chair. 'So you're following the guy's cards. How come the dude don't know?'

'Know what?' said Walter.

'Somebody's watching him.'

'How come he don't know? Everybody suspects. Nowadays everybody thinks somebody's on to their shit. But if you ain't losing money,' he said, 'if your money is still, you don't do anything about it. And we ain't taking his money.'

Ty said, 'If we got a computer, say at a library, could you see him?'

'No.'

'I thought that was the point,' said Ty acidly.

'I know,' said Walter. 'It's complicated, man. We were tracking more than one guy. It ain't like I had just one password. I don't know what his was. I ain't got these all memorized. And we was faking IP addresses, everything. We had a whole setup.'

'What computer did you use?' said Ty.

'At school.'

'No wonder you still in school,' laughed Ty. 'Tell me how come Fin ever had you standing yard. You a smart boy.'

East opened his mouth, shut it again. It was more questions than he'd heard Ty ask in years.

Walter replied, 'I stood yard so I'd know the job.'

He coasted to a stop. The highway ended at a stop sign. Ahead, a maze of road signs peppered a luminous guardrail that kept cars from hurtling into the woods. Walter had been running squares, East knew from watching the roof compass switching *N, E, S, W.* Just going around the block, keeping the lake in the middle. And they'd been riding almost two hours.

'We can decide whatever we want,' Walter said.

It was East they were waiting on.

He stirred. It had been easy to say *go* in the light of the pay phone, tethered some way, however, to LA, to The Boxes. But here in the dark, the van filled with the things he didn't know.

Something about talking again seemed difficult. 'Should we call them again and see what they know?'

Walter shook his head. 'Maybe. But not till morning at best. School's closed. And I don't even know who's watching things. I don't know who's in jail and who isn't.'

The turn signal pulsed in the ditch, shotgun side.

'If we went back,' said Walter, 'we could see if anything is going on.'

'Back in them pine trees,' East said hopelessly. 'With nobody there.'

'Maybe we'd find something,' Walter said. 'Maybe if we broke in. Something that would tell us.'

Ty said, 'I *did* break in. At least, I popped a window up.' Walter turned in his seat. 'Why didn't you say something? Was there any alarm?'

'If there was,' said Ty, 'I didn't hear it. If there was, cops already came and went.'

'You think we should go?' Walter said over his shoulder. 'Ty?' Ty said, 'Me? I seen it already. Doing my job. You two make up your minds.' He lay down theatrically, retired.

'Yeah,' East decided. 'Circle back.' He had been hugging his knees, and now that he let them go, his whole body hurt. Beaten up from inside. Heading back to the house did not make him happy. But Ty was right. You did your job.

Wilson Lake. Reflectors on every post, every driveway, eyeing them. The driveway of 445 Lake Shore empty but for the cold black truck.

Walter idled the van at the lake parking lot while once again they loaded up and got ready. They slipped on the thin, dark gloves. Once again they walked the back track off the road.

The grass had gone quiet, and the branches slapped back when Walter caught one in the dark. Ty led them through the field of pines to where they saw the yellow back porch light. A single moth clapped at it, ineffectual.

'There's the phone box,' said Ty. A gray box below the kitchen windows.

'So?'

'If you got an alarm, it comes out in that.'

'Some alarms work cellular,' said Walter.

'Ain't no signal up here,' Ty said.

'How do you know that?' Walter said. 'How do you *know* that?'

Ty had Walter spooked now.

The phone box was cobwebbed. Ty pried the lid up and pinched free the plug.

'If we're going in looking, what you want to find?'

Walter said, 'Anything. Directions? Ticket receipt? A note? We'll just look. But we ain't going in there to break and fuck things up.'

'Of course,' said Ty.

'Take your shoes off,' said Walter.

The window Ty had popped was on the middle of the back side, over the sink. There was a security lock on the frame, but it left enough room for Ty to squirm his head and shoulders in.

'Maybe they'll have a flashlight,' Walter said. 'You'd think we'd have a flashlight.'

Ty kicked his shoes off. 'Lift me up.'

Walter clucked his tongue at East, and East started. Together they made stirrups of their hands. Ty climbed them and got an arm inside and went moving things – a bottle of soap off the sill, two glasses away down the counter. Then he began wriggling in. It was tight. He yelped at something. East passed Walter Ty's foot and went to help, felt at Ty, at the metal framing of the window. He found what was catching: his brother's ear. He touched it, little stub of cartilage, strangely warm, and for a flash he thought of their mother's face.

'Damn, that hurts,' Ty groaned from inside. East pressed the ear, flattened it, helped pass it without abrasion through the hard, slotlike opening. And let Ty's head go. In. Ty's head was in.

East threaded his other arm around and began keying Ty's shoulders into the slot, feeding his body in, inch by inch, rib by rib. His waist and legs wriggled in midair.

'Fuck. Ouch. All right,' Ty said from inside.

'You want us to stay back here?' East said.

'Yeah, let me look. Then I'll let you in.'

'All right.' East and Walter braced Ty's thighs as he wormed in in midair. His body seesawed, and his hips disappeared over the sill. Then the pair of headlights swung into the driveway.

13

THERE WOULD BE A few more seconds where the car would be running, seconds where they might not be heard. East had Ty's legs in his hands. Ty was still pulling, wriggling in.

'We got to pull you out,' East whispered fiercely through the window, past his brother's body.

'What? No!'

'They're here.'

'I just got *in*,' Ty cursed.

The pair of lights swung away as the car picked its way up the driveway. Then they stabbed again across the open *A* of the house. The lights bounced off the countertops, the faucet. Then the car stopped – it was something new, little high-intensity bulbs – and the lights were doused.

'Now,' said East, and he caught Ty's hand and hauled him back, up over the countertop and out the window. Ty's head bounced on the sill: '*Ow, ow, ow, ow,*' he complained.

'Shh.'

'The screen. The screen,' said Walter.

'Forget the screen,' East said. He slid the window down and scooped Ty up with him. They scuttled into the pines together. This little square of a yard, the house lights would fill entirely.

'Where my shoes at?' Ty whispered furiously.

'Shh,' East replied.

The doors of the little car popped open. Two people got out: a full-grown man on the driver's side. Someone else on the other.

'What we got, a girlfriend?' said Walter.

Ty watched intently.

East picked up a pine bough, the needles dry and brittle but still arrayed. He held it over his face, peering through it. The man was coming to the house, thumbing through keys.

He stopped, the man, at the front door and caused an overhead light to come on. They could see him – large, a black man. East wondered: *our black man?* The man opened the door and moved through the open space to the kitchen. On the counter he laid a satchel or briefcase. The lights he switched on there were furious, bright, paint-store white: yes. They threw a glare that filled the yard, that counted the trees. East flinched at it.

Were they covered? Deep enough? That last-second dilemma of hide-and-seek: could you find a better place? Or did moving expose you now?

Slowly the man stepped back out of the kitchen, into one of the sides of the house, soundless – like watching TV with the mute on. Into the kitchen next came the girl. East watched her reach up. She took a cup down from a cabinet and a plastic jug of water from somewhere below and poured a drink.

Dark. Black dark. Hard to make out her features or her age. 'No water,' Ty said. 'They're just camping out here, man.'

'Was that him?' Walter said. 'East?'

East stared until his forehead hurt. 'I'm not sure yet.'

'Best make sure,' said Ty. 'If I shoot, he ain't coming back.' Madly

East tried to flip through the pictures in the back of his mind. To see again what Johnny had shown them that morning. He could bring up the man's suit, his heft. Could remember nothing of his face.

Silently the man and girl moved around the lighted house, specimens in a box. So blindingly bright. East felt his stomach begin to knot.

'Just knock,' Ty muttered. 'If he answers, ask is he the judge we're here to shoot.'

'What about the girl?' whispered Walter.

'Don't shoot her,' said East.

'She ain't a target,' Ty said, 'but she better not fuck with me.'

'That's cold,' Walter said, 'shooting the dude in front of her. Because he looks like, you know – her dad.'

Ty didn't say anything. East held the fallen bough close. The dry needles prickled across his cheeks.

'You decided yet?' said Ty impatiently.

The neighbors' houses were distant, dull shapes. The stars wheeled above them, forgotten. East chewed a pine needle. Strange, bitter, sweet, like orange peel somehow. His eyes tightened on the blaring light.

The girl accelerated things. Two people there: one person you had to peel away. To ignore, to not shoot. But that's how it worked. You thought you had the rhythm, that your pace was the world's pace. Then someone busted a move. Someone drove up in a fleet of black-and-whites and disrupted. Someone opened a door. The world would have its way with you. You and your plan. There was only that lesson to learn.

You could pretend that it would not, that all your breathing and all your insulation would protect you. Ask Michael Jackson. Ask anyone in LA. Earthquakes rattled up out of nowhere. No radar, nobody yelling *Incoming*, no warning text on your phone. Only the house jangling, things falling off the wall. East was fifteen. He'd never been through a big one.

Stop. Stop it, he told himself.

He spat out the pine needle and began creeping, moving left along the line of woods around the house. The thrown light was as bright as a ball field: he had to stay well clear. Dark clothes, dark shoes, dark branch, dark skin. One night Sony had brought along his sister's astronomy book from school – she went to a special all-girl science school she had to ride an hour to get to – and they observed the stars they couldn't see in the LA sky, they studied the words that weren't used in The Boxes.

Albedo. Can a body throw back light? It might have been the last word he'd ever learned. East's albedo was near zero. Not much bounced back off him.

He'd been tracking toward the front of the house, but then the man appeared again at the back, in the kitchen. He lit a match, got the pilot going on the stove. He poured water from a bottle into a silver kettle and set it down. The light over his head drowned his face in shadows. Graying hair. Maybe fifty. Solid, thick shoulders. He washed and dried the girl's cup.

East stopped and sighted through the bedroom windows. Through one he could see the girl stepping into a bathroom on the other side. Light spilled into the hallway, then the door narrowed and snuffed it out.

Give me a minute, he'd told Ty. Because from what he saw, he could tell nothing, could conclude nothing.

Then the man was moving again, stepping to the front door. East watched him flicker past one window, then the next. At the front door he rummaged in his pockets. Where was Ty now? Ty was waiting. Waiting on him.

The man couldn't find his keys. He stopped, retraced his

path. Back to the kitchen. He reached, took the keys from the countertop.

The stripe of light at the bathroom opened again, and the girl stepped out. She went to the kitchen. Turned the tap, but the faucet gave no water. She reached again for the gallon jug, then the just-washed cup. As she poured the cup full again, she looked out the window, and East saw her eyes. Her face swam, seemed to look at him sideways. The face was the Jackson girl's face. The one he'd watched die. He caught his breath and looked away for a moment.

Yes. Just the girl, just the man. Nothing more.

Where was the man now? He'd come out the front. He was at the car! In the open air, away from her. Keys in his hand, even. East peered back along the trees' edge, but Ty and Walter weren't there where they'd been. Everyone was moving now: without anyone saying *Go*, it was happening. East slipped left, farther toward the front, past the bedrooms, past the short brown stockade around the air conditioner. One lone pine stabbed up out of the earth, away from its pack. Then he was near the black truck and the car – a little Volvo wagon, snub-nosed, Illinois plates.

The man fobbed open the doors and lifted suitcases out of the back. He wrestled with them – big ones, not the little tote size, but monsters. He couldn't make it with both. He put one down on the beaten dirt and entered with the other. East watched him disappear inside.

The other suitcase sat beside the car, unattended. Uncalculating, straight and quick, East rushed behind the truck, around the light that spilled out the front door, to the suitcase. Was there a tag? A name card? He reached for it, the pine bough still in his hand. Looked for a name card, something on the handle, down the side. Nothing.

Then he found the golden stitching on the highest flap. Faint in the house's glow: a monogram. cwt. For a moment his brain buzzed, pulling up the name of the man they were hunting. Then a shriek echoed inside the house: it all clicked in. Carver. Thompson. The right initials.

The right man.

The girl. 'Daddy? Daddy? Someone –'

She came running. Not at him – not to shut the door. He saw her eyes. Never mind the initials – this suitcase was what she wanted.

He straightened, raised the pine mask idiotically to his face.

'Daddy!' She burst through the door, came outside.

East's heart hammered. Discovered now.

The father's first cry was faraway. Then he came barreling, yelling now: *Melanie! Melanie!* East spun away – where was his gun, even? He kept his face hidden, for being spotted by her was not like being spotted by him. She was a witness; he was the target. He was the one who knew too much. East cleared his throat, but as he did, she reached her suitcase, and he heard the other pair of feet sliding to a stop on the piney ground: his brother. Arrived.

Ty said, 'Here we go, E. Is it him?'

East nodded. 'It's him.'

The judge stopped at the door. East watched him stare and then smile. Half laughing, a curious voice: 'Do I know you boys?'

Ty's arm came up and a growl rose from his throat, a reproach. Then he fired through the screen door. Two shots, three. East heard them punch the man, heard the long, failing gasp.

The girl tugged the suitcase and shut her eyes. Opened her mouth, but nothing came out.

Her father hit the floor. Walter arrived.

'He finished?'

Ty leveled the gun at the girl, who hadn't unsqueezed her eyes. She clutched the black handle.

'Not her,' East said.

Pock. Pock. Twice his brother shot. The noise ripped the black yard. 'No,' East said, but already she was falling, the suitcase toppling over her.

Walter's face was pale, stretched. 'Is he finished, I said.'

'Three in the heart,' Ty said. 'That'll do. He's the right dude?' East dropped the pine bough. 'He's the one,' he murmured. And the girl. The girl with her face going still in the lamplight.

In the dark, she had the Jackson girl's face. That same all-seeing look, into a world where nothing moves. East stood near her. 'I told you not to,' he said.

'My call. I did it. That was what we said,' said Ty. 'No time to talk about it.'

'You want to lose that gun, man,' Walter pointed out.

'No,' said Ty. 'Ain't the way it works. Right now I got to find my shoes.'

He sprinted, dirty socks, back to where he'd mounted the window. East staggered away. The gunshots still echoed around the spaces of his brain. Seconds were passing.

Lights in a house deeply set behind pines. But they might have been on before.

Ty's feet scrambling in the needles behind the house. Every sound carrying sharply now, every breath leaving its shape like ghosts in the air.

'We got to go,' Walter urged. 'East. We got to leave.'

'I know it.' East's neck crawled. He did not look at the two dark piles, the man behind the door, and the other, under the black suitcase toppled over. He stared down the cleared channel beside the lit, empty house.

'Fuck!' Ty said in the useless dark.

Walter's eyes swiveled. 'East?'

'Did you do something with his shoes?'

'I didn't do nothing,' Walter protested. 'He kicked them off.

193

Maybe we should get a head start? East?' Backpedaling already, finding the road with his feet.

Then mad, flying footsteps, and Ty was coming, the stripes of light painting him as he sped beneath the windows. In one hand the shoes, in the other the gun. 'Go!' he panted. East turned: already Walter was pumping down the road. No other noise, no movement, no response. The quiet banks of mailboxes marked them passing by.

Quickly they made their way back around the stony road, thudding heavy of foot as it swept downhill, the pines less dense on their left between them and the lake. Their breath came and fled in quick mouthfuls. Around the lakeside curve, the parking lot came into view, the lone light on its pole stained yellow, a glimpse of their blue van shining beneath the trees. Numb, East hastened his steps. *Get away, get away,* his mind drummed. And also: *what happened?*

No talking, only the question the girl's face made.

Then he saw the other car, an old boat of a Chevy jacked up on fat wheels, parked near the van, black like the pines in the yellow light. And two kids swarming around the van. Trouble.

'Look,' he said, pointing.

'Mother fuck,' said Ty, taking the lead. 'All right. Guns up, and spread out. I'm a handle it. But be ready.'

'It's just neighborhood kids,' said Walter.

Ty's scowl locked down. 'Do what I say, Walt.'

He fanned left, and East began a slow run across the lot, taking each yellow-lined parking space in two steps, Walter coming up behind. Ty's gun made a heavy *click,* and East pawed at his pockets for the little gun. He found it clumsily, fumbling at it as he ran.

As yet the kids hadn't spotted them. One might have been the ghetto-lake thug from yesterday. Meaty shoulders, moustache.

'That one got a gun,' East panted. Guessing. But just as much, telling Ty: *Careful.*

Ty raised his hand and squeezed a shot into the trees. *Pock.* The white boys saw them now. They clutched at each other, then broke for their car. The rattly engine roared. Ty followed them left, and East went for the van, slapping his pockets for the keys. 'Hey!' Ty was yelling. 'Hey!'

The dark car burned rubber. It leapt toward a gap in the trees. Instantly its lights were gone, just its whine climbing the road away from the lake. East reached the van, panting, key ready in his fingers.

But it wasn't any use. The kids, they'd fucked it up. Walter came wheezing up behind, goggle-eyed. 'Oh, shit,' he groaned. 'Oh, shit!'

East breathed and circled. One side window had been popped off its buckle. It hung askew on its hinges like a flap. That had gotten them in. They'd pulled out everything – the clothes, the food, the first-aid kit and blanket. The case of water bottles, scattered on the ground.

'They took my game, man,' Ty swore from the back.

'We got the money, right?' said Walter. 'Y'all still have the money?'

'They got my *game.*'

'We have to leave,' East said.

'Look, though,' Walter said. East stepped back. The problem wasn't apparent. But down the hidden side of the van, the woods side, it said something in spray paint. It said, FUCK YOU NIGGERS.

'Bashed out the taillights too,' said Ty, shoes still dangling in his hand.

Walter chewed his lips. 'We can't drive like this,' he said. 'Like, hello, help us out, every cop in the world. Right at the same time they're finding bodies.'

'But right now we need to go,' said East. 'Get in.'

He found a four-lane road westward and took it. Avoiding going back through town, where people would see them. Neighbors. The wind cut in through the broken side window, swirled through the van, searching. Ty was trying to rig a sling for it with the Ace bandage roll from the first-aid kit. East waited until his breath was steady before he turned around.

'The fuck was that, Ty?'

Ty, working on the window, was serene. 'What? You hollering at me now?'

'What happened?'

'What happened?' Ty stopped and glanced forward for only an instant. 'Mission accomplished, son.'

'The girl. I told you, don't shoot the girl. Why don't you just kill everyone you see?'

Ty said, 'Thinking on it.'

East banged the steering wheel. 'Just evil. Evil! And those dudes. Run right up where they can see you. Why don't you just tell them how many people you shot lately?'

Ty paused ironically. 'Sure. Say. Maybe you're right. Maybe we should be subtle. Driving a van with *nigger* wrote down the side.'

'People can't see that in the dark,' East snapped.

'People can see whatever they want.'

It was what Ty did. Move East off the subject. Though East couldn't bear to move back. It was like a furnace behind them, something blinding hot.

Empty dark road before them. No lights or shapes. East fought his eyes – they kept searching the pavement rushing under them. Had to keep looking down the road.

For all the planning, they had nothing now.

'We got any help from here on out?' he asked Walter. 'Or are we on our own?'

Walter opened his hands slowly and closed them.

'Ty?'

'You got a car,' Ty said brutally. 'You got a gun. Make your way.'

'You got to change cars,' Walter said. 'We're just gonna have to get a new car.'

'Could call Abe,' said East. 'See if he can hook us up.'

Said Walter, 'No. Listen to me. We're on our own now.'

A little town was coming up, and East slowed for its speed limits. The van passed through the center of light – a gas station, bright as the vault of a refrigerator, and two late-night girls out pumping gas, brown hair fanned out over their fur hoods. They turned, watched the van roll past, painted words like a banner on the side they could see.

Fuck you niggers.

If nobody knew who they were, still, everyone would remember seeing them. When it came to connecting the dots, everyone would draw lines.

They had most of a tank of gas and a few hours before daylight.

Two more towns and East found a gas station with a blue-lit phone on its outskirts. He pulled in. 'I'm gonna call,' he said.

'They won't know anything,' Walter said. A beaten-down quiet in the middle of his voice. 'Do what you want,' he conceded.

Ty had gone silent in the back. Sunk back into his bench. Like a monster who rises out of the sea and then submerges.

East climbed out with a handful of quarters and gritted his teeth at the loud sexy recorded lady. Then the bloodless operator who tried to connect.

A red light blinked ceaselessly over an intersection.

He looked back at the van, battered now – they'd smashed the plastic grille trim with something, those kids. Taken out one of the front turn signals. *This,* he thought. *This is what it's like.* It hadn't been his bullet, but he'd said, *It's him.* He'd risked his life to prove it. *Get him* was going to be the next thing he said, if not for the girl standing there.

He didn't want to think about the girl right then.

'Y'all did it?' Abraham Lincoln said. Surprised. 'I mean, the whole deal?' Like nobody had any idea.

Some sort of muttered consultation kept East waiting, looking sideways out of the wind. Finally Abraham Lincoln came back on the line. 'Okay, thanks for calling.'

'That's it?'

A long silence.

'If it makes sense, just go on home,' the voice said.

They sat in the lot near the blue pay phone's glow, a bone-dry wind scraping under the van. It rocked them side to side like a cradle.

Walter sighed. 'So we're here. Making it out is up to us.'

East watched the red eye of the traffic light switch on and off. 'One idea,' Walter continued. 'Go on. Find a store, buy some paint and tape, fix the window and the taillight. Paint the van up. Another idea: we ditch the van and get home some other way. Plane. Bus. Whatever. We might not have ticket money for three. But two of us could hole up and one goes home and wires back.'

If he'd brought his ATM cards, East thought. If he hadn't come clean the way they said but brought something extra. Like Ty did.

'Better idea,' said Ty. 'We carjack some bitch and get out of Dodge.'

'I thought about that,' said Walter. 'That guarantees us attention, though. That gives them a car to look for, a car to hunt.'

'Got to get rid of this van,' Ty said. 'For real. It ought to be burned. Soaked in gas and burned.' He ejected his magazine and reloaded in the dark.

'Let's not waste time,' East said. 'Decide right here. Can you call someone, man, and fix us up some tickets?'

'Today?' said Walter. 'Not *today*, East. We got us a dead man. Federal witness. Three boys getting on a plane. Nobody wants their name on that purchase. And if they figure it out while we're still in the air, we're fucked. We're locked down. You like those chances?'

'We'll keep on, then,' East said. 'Do something about the van before daylight.'

'Not soon enough,' said Ty from the backseat.

'Ty,' said Walter. 'Don't you want to get rid of that gun?'

Ty said, 'This gun's the one thing I got.'

Westward they kept on, cutting a corner off Minnesota, then down into Iowa. Roads nobody hurried on, roads where they weren't expected. Soon the sun would come up. Walter laid his gun on the dashboard, but it kept rattling, sliding around. So East pocketed it.

Fuck you niggers. They carried it with them through a dozen little towns. First the tall, ghostly farmhouses, then the little shops with their new trades hand-painted over the old signs. AUTO BODY, BEEF JERKY, TAXIDERMY, ASISTENCIA CON LOS TAXOS.

The occasional truck in the oncoming lane, pushing its blast of air.

'It's getting light,' said Walter. 'If you see something that's open, let's get some paint.'

They rolled by one large discount store in a shopping plaza, a thousand parking spaces deep. The letters were stripped off the concrete façade. Given up for dead.

'I gotta take a leak, man,' said Ty. 'Gas station right up here, man, please.'

'You might want to park a way off,' said Walter.

'We need gas anyway,' East observed.

Maybe they'd been lucky. Maybe they should have expected to be stopped long ago. East walked into the little station shop and found a roll of red tape for broken taillights. FOR TEMPORARY USE, the package said. The cashier wore a red sweater the color of Christmas and a strange thing on her head. It appeared to be a pair of stuffed antlers. She was a big lady, big diamond ring, somebody's mom.

'You got any paint?'

The lady shook her head. 'The new ordinance.'

'What new ordinance?'

'When certain people,' she said loudly, as if it were a rehearsed speech, 'spray paint all over the middle school? They won't find it quite so easy next time.'

East looked away then. He paid for the tape.

'Thank you anyway, ma'am,' he said, his best manners.

The lady put the tape in a useless plastic bag. 'You're welcome, hon.'

Outside, the only person was Ty, standing in the cold in his socks. It was as if the cold and the van had driven something into him, because his eyes were big, and he quivered slightly, the way a cat does watching a yard mouse. The moment East saw him, Ty took the gun out. A car was pulling in, a low white sedan, Infiniti. Ty stepped right into its path and brought the gun up.

The tires chirped, and the sedan stopped short.

What? thought East. Helplessly. For, he saw now, agreeing on a plan, he and Walter, meant nothing to Ty.

Nothing he said or did meant anything in Ty's mad story of the world.

He wanted to deny it, to return to the starting block and start over. No. In the station's noisy light, the Glock was a dark fact. The runners weren't stopping. Ty circled, taking aim on the driver, hollering, 'Man! Get the fuck out the car!'

14

THE BOY WEARING DIRTY socks yanked the driver out of the car. He thrust the gun against the man's face until the man was up against the pumps, teetering.

'What are you doing, man?' the older boy demanded, one eye a bruise, the other wild.

The younger boy ducked inside the car to look. No wife. No babies. Just this early businessman in his buttons and tie. Unlucky. The boy popped the trunk release and stood up. He gestured with the gun arm. 'Get in the trunk.'

A gold tie. Gold with a pattern of bright blue pearls.

'Oh, no,' the man said. Low and collected, even indignant. 'I'm not going in there.'

'Give me the keys,' said the younger boy, 'and get in.' He leveled the gun again.

'No,' gulped the man. He appealed to the taller boy, to the cashier inside, with his eyes, one raised hand.

The younger boy raised the gun up and shot one hole through the canopy. The echo bounced down, metallic.

'We can't do it like this,' the older boy said. 'It's crazy. You need to chill out. We can't come with you like this.'

'Think I need you?' said the younger one. 'You ain't fit for nothing but standing yard.' To the man he said, 'I'm a say it just once. To me you're just one more bullet.'

The older boy thrust in then between the young one and his prey and shoved, made the gunner bounce off the car, nearly fall. The younger one found his footing and turned. The businessman pressed himself hard behind the gas pump.

'Oh,' said the younger one. 'So now we see.'

He raised his gun, and the older boy, a gun in his hand though it hadn't been there until then, shot the younger in the chest. The younger boy uttered a short cry, and he fell. In a flash the older boy was on him, pinning the arm and taking the gun, rifling the pockets, taking a cache of bullets bunched carefully in a greasy wrapping. Opening the boy's pants and taking a fold of twenties out of the vent in the underwear. As if he'd known it would be there. He stood again and shut his eyes.

'Jesus,' prayed the businessman. 'Sweet Jesus.'

'Shut up,' the older boy said. He turned. Then something overtook him. He bent over the young boy's body, put something back inside the boy's pants. He buttoned them and stood again, looking down. The boy on the ground opened his mouth, rolled his head back. The muscles of his neck quivered in the night glare.

A fat boy in a van behind sat stricken at the wheel.

In the floodlights' glare, the older boy's face was a mask, angles of hardening bone, the eyes shadowy holes. He faced the man with the golden tie. 'Run, God damn you,' he said.

'Sweet Jesus,' the businessman pleaded. In the station the woman with an antler headdress held her phone and stared, holding, holding.

15

WALTER SOBBED. 'I SEEN it,' he blubbered. 'I seen there wasn't nothing but this. We knew you would.'

'We who?'

'Me and Michael,' said Walter. 'We knew it was gonna happen like this. Mike, he says, one of these brothers gonna kill the other. I thought he was joking. I said, that's bad news for Easy. And he said, naw, my money's on East.'

'Bullshit,' East said. 'You making it up. Like everything.'

'No,' wept Walter. 'It don't matter.'

East chewed his lip.

'I'm sorry, man,' Walter sobbed. 'I saw it coming. I told myself, no, I couldn't do nothing. I didn't get out the van. I couldn't do nothing. I couldn't stop you.'

'Stop me?' East said. 'Ty's the one out of control.'

'You the one who shot him. Who was cold to him the whole way.'

'I'm not cold to him.'

'You were,' Walter insisted.

East raced through the dark, dread like two hard hands working his guts, reshaping them, remaking his body. He felt every poke, every lump of food inside him, every stone on the road coming up from the tires to his seat. His road-shocked mind could not even keep time.

He had run from police before: standing yard, after fights, after hurling stones at the windows of stores, hoping something would break. Flight, they called it. One part fear, one part the blindest excitement you'd ever known. It freed you from time, from who you were or the matter of what you'd done. You darted, like a fish away from a net, like a dog outrunning a dogcatcher.

No flashing lights behind them. But no time either to think of his brother, or the other two, knocked down along their trail. And Walter's grief was unending: his brother's stoniness, just taking other form.

'I'm sorry,' he said once. But this just started Walter sobbing again.

None of us was perfect, East thought.

'Do you think I killed him?'

'You shot him in the chest, East.'

'Yeah.'

'Well,' Walter said, 'that's how you kill people.'

Once, when Ty was about six, East had been sent to enforce his mother's word. Back then their mother's bedroom was sunlit and clean and the TV sat small and quiet in a corner – later, it took over the whole apartment. It was time for the TV to be off, their mother said, and Ty wouldn't turn it off – SpongeBob or something. So East turned off the TV for him. Ty jumped up and hit him and turned it back on. East repeated their mother's warning and pulled the plug out of the wall. Ty threw the remote and hit East in the head. When East got back from checking his head in the mirror, was he cut, the TV was back on. Louder than ever. East picked up Ty and locked them both out of the bedroom. He caught hell for it – that old broken lock, if you locked yourself out, the only way back in was to take the door off the hinges.

He toted his brother like a laundry sack, one arm locked around his chest and the other around his hips. Ty caught the hand that had him at the collarbone and bit the fourth finger of East's left hand as hard as he could. First East screamed in anger and shock – it didn't really hurt yet. Screaming stopped things: startled them, embarrassed them, gave them satisfaction. With Ty it only stilled East so that his teeth could get a better grip. That was when it began to hurt. East had stopped screaming to begin to fight his brother then – put him down, free his arms up, begin wrestling himself out of a set of teeth that only clamped on tighter. That was when he began to imagine simply living as a sort of undying battle. Sometimes in the right kind of light, he could still see the indentations – the chain of little tooth marks circling – in the brown of his skin.

Different roads, different land, but East, half dreaming at the wheel, imagined the days in rewind: his brother, restored. The van, undamaged. The wooded house, undisturbed. The red moustache with his gun, bored and lonely near the swings. Back out the roads, without the guns, without all the food. Michael Wilson waiting for them by the foot of a bridge somewhere, welcoming. All forgiven. Like sometimes when he would sit up chilled and guilty from a horrible dream and stay there, the black string humming inside him, trying to breathe, to reassure himself that nothing had happened. But there would be no reassuring. Walter's weeping made sure of that. He looked down at his hands, still clad in the dark gloves they'd been issued.

He stopped the van just one time, to reach behind him, under the middle bench, and find the empty black shoes, sticky with pine sap and crumbly soil, a bud of pine needles caught in the laces. Maybe wet with something, maybe just cold, as the air was. He couldn't look. He rolled his window down, gunned into the oncoming lane, and let the shoes tumble into a ditch dark with reeds and litter, things that had grown there and things left behind.

Outside it would soon be the plain blue morning. The banks' signs gave different temperatures: 28, 31, 36. Air whistled in around the side window where Ty had managed to sling it in place. East scanned the roadsides for a store. An idea. Anything.

'We gonna paint this thing?' East proposed.

'Whatever you want,' Walter replied, drained.

A small-town discount-store palace. Something about the big crumbly fort of the store, perched atop an old, sloping lot the size of a football field, promised to fix everything. There was a junction here, and around it had grown up a battlefield of paved spaces, a few of the buildings still doing business, some of the lots empty as if the sky had swiped them clean.

Walter sat straight. 'Park up behind that Denny's there,' he said. 'Get between them trucks so we don't stick out.'

The painted words along the blue side of the van were a dark, chalkboard green.

'What you want to do?' Walter asked, his white breath floating away.

East assessed the van. 'Paint it over. Quick spray-paint job, good enough. And some duct tape to hold this window in. Tape the taillight red. And get going.'

Even at sunrise the store was busy – early-morning women with hair tied back. Single, angry men lugging detergent or powdered milk. Everybody tired, even the people getting paid to be there. Everyone with eyeballs, noticing the black boys. The lady with chin-length, orange-dyed hair, bright sweater, staring in the candles aisle. East felt small, tried to stay small. Fluorescent tubes twenty feet up. Pine chips and needles still dotted his sweater, and a rank, anxious sweat ebbed from his skin.

He felt wired, sick without sleep.

'Back there,' Walter said. 'Paint and painting supply.'

The aisle was dazzling. Most of the store was patchy, stock falling over, end caps picked clean. But the paint aisle was straight, tight-packed.

'Help you guys find something?' A twenty-year-old kid poked his head around the corner. Mexican goatee, tattoo on his neck.

'We're all right,' Walter said.

East noted the kid. Gang stripes on him. Even here. He eyed them with a calmness that set East on edge.

'Right here if you need me,' said the guy, and East could hear the R kick and rumble like a motorcycle. Like the south side of Los Angeles. This guy was from home.

'Thanks,' East said, nodding. As opaquely as he could.

Walter, studying the spray cans: 'This will cover. Should we use primer?'

'No,' said East.

'What would Johnny say?'

East said, 'Johnny doesn't ever want to see this van again. Not now.'

'Primer is cheaper,' Walter said. 'One can or two?'

'One. Jesus,' said East.

Walter picked out a spray can of primer gray. Shook it once, the agitator bouncing around the hollow can.

The paint man passed suddenly behind them. '*Váyanse con Dios*,' he whistled, making his accent plain. East watched him disappear around the end of the aisle.

They walked, Walter muttering to himself the whole way. They had paint, tape. Walter pulled a box of granola bars off a shelf in the aisle.

'We don't need that,' said East moodily.

'Good price, man.'

'Impossible, man, you out here trying to save a dollar.'

'I like to eat, East,' Walter said. 'I like to live.'

The cashier barely looked at them. East saw it now: the whole front end, the ceiling was dotted with cameras. Everywhere they went now would be like that.

'You think they had cameras going at that gas station?'

'Who knows?' Walter said. 'I don't know if we should even get back in the van.'

Outside, again, their breath rolled forth in sunrise plumes. East took the spray paint and shook it ready. 'Where you wanna do this?'

'Anywhere. Not here,' Walter said.

Then they saw the police cruisers. Behind the Denny's. Behind and around the van. The blue lights cut the air, and the red ones flashed high and stuck along the trucks, along the light poles. The cops milled, their uniforms and sticks on, all their cruisers churning smoke into the air.

'Man,' Walter said.

Then, without a word, he turned the other way.

East froze for a moment, paint can in his hand, dumbfounded. So this is how it went. Downhill. Maybe the police had just arrived. Maybe they hadn't thought to fan out yet, or were waiting on backup. Maybe they hadn't approached the van, were just boxing it in, not sure it was empty. If you only had a minute, you clung to that minute, you were thankful for it, you made an hour of it, did what you could. Downhill to the road, putting cars between them and the scene developing. Not toward anything, only away. The van after a week called out to him: *Defend me.* The way he'd guarded the house. A fool's voice. Gone.

They had the guns in their pockets and the money. Not the map, not the pink flyer, not the blanket, not the water, not their clothes, not the gloves, not Walter's directions in his inscrutable scratch. Not the heat.

No need for paint now. East ditched it in the back of a truck.

'Pick a direction,' East said. 'I'm with you.'

The lot was studded with stones, protuberant like eyes, like once they'd been moored in concrete but the concrete had worn away. East and Walter left it and crossed a storm ditch, slick with frost. He stole a glance: now he couldn't see the van or cops. Just flashing. Just the store. Now no longer the store.

'Quit looking back,' Walter said.

They reached the highway's shoulder. 'Cross here?'

'Down there.' Walter indicated the next intersection.

East checked the stoplights. 'Got cameras on the lights down there.'

Walter waved his hands, helpless. 'All right, let's go here.'

They sighted a hole between cars and took it. Across the street, the buildings were smaller, squashed between the highway and a running ten-foot fence. Hemmed in. Gas stations, doughnut shops: people and big windows everywhere.

Walter breathed his chugging breath. A little fire truck, a pumper with lights on, roared behind them. Going up the left-turn lane toward Denny's. *Ought to be burned. Soaked in gasoline and burned*, Ty had said.

A stitch pierced East's side. Walter was panting already, his eyes worried like a dog's.

The first gas station. East evaluated the one truck parked at a pump: nondescript but old, tires knobby. Tough but slow. They hurried on. Next, a sort of post office. Closed as yet. Then a Laundromat. A beauty shop. Closed. Then a row of drive-throughs. East looked again to his left at the wire fence.

Barbed on top, flecked with trash. Behind it, nothing.

There was nowhere to walk to, no hiding place. It was going to have to be here.

East closed his eyes and gave Walter a moment to catch up. 'We got to go gunning, right?'

'We could call,' said Walter, wheezing.

'And say what?' said East. 'Ask for some Superman shit?'

'You're right,' said Walter. 'Calling's no good.'

'We got to go gunning.'

'Yes,' Walter agreed.

The time. In flight you used it. The space. Like a gunner checking a house. They examined the drive-throughs. The first was burgers. Hopping: two lanes in the drive-through, each one backed up. Nice, fast cars there: a sport Lexus. But any move you made, there'd be ten people watching.

The next was doughnuts. They studied the building, ugly and square, a little box of concrete with painted-on stripes. One asphalt snake around the back and up to the window. And a brawny green hedge five feet high all around.

'Let's look,' East said.

They cut along the outside of the hedge until they stood across it from the black-eyed window. There was a gap a foot or two wide where the lane drained into a steel grate in the pavement.

'Come right through there,' East said. 'Wait till it thins out and a car comes. One of us blocks, one talks. Climb in and go. But time it right.'

'Did you ever carjack before?'

'Never done it,' East said. 'I'm a yard man.'

'And a proud one,' said Walter. 'How we keep the girl in the window from seeing?'

'Get it before the window, maybe,' said East. 'In the back.'

'What about the driver?'

'What do you mean?'

'Take them or leave them? Ty was gonna put that dude in the trunk. What do you want to do?'

'I don't know,' East said. 'I guess I don't know.'

Glumly they examined the hedge. 'It ain't perfect,' Walter decided.

'Keep looking?'

'I don't know,' said Walter. 'We ain't gonna find anything perfect. Not on this side. We can't go shooting no matter what. It's gotta be quiet.'

'If we have to,' East began.

'East. We ain't in the woods anymore. There's a hundred cops right over there. And the longer we stay here, the blacker we get.' He gave East a worried look.

'All right,' East said. 'What? You think I'm trigger happy?'

'You shot your brother,' Walter said bleakly.

'He was losing his shit.'

'When we shot that judge, what, six hours ago, I didn't think we were going to jail. Now I do. For a while, everything that got in our way, we were on top of. But now it's a losing streak. And we ain't got your lucky brother to fall back on.'

'He ain't lucky.'

Walter said, 'You can say that again.'

They took up spots behind the hedge. Through the gap, they could watch the cars coming, look without being looked at.

Two cars came at once. First a van, tinted out, green, heavy, anonymous. Ideal, East thought, but impossible, for right behind it was a little Suzuki or Isuzu or something, a woman at the wheel, some sort of earring glinting near her ear. Right up smack behind the van, a witness. She missed seeing them entirely. But her child, a stout little thing with red on its chin, stared them through.

'I don't think this joint got a camera,' Walter said. 'I think we could stand right up in the back if we wanted.'

'And what?' said East. 'Just turn around and go out the way we went in?'

'That might work.'

The next, a pickup, held two men and a boy. A full gun rack in the cab. 'Not that one,' Walter said.

'No.'

The following car showed up so suddenly, it seemed as if East had been sleeping on his feet. Impossible, but maybe. Walter touched his arm, and he saw. Light brown Ford with after-market mud guards and golden seat covers. An old black lady, alone.

'She looks nice,' said Walter.

'I ain't making that lady get in a trunk,' East muttered.

The Ford pulled abreast and waited at the window. Suddenly Walter pushed through the hedge, the trimmed branches plowing at his clothes. He straightened his sweater and held his hand up in greeting. Like this was his great-aunt.

Crazy. East shivered. He had half a mind to run.

The old lady turned her head. Pouted, appraising him, through gold-trimmed glasses. Slowly her old power window whined down, and she said, in a high, chipped voice, painstakingly clear, 'Do you two young men need some sort of *rod* somewhere?'

'Ma'am?' said Walter.

'I said, are you young men waiting for a *ride*?'

Walter said, 'Yes, ma'am. Thank you, ma'am.'

The lady's sunny expression dimmed a bit as she peered around Walter at East, still hiding in the hedge.

'You with him?'

'He's my cousin, yes.'

A silent *humph*. 'Well, come on.'

Walter pivoted, shaking his face at East. 'Come *on*.'

East wavered, then squeezed through the hedge. Squeezed his eyes shut like a kid jumping into water. The little branches tugged and ripped at him. Walter was twice as wide, but he'd come through easier.

'One black lady in the whole state,' he whispered, 'and you gonna steal her car.'

'She *offered*,' Walter hissed.

Across the roof of the car, the drive-through window folded open on a white girl with a round, pimpled face. 'Good morning, Martha!' she hollered. 'How are you?'

'Oh, I'm fine, fine,' said the old woman. The cashier girl took the lady's money cheerfully and handed her down a dozen-doughnuts box with a gold seal on top. 'Have a nice weekend – till next time!' she shouted. Sparing Walter and East one odd glance.

East stood at the back door, and the locks hammered up. The old lady set the box of doughnuts next to her on the seat, and she peered out at Walter again.

'Was you coming?'

'Yes, ma'am.' Walter nodded vigorously. 'Let me talk,' he murmured at East.

'You better,' East said.

Already Walter was taking the front seat, chirping his thanks. East lowered himself into the clean-swept interior. Extra rubber mats, one floral umbrella on the seat. The faint smell of lubricating oil. He reached for the belt; it clunked as he unrolled it. The old spring was soft and would barely click in.

In his pants, Ty's gun. A spur.

'What is your name?' the lady inquired, not going anywhere, not quite yet.

'Walter, ma'am.'

Just like that, thought East, real name. Why not?

'A,' said East. 'For Andre.'

'My name is Martha Jefferson,' the lady said. 'And where are you two headed today?'

'We'll just ride, ma'am,' Walter said. 'If it's all right.'

The lady paused. She had that grandmotherly pout for thinking. 'In my experience, a young person doesn't just ride. A young person has a good idea *where* he's going.'

'We've been going, but we're just stuck here,' Walter said. 'We need to get along.'

'You in trouble?' said the woman, narrowing her eyes. 'Or *are* you trouble?'

'We hope we're not in trouble,' Walter said.

She laughed. This pleased her. 'Are you runaways?'

'No, ma'am,' Walter said.

'Hoboes?' Her giggle a creak, like an old wooden chair.

'No.' Walter giggled back artfully.

'Are you college students?'

'Yes.'

'No you're not. Too young!' But at last, with this interrogation, she put the car in gear. Old but not simple, East observed. 'Are you robbers?' she asked merrily.

'No, ma'am,' said Walter again.

'Not here to rob me. Well, what, then?' Martha Jefferson said. Like sweethearts flirting, East thought.

'Together we could rob some other people if it helped you out.' The old lady creaked with mirth. 'Aw, no,' she said. 'I be all right.'

Now she'd put her sauce on.

'This morning,' declared Martha Jefferson, 'I am headed to the airport in Des Moines. I don't know if that helps you. But I can take you to the highway if you don't want the airport.'

'We would ride all that way with you,' said Walter. 'With thanks.'

Formally, Martha Jefferson agreed, 'Then I will take you.'

'Yes, ma'am.'

East looked out. They were passing the Denny's. Police cars all up and down the lot. Then Martha Jefferson turned at the junction, and it all fell behind them: that van, that everything. East did not turn to look back.

'Chilly day for just a sweater, Mister Walter,' the woman said. The box of doughnuts wafted their smell into the car's box of air. Was she ever going to break into them? East thought rudely. Walter broke open his box of granola bars and offered one to Martha Jefferson first before passing one back. East unwrapped his and let a first, dry bite moisten in his mouth slowly, feeling it as much as tasting it, the chunks of it coming apart, turning to starch on his tongue. How something plain could open up like the whole world when you were starved. He was asleep before he could take a second bite.

He awoke. The little digital clock stuck to the dash said 9:20. No idea when they'd begun. Outside, the highway flowed by. They'd come through here before on this highway, heading east in the dark.

Walter was saying: 'I'm going to study electrical engineering. Electronics. Wiring. Installing. You know. If I'm good, I can get a degree and begin to design. I could work up in Silicon Valley, you know. Not programming but helping on the engineering side. And if not, I can just install and repair. Computer. Cable. Alarm systems.' On and on.

'You got it all figured out,' said Martha Jefferson, admiringly.

'I'll come out okay either way,' said Walter.

'It's that kind of world. You have to plan for either way.'

Walter said, 'Amen.'

'My grandson lives in California, too,' she revealed.

The highway sang under them, and the two of them talked, like relatives, like people sure of their homes, till East felt himself falling away again. Walter was a good boy. East dreamed he was alone in the van, alone in a storm where he could see nothing ahead of him, knew there was nothing ahead of him. No one had seen Walter. Walter was a good boy. He slept until he felt the gentle lift of a ramp, and again he awakened, and a parking garage surrounded them now. Outside, the airport sky, cluttered, gray. A plane arced up behind a gray-windowed tower.

'Let me get it for you,' Walter was saying. 'Here's forty to cover it.'

'No, no,' said Martha Jefferson. 'I'm only gone the two days. It ain't but five a day.'

'Gas too, then,' winked Walter. He tucked the twenties into her purse, and again she *humphed* silently.

What was the act now? East had missed the whole conversation of lies. Keep his mouth shut.

'I knew,' the lady said, 'you was good people.'

Walter. A good boy. East's stomach felt hard and scraped out. He felt as if he'd been punched in the chin with force. He wondered how he smelled. Shuddering, the old Ford pulled into a space near a ledge that looked down two stories. Walter leapt out, fetching the old lady's weekend bag from the trunk.

Then East was trudging behind him, the dumb cousin. The airport. Wasn't this what Walter had said to stay away from? The world was a gray smear. The patterned carpet running forever reminded him vaguely of the casino. Dog-tired on an invisible leash, he just followed.

People crossing his path were thin, wore black and gray, ears clipped to their phones. Long yellow and white lights blared above: they told him nothing.

'You're meeting at the gate?' Walter was saying.

'My sister? Yes, dear. But we couldn't get seats in the same row. Couldn't get that,' the old lady said. 'She's right in front of me, though. Oh. Oh, goodness.' She stopped with a jolt. 'We forgot the doughnuts.'

Walter stopped too and grinned.

'She gonna have a fit!' he scolded Martha Jefferson.

Martha Jefferson laughed aloud. 'She will!'

Walter turned on East in mock fury.

'Andre! Why didn't you bring the doughnuts!'

Andre. Right. Wearily East regarded Walter.

Either it was exhaustion or it was being on the outside, but he could see what they were playing at. As if a pair of sunglasses had been removed and now the light of day was bright and strange. Playing three black people, comic and noisy in an airport. Like a skit in school, the boys playing wolves, the girls playing lambs. Acting out what all these people expected them to be. Better than what they were.

He understood it, and yet did not know his lines.

Martha Jefferson said, 'She'll be so *frustrated* with me.'

'I could –' began Walter.

The old lady, with searching eyes, asked, 'Would you?'

Walter said, like a faithful nephew, 'I will. I'll go right now. Andre, walk Mrs. Jefferson through to security now. I'm gonna be back before you go through the line. But you can't go through the line – you're not a passenger. Got it?'

East's stomach rolled. He nodded. Walter took Martha Jefferson's bag off his shoulder and traded it for her key ring.

'Andre. You can't go in the line,' Walter said. 'You hear me?'

'I won't go in the line,' East murmured. *Jesus.* The lady was looking him up and down. Again East wondered how he smelled.

'I can carry your bag if you like,' he offered.

'Very kind,' said Martha Jefferson, but she kept it on her. He was the one she didn't like the looks of. All right.

Together they trudged off toward the security line.

A smattering of people funneling into line. They paused and shuffled, eyeing phones or conversing in low voices. Steering their luggage, casual but alert, along the switchbacks. East and Martha Jefferson came to a stop just outside the cordoned area.

A few of them watched the old, stern-faced Negro lady and her ragged boy. East was bilious. Acting sleepy was the best he could do.

'You can't go through, you know. Through the security. Not unless you have a ticket,' Martha Jefferson reminded him.

'I know,' he responded dully. 'Walter said.'

How long was the fat boy going to be?

He understood that he was standing by her now not to be quiet and kind, but to hide behind her. He was raw. He could barely stand. And Walter was dashing about, carrying things. Out in the parking lot now without him, a set of keys in his hand. Inventing things. He was standing by her to be the sort of boy who traveled with his great-aunt, who didn't have blood on his shoes. Late coming to the play, but happy to be in it.

As long as Walter came back.

A black couple inched forward in the line, one midsize son with his face in a video game and a little girl in braids, up on her father's shoulder. She eyed East with dread.

'I hitchhiked one time,' Martha Jefferson reminisced. 'I'll never forget. Course, it was in Louisiana, long ago.'

East was going to say *Oh,* but he hiccupped instead.

'You okay?' said Martha Jefferson.

'Fine.'

'You don't look fine,' said the lady. She stepped back, and East lacked the strength to argue. There wasn't anywhere to go. The little girl stared sideways. She closed her eyes and became the Jackson girl.

His stomach flipped, and instinctively he turned toward a trash can. He fought his jaw muscles, but they pried themselves apart, and he vomited into the cups and wrappers with a long, despairing cry.

'Oh, Lord,' the lady was saying. 'Look at you now.'

Yellow heat in his mouth. He spat out the rest and felt in his pockets for something to wipe his face. Nothing. Just a granola bar wrapper, a key, a fold of twenties, and a gun. He cleaned himself with the back of his hand.

'I *told* you,' said the lady. Though she had not told him anything. But he saw that she was not speaking to him; she was speaking to the people in line, now gazing from their cordon at this small misfortune. He saw that she was not going to help him out like a grandmother might. She stood back, marking their distance.

At last, Walter. Bright fat idiot angel, he carried the box of doughnuts with its golden seal before him like a prize. 'Here you are,' he sang, flashing Martha Jefferson's key chain and helping her guide it back into her purse.

He looked around, seeing that something had happened. It was on everyone's faces. 'What's wrong?'

'Your cousin is sick,' announced Martha Jefferson.

Walter touched East's forehead, his hand there heavy and soft. 'I'm okay,' East said.

A guard was coming up to see. The line slipped forward. The little sideways girl on her father's shoulder watched East again.

Walter said, 'Well, maybe we should *go* then, Andre.'

Martha Jefferson agreed silently, stirring toward the line with her eyes. She was eager to be rid of them. Even Walter. She knew how to do it: she did it with such public sweetness. 'You *have* been good to meet. Such lovely young men.'

She and Walter beamed brightly, falsely.

'So happy to have met you,' Walter said.

She fluttered. 'And I, you.'

Walter handed the box of doughnuts over and then gasped at it. 'Oh!' he exclaimed. 'But, Mrs. Jefferson, are they going to let you take this on board?'

Mrs. Jefferson smiled, a final smile, not for them. 'Well, it isn't allowed. But don't worry. They know me. Everyone in the sky knows me.'

East, bleary though he was, saw different. Nobody knew this lady at all.

Walter: 'What is it?'

East's stomach was tumbling to a halt. 'Like food poisoning. Something.'

'You're panicking, man. Your body's fooling with you.'

East let this go. In the vast men's bathroom they washed with squirt soap and dried with brown paper. Morning businessmen made hurried passes under the seeing-eye faucets. East stood there a long time. In the mirror he was a different mess than he'd ever seen before: an eye still dark and swollen from Michael Wilson. He'd forgotten about it; he hadn't had time to hurt. Now, clean, the eye was fat and tender. No wonder Martha Jefferson had looked at him funny. His skin, even after he scrubbed it, was puffy, black, and greasy. The cold water brought his focus back a little.

'I was going to pass out,' he grumbled.

'You did. You slept the whole way.' Walter glanced around at the other men. 'Can we go out? We got to talk.'

East nodded. The bouncing daylight outside the bathroom braced East, brought him back into space and time. He and Walter made their way to the exit. *Iowa,* he mused. Back in Iowa now. Behind them like beads on a string lay the other places: the van, his brother, the wooden house in Wisconsin. And The Boxes, the boarded-up house that was his. Strung out behind, not far, not long, but behind. Links in a chain. Behind, like his black eye, the bruise clouding over.

The noxious air of taxis idling. They found a bench, and Walter dug in his pocket.

'What is it?'

A single key. 'Hers.'

'Whose?'

'Miz Jefferson's. She had two. This is a valet key. It will start the car – I tried it. Just won't open the trunk.'

East held the key in his fingers, examined it.

'And she won't be back for two days.' Walter looked down the line of cabs. 'Likely won't notice it's gone till then.'

East whistled. 'Smart,' he said quietly.

Walter laid his legs out straight and crossed one over like an old cigar smoker. 'I know,' he said. 'I impress myself.'

'Walter,' East said. 'We gonna get caught?'

'I been thinking on that,' Walter said. 'Looks like police got the van. Question is, why? Because of Wisconsin? Or because of your brother?'

'What does it matter?'

'It does,' Walter reasoned. 'Two very different things.'

'You gonna tell me they upset about Wisconsin,' East guessed, 'but they don't give a damn about my brother?'

'Well, there's that.' Tightly Walter smiled. 'Maybe you're right. Maybe they don't hunt the one at all. But they gonna hunt them differently. If it's just Ty they're looking for here, and they found the van, then we're just black boys who shot another. Probably didn't go far. Police are looking in that area. That Denny's, even. Not an airport. You follow?'

East nodded.

'But if it's Wisconsin, then they tie in Ty, maybe – there were witnesses, they saw us, man, they got a plate, probably an APB on us all night – then they find the van, that makes a direction. One, two, three. That points west. This way. The way home. Got me?'

'How you gonna know for sure which it is?'

Walter laughed. 'Ha. I'm not. East, I'm guessing it was because of you and Ty. Because of the witnesses. I'm guessing it's your bullet they're following.'

East sat back. The black string jangling inside.

'But the van isn't here. That's lucky – we drove it a few hundred miles last night and ditched it. We made a mystery jump. And we didn't dump it near an airport. And we didn't steal a car they can look for. That don't tell the cops we're looking to hop on a plane.'

'But we're not,' East said, 'looking to hop on a plane.'

'Well, I was thinking about it,' Walter said.

'You what? You said it was dangerous, man. Even walking in there.'

'Everything's dangerous now,' Walter said. 'Right? But we got cash. They can sell us walkup tickets. They gotta check our IDs, but they're clear, and we can drop them the minute we get to LA. Kill these names off and never look back.'

Walter sat up out of his crouch and looked around, face wide open, as if they were waiting for a ride, as if he was unconcerned.

'What's it cost?' said East. 'Do we have enough?'

'Don't know,' said Walter, 'but it sounds good to me. See the country from up top. Be home this afternoon.' He traced the idea across his pants and stopped it with a dot. 'Nobody knows where I've been all week,' he confessed. 'Probably worried.'

'Oh, you got people?'

'Yeah,' Walter replied. 'Of course. I got people.'

East watched the airport cop down the way, forty yards, directing people with suitcases.

'Quicker we drop these guns, the better, then,' Walter said.

'If we're done shooting.'

'How we gonna know if we're done shooting?'

'I'm done shooting,' said East. He got up and strode over to the nearest trash can, poking around until he found a good fast-food bag, stiff white paper, a little greasy. He picked it out, straightened it, then palmed the little gun into the bag. He walked it back to Walter.

'See if you can put your trash in here. Be cool with it.'

Walter emptied his pockets on the bench beside him: granola bars, van key, the money in a clip, paper napkins clean and used. He covered his pocket with a napkin and fished the gun out into it. Into the bag it went. East crumpled the bag and took it back, tucking it into a corner of the trash can, just so.

'Feel better now?' said Walter, up on his feet.

'No.'

Walter frowned. Disappointment, maybe. What mattered to Walter, East saw, was solving problems. Inventing. Wasn't anything in East's stomach that Walter could solve.

A police car went by, white cop, black glasses, who knew what he was looking at. Airport security. Passed without slowing.

East's mind hurt and he could see only a part of it: the part that was made up. Nothing in him wanted a plane. He didn't trust it. Or maybe he didn't trust himself. Sick, tired, out of control. That person he'd always reined in, in himself or others – noisy, violent, fractious – he felt behind him, or just beside him, or attached, like a shadow. Outside him, maybe, but double. Visible.

He'd never been on a plane. But all he knew about them – the getting on, the staying put, the thousand people packed together – was not going to happen today.

'I'm gonna make it on the ground, man,' East declared. 'You take your plane if you want to. If you think it's safe.'

Walter said, 'Really?'

'Yeah.'

'It's safe. I mean, this way,' Walter said, and he could not help looking guilty. 'For me. Nobody saw me, man. In Wisconsin, because I was running behind. Or with Ty, because I stayed in the van. They just saw you.'

East toed at a spot on the pavement. 'All right.'

'I mean –' said Walter, then gave out.

'Come on,' East said. He wanted to be done with it, finally alone. 'Let's see how it goes.'

He observed the line to the counter from a bench some distance away. What happened at the gate was out of his hands. He liked Walter. Walter was handy in ways he'd never imagined being. But there wasn't anything he could do for Walter. Across the country they'd come together – a team. A crew, right? Now scattered to the wind. They'd put bullets in the right guy – finished the job. But all East felt was beaten. That's what it cost. The week was a wound he hadn't even steeled himself to look at yet. Yet he felt it bleed.

He had a hundred dollars in his pocket. Walter had the rest. He was thinking about that thin hundred and the little clutch of ATM cards he hid under the block of wood in his bedroom, that he'd agreed not to bring, that he'd hidden away so he could follow Fin's rules. He wondered about the home Walter had, that steady place with a computer and a library, maybe a piano or a cat, and the people he had there. Who would be in LA when he got back, or when he didn't? Who might be wondering where he was right now, and, if Walter got taken down at the counter, or at the gate, or pulled off the plane, would wish they were here where he was sitting right now, watching Walter make his mistake, watching him crawl up to the backlit ticket counter with his teacher's-pet grin and his pocketful of twenties? Overconfident. Or maybe just lucky.

Rather be lucky than good, people said. East felt neither.

What East had – the house in The Boxes, a crew, the everyday job with Fin's gang, and Fin himself, maybe even his place under the office building, and Ty, whatever Ty had meant at the end of that invisible gravity that bound them unhappily to each other across the blocks and years – all that was gone. All defunct. The streets would be there, and the business, and he was skilled. But he was known too, one of Fin's. Even if he caught on with another outfit, he'd be secondhand, a refugee. Never a citizen. Nothing he'd ever done with Fin would make way for him.

He'd start again from the bottom, like a kid ten years old.

Watching the ticket counter in Des Moines, he thought of LA, the smell of the steady flowers mixed with the smell of sun and desert and cars and food frying. The people he knew, the ghost that was his mother, the guys who had scattered. None of it was anything he'd buy a plane ticket back to today.

That was the business, and the business was closed.

Walter's agent was a young man, thin, a thin moustache, a face without fat on it. East could see that the man didn't think much of Walter – fat, black, wrinkled clothes smelling of nights and days. Raggedly cheerful. All his brilliance invisible inside. The agent listened, his lips pursed on the edge of a grimace. Tapping his screen, asking, checking the license, asking again. Soundless from here. Eyebrows working like two small animals.

A moment passed when he was hoping the man would reject Walter. Would stop him dead at the counter, would take him down. So East could retrieve the guns. So East could blow holes right through the ticket agent, renounce himself. Throw everything down in an avenging storm.

He shook his head to clear it. A printed document came over

the counter. Walter nodded again. And he stepped clear.

Are we gonna get caught? he had asked Walter.

The fat boy hitched his pants on one side and sauntered back to East, incautious, a little proud of himself.

'How much it cost?' East said.

'Man.' Walter whistled. 'Three hundred and some. A lot. You buy at the last minute, they get you.'

Grimly East remarked, 'We got to plan ahead next time.'

'There's one person,' Walter said. 'That girl at the doughnut shop. She saw us both. She saw us get into the car. She knew Martha Jefferson, knew she was going to the airport. If they asked her about us, man, she could trip us up.'

'But you got your ticket,' East said. Beyond considering possibilities. 'You're gonna go anyway.'

'I'm really gonna go,' Walter said. 'Let's find someplace to talk. I got to be at the gate in twenty minutes.'

They sat apart in bathroom stalls, trying to purge, then huddled together at the sinks. Around them the businessmen cast down their eyes, wet their hands in the basins. Walter slipped East a wrinkled wad of bills. East counted it out. Seventy-one dollars.

'You take it,' Walter said. 'Give me back a twenty I can show. Get me on a bus or whatever. Get me home.'

East fed him back a twenty. Now a hundred and fifty-one dollars was his stake in the world.

'Here,' Walter said. He gave East a slip of paper from the airline counter. A suitcase tag, a 310 number on it and an elasticized string. 'Give me till tonight, man. Then call me. I'll take care of you, man. I swear it.'

East laughed hoarsely. 'You gonna take care of me? Really?' Walter stammered. 'East. Why I'd wrong you? I mean, you're a bad man now, right?'

East lowered his head.

'You tell me where you're at. Town and address. I can buy you a ticket: plane, train, whatever you want. I can rent you a car. I can wire you money. I can probably find you a house to crash in.'

'All right,' East said. 'I know it. We better ditch these van keys.'

'Oh shit. You're right,' Walter said. He grabbed a series of paper towels from the wall, dried his hands, and they wrapped the two keys up in them. Tossed it out.

'What happens to that trash?'

'They burn it. Some incinerator somewhere. They'll wind up in the ashes. But nobody ever looks at that shit,' Walter said. 'Whyn't we get out of this bathroom? I'm tired of the smell in here.' Suddenly he was smiling, lighter. 'E, man. We finished it.'

They walked together into the spilling white carpeted light of the terminal. People flowing around them. East barely noticed them.

'This was terrible,' Walter said. 'I hated it. Hitting the dude. But I'm glad you were there. It wouldn't have gone on without you.'

'I know,' East said.

'We did it,' Walter said. 'I got to go.'

'Be careful.'

'I will.' Walter slapped East's shoulder. 'Love you, man.'

He slapped Walter back and started walking. He burped; it came up raw, bitter. *Love you, man.* He didn't love Walter, and he didn't say shit like that. He made sure of the bills in his pocket and he looped the luggage tag with the number through the hole in Martha Jefferson's key. And he made his way out toward the garage. But before he left, he looked back. Walter was in the security line, watching him, his pants sagging already below his belly but the ticket clutched in his hand. East raised a hand and Walter smiled back. There. That much was enough.

He returned to the trash can out front and fetched the greasy white bag he'd stowed. He could feel its contents, the two loose weights inside. The popgun he'd shot Ty with and the other, the Glock that had killed Carver Thompson and his girl. The two guns with history. The third, the Taurus that no one had fired, the clean one, he'd left on his brother, tucked it into his pants at the end. He tightened the bag and clutched it to his hip.

'Can I help you get somewhere?' sounded a voice over his shoulder.

Maybe the airport cop had seen him. Maybe it was taking trash out of the can that had brought him hovering. Maybe it was just the way East looked. Or felt.

'Naw, man,' he drawled without looking. 'You can't help me.' Then he was moving again, off into the garage. He was a bad man now.

First he drove south. South was away from the police and the van; it was away from Wisconsin; it was neither here nor there. Farms by the side of the road, naked highways, no trees. Sometimes he glimpsed ghostly barns lost on plains, herds of pigs thwarted behind wire.

His eyes felt caked, sticky, like they'd rolled around in the gutter before he'd popped them back into his face.

Brown signs pointed the way to a state park: picnic, camping, river access. Something in his mind started at the idea of a river – it promised crossing, crashing, the cold water dividing this from that. He turned off the highway down the old, tree-lined road.

A cruiser rolled by. STATE PARK RANGER. Cop of a different color is still a cop.

Then he neared a little farmhouse a quarter mile before the wooden park gate. The old house stood gray and alone on a big swath of forgotten land. Weathered past color, the way the gun barn had been. Weeds the height of a man had grown up all around. Two signs advertised it for sale, but sun had baked their red to pink. They'd been there awhile.

He nosed Mrs. Jefferson's car in. The drive circled around to the back. He could almost bury the car in these weeds. There was a space beneath a tree where small gray birds dove in and out. Birds so small they might have been babies. He hid the car in the shadows there, tucked the greasy bag under the seat, and watched the birds until he fell asleep.

OHIO

16

WHEN HE AWOKE, IT was coming out of him like magma, like a volcano, punching a hole through the rock, spilling down his face. The black eye giving forth its flood. The back of the house, the abandoned oil tank, the meadow of weeds, the belly of the tree. A place where people had lived and left. He sobbed until it gave out. But he knew as it did that it had changed nothing. No words, no pictures, no thought. It was just a trick of the muscles, a release of the glands.

His skin grew dry and cold as the car cooled, and it was night when he woke up again.

Not afternoon dark but night dark. The stick-on digital clock on Martha Jefferson's dash read a quarter past eight. So he'd been asleep for six hours.

Not a night's worth, but a good sleep. He hadn't had a night's sleep since they'd left The Boxes on Tuesday.

If he was right, it was now Friday night.

He stood and pissed into the roots of the tree. A choir of small voices chirruped in the darkness. Something moved, and he startled. Wind. Weeds and wind. The back of the house, nobody's house.

He waited outside.

The car was old but well kept, well tuned. It rolled smoothly on the polished, rolling, back roads. Like the van, it was better than it looked. East filled the tank at a station where two empty roads crossed, each road a story lit by the station's glow. He wiped grime off Martha Jefferson's windshield and dried the runoff with a paper towel.

He was sorry to do the old lady wrong. But he wasn't going back to Des Moines, Iowa – to the airport or anywhere else. That lady had had a good look at him; she had heard him sleep. She had his measure. There was no guessing the things she knew about him, or what Walter had said while he snored. It was not impossible that after everything, Martha Jefferson would be the one who called him to account, for sleeping in her backseat, for stealing her car away. So he polished her windshield clean, and the cold biscuit sandwich he bought out of the cooler, he ate outside the car – no crumbs, no wrapper.

He switched on her radio, but it was all static. Loath to disturb the station knob where she had it set.

Each time a junction opened the four directions for him, he went away from home. He went east.

He passed signs for Chicago at four o'clock in the morning. For a moment he considered it. Chicago: everyone knew that was a town for gangsters, Michael Jordan's city, full of people and ways to make money. He had guns to travel by. But the gray-yellow light of the city under the clouds brought back Michael Wilson's crawling into Vegas. *Just a taste.*

The billboards advertised everything, promising everything.

The long, steamy reach of the city flanked him for miles, gray factories lit by orange bulbs on his left, huge skeletons of iron that had held trains or loaded boats or moved the road over rivers or launched rockets into the sky.

In Indiana, on a larger road now, he had to stop with other cars at a booth and take a ticket out of a box, like at a parking ramp. He sat still and read it. It was going to cost him four dollars somewhere down the road. Someone behind him honked.

Booth, camera, stolen car. Keep doing what the others do.

Then the last signs of the city dropped away, and he was back in darkness, the highway narrowed down, the starry blocks of houses placed just so behind the trees.

At sunrise he'd reached the end of the state. A gauntlet of booths blocked the road; cameras everywhere now. He pulled in slowly where it said CASH and surrendered his ticket. 'Four sixty-five,' the woman said.

He'd barely heard humans speak since he'd left the airport the afternoon before. A sign advertised the last exit before a new toll pike. It was Ohio now. He took the little road south, Highway 49, then again turned east.

About eleven o'clock in the morning, in a small town with a sagging water tower, where the sun had quieted itself behind clouds, he had gone far enough in Mrs. Jefferson's car. His tank of gas was nearly gone. He had crossed three state lines.

On the main street, he located a little corner police office. Meters out front. He stopped in a space and made sure his money was with him. He took one gun out of the bag, rolled the bag shut on the other, and shared the guns out between his two front pockets. He left the key in the center ashtray and left the car unlocked.

For a moment he felt a panic. Was this an error, giving the car up? Walking out again into the winter?

One-hour parking. It would be found.

Ty would have pulled it behind a building and set it ablaze. Quietly he dropped a quarter into the meter and walked away.

17

OUT OF TOWN HE walked on tipped, sunken sidewalks, passing bacon-smelling restaurants and used-car lots laid out precisely, wheel facing wheel, headlights polished and aligned, everything eyeing everything else.

In a low gray midday, the windows of the buildings were mirrors, glass glaring back, insides invisible. The lots lay squared and similar, and seams and borders separated every this from every that. A fence, a rail, a line of grass or littered shrubs like the alley where they'd waited for Martha Jefferson. Or just a line of curb coated in tar. Each place marked the line between this and that, here and there. Each one he passed ticked off the passing from then to now.

He heard the motor first; then tires scratched the pavement behind and stopped at his heel. Little fat-tire police car with the windows rolled down. A moustache, bristling.

'How you doing this morning?'

East stopped. Helplessly he imagined the parking meter – it had to be still ticking. Not that. An age of dealing with cops had taught him what not to do.

'Fine,' he mumbled.

'Going anywhere special?'

'Just a walk.'

The cop looked skeptical and East squeezed his shoulders together, mute.

'Know anybody in this town?' the cop added. They asked a question, then stared into you like a fishing hole, like sooner or later the truth would swim up.

'Not really.' East stood still, hands down in his pockets, where now there was only a small fold of bills and the bent California shapes of some guns.

The police radio burped and whistled. The cop glanced at it, then stilled it with a hand.

East gazed down the road and said, 'You got what you need?' The moustache stared through him. Like a gaze you could actually feel, could round on if you wanted to sleep tonight on a concrete floor.

'You take it easy,' the cop said. Not a farewell. An instruction. East volunteered nothing. Behind him the engine flared. The tires didn't crawl but cut a hard U-turn. So somebody had sent the cop out just to take a look at him.

The town smelled like corn cooked too long. Up the road, the two-lane broadened out as it sped up – flat shoulders spreading, cars at fifty or sixty, tossing up black grit and cinder tornadoes that bit his ears. He burrowed down in his sweater. No trees to hide behind, no woods line to trace – this would be straight country walking. Out where anyone could see.

A mile of level fields. Stalks sawed into splintered bits, scraps of wind-trash bright in the ruts. He heard Michael Wilson's laughing voice: *Country.*

A sign said it was four miles to the next town.

At a junction gas station kept by a teenage girl, he bought a long sub sandwich and a stocking cap. The caps said BROWNS and came in two colors, orange and brown. He chose brown. He chose ham. Inside him, his stomach was a drifting ship. But he should eat. He knew that.

By the door, as the nervous girl prepared his sandwich, a map with a yellow tape arrow showed YOU ARE HERE. No Wisconsin, no Iowa, none of those places on a map that meant what they had done. Just this state, just Ohio, the town where the brown car slept somewhere to the west. He didn't remember the name of the town. He just wanted away. This was running. From the police and from the spinning inside his body, the yaw.

The girl patted his ingredients together through plastic-bag gloves. When he asked for more tomatoes, she took her phone out of her pocket and laid it on the chopping surface, near onion half-moons, within reach. Her movements sharpened: she pressed the sandwich and sliced it with the quick blade, and then she was done with him, everything but the making change.

He knew he must look horrible.

He took his bagged sandwich and used the little restroom. Everything looked like it had sat for years in rusty water. He would have liked to take a shit, but his insides were dry. The fountain, *Halsey Taylor*, was just a husk.

When he stepped out, the girl was half-hidden in the back room, on her phone. She saw him and disappeared completely. He would have liked a cup of water.

Outside was a picnic table made of concrete with stones inset, under a hard steel umbrella. It was winter-cold, and the umbrella had once been white with a large red logo, but now the red had faded in the sun and was mostly rusted, and the rust had dripped down and begun to stick at the edges of the stones, like cuticles. It was the least comfortable table he'd ever seen, so he ate the sandwich as he walked, shedding bits of food, bouncing them off his trousers and onto the gritty shoulder of the highway.

In the bottom of the bag, a pawful of napkins, maybe twenty. A long slash of orange in the southern gray sky like a headache, like a crack.

The land changed, from flat and open to woods brooding over a series of prone, steplike hills. People here had hollowed out deep spaces – a long drive back from their armored mailboxes to their houses in the trees. Some were big and pointed, full of shapely windows; others were little boxes made of cinder-block. In front of or beside their houses the people here arrayed their cars and pickups and boats, and some kept dogs on leads or in stockades.

On the shoulder where he walked, East felt the eyes of every driver on the road. He would have kept to the woods, but the last thing he needed was some person's dog latching on.

Here and there he saw a horse or cow. Or raised boxes in a little cloud. Meat smoking, he thought – or something. Then he got a good look and saw one clouded by bees. Bees: one time back when he still went to school, they'd shown a movie about them. Little colonies, getting along, everyone doing for the queen. Some teacher tried to start a hive up on top of the school – got beekeeper suits and everything. But then a boy had been stung fifty times and had gone to the hospital, and that was the end of lessons with bees.

He kept walking, getting far from the little town, the little car. That car was the bone that connected him to Iowa. In Iowa, the van was the bone that connected him to Wisconsin. Somewhere the judge and his daughter lay, and somewhere his brother lay, unable to say his name. Bones. Walter and Michael Wilson, on the ground in LA or anywhere. They could be anywhere. Walter would keep it airtight. Michael Wilson: all East could hope was that he stayed out of trouble, stayed free of anything where telling what he knew was something he could bargain with.

He wondered who was watching. Not about the police – of course they were. Of course they looked funny at every step he took. He knew how to walk around the police. Even carrying the gun in his pocket, he didn't fear being stopped by them.

It wasn't just the police that worried him. It was the stop he wouldn't see coming. The little town centers had been swept and were quiet, older white men catching him in their eyes, holding him there a moment: *single skinny black boy walking nowhere. Had a cap on.* Enough to remember him by. Enough to provide a description, or to find him again. They said 'Hello there,' and East nodded, walked by. Grateful for daylight.

It was on the unswept edges of town that East noticed the litter of the life – the little circles of stamped-down wrappers, abandoned bottles. He veered off his line on the shoulder of the road to look: yes. The vials and pinchies, the little knots of activity, torn-off matchbooks, plastic ice cream spoons scorched half through. *Firing up a plastic spoon,* he thought, shaking his head. Over in the blacktop refuse and colorful trash that waited outside the border of the lot for nothing, splotches of vomit and the warm, sad smell of piss.

Right out on the edge of the main road they were doing it. It was these people he needed to avoid. He had had plenty of friends who'd used, who'd become deep U's before they were teenagers. He could resist them. But he had no friends out here. He wondered how young they would be.

The old lady's face returned to him, her pointed voice, and he heard her talking to Walter as he walked in the cold. He saw her looking at him. Or sometimes it was the face of the Jackson girl, leaking blood and going to sleep on the street, or the screaming mouth of the girl in Wisconsin. Her body, under the toppled suitcase. All of it inside him now, screaming to get out. Everything.

Another mile, he thought. Another mile.

As he passed a gas station, two men asked did he need a ride. He looked up, but then one was talking to the other, even though they were both looking at him. Two of them, one of him. He put his head down.

His sense of the direction was partial. But the winter sun kept slipping to the right. Soon he could walk under the cover of darkness.

A while after every intersection, the highway sign said EAST. So he kept on.

Inside he was used up, but his body pleased him, as if it were a specimen he were observing. Even after hours of walking, his body was light. When it rained lightly, the rain did not chill. He breathed it, absorbed it with his skin; it sated him, and the wind dried what it left in his sweater. The wind pushed him. His legs, so soft after driving, came back warm and good and hard. When he bent to retie a shoe, they quivered like engines idling.

How long he had walked he had no idea. It grew dark and colder, and he would have to decide. It was going to get a lot colder. He could see the plants shrinking, small plumes from chimneys. A regret hit him: couldn't he have driven the car one more day? Couldn't he have driven this all in an hour?

No. He had to keep telling himself. The car, he'd had to leave it behind.

By now it had a ticket. By now it was in the computer. Unless it was Sunday and the meters weren't enforced. This too he wondered about. He forgot what day it was.

Signs promised the next little town a mile out – churches, Neighborhood Watch, a billboard for a Chevy pickup built in

America. The trees walled off the neighborhoods from the last ruined fields. The first liquor store, just outside the line. The streetlights began just beyond it, windowpane-yellow under the trees.

As he walked past houses again, his body came back into focus, took on color and shape. People crossed the street – walking together, older, twenty, dressed loosely or lightly, jackets open or sweaters and scarves. Dressed to walk outside but not for long, drinking from paper cups in the cold, disappearing into houses or coming out, holding hands, worrying, laughing. East stared at the big old houses with flags and open windows, even in the cold. At last a large stone sign the size of a bedroom wall announced it: it was a college. These were students, like Michael Wilson once was.

He couldn't stop looking. The way they walked – they met and bunched on the sidewalk, sat on the porches. They crossed the highway carelessly, and cars slowed for them. So sure of their world.

He broke from the road and followed a group of six that was cutting across a parking lot. Shiny sedans like he hadn't seen since they'd left LA: Volkswagens, Acuras, Hondas, Hondas, Hondas. Two students split off toward a building with a hundred long, lighted windows. East stuck behind the larger group. Three boys and a girl. They crossed between buildings and across a green field. Like kids rambling a neighborhood. At last they approached a large squarish building. East caught up and followed them in. A gymnasium: a desk said ALL VISITORS MUST SHOW ID, but the boy at the desk was on his phone. East ignored him as the others had, and the boy never looked up.

Inside, the four students turned left into a noisy arena: girls playing volleyball under blue-white lights. East followed the polished hallway. He knew what he wanted: MEN'S LOCKER ROOM.

Inside, on a toilet, he sat and waited until he stirred inside, that ship, that load, until he could rid himself of it. Then he followed the sound to the showers – quiet lights, two older men cleaning off, pump tubs of soap and shampoo on the wall.

He opened an empty locker and stripped off. He hung the pants with the two guns gingerly. If someone were to find it now. Well, if someone were to find it ever.

But his money he drew out and took with him into the showers. The tiles, square and divided by the lines of white grout, rectangles from here to forever, were gritty under his feet. That was his feet's grit. His body was caked with it, the grime of a week, all the way back to The Boxes. His body reddened in the scalding water and hurt the same inside and out, softening like meat under a hammer. He kept his head in the stream and tried to wash it clear.

In one locker, a forgotten pair of clean socks. A worn red T-shirt lay atop a locker. It had a dusting of sawdust, but that shook out. The breast read champion.

He wadded up the last bitter Dodgers T-shirt and stuffed it into the trash. Farewell to baseball. Farewell to all that white people's love.

His shoes, when he tied them again, seemed ragged on his feet. Dark drops on the toes and laces – he hadn't noticed them before. Spots. They could be anything. He padded the hallways, keeping quiet. No one stared, particularly; no one ejected him, yet. Weight rooms, a pool where the very air looked blue, the big gym where the game had ended. The crowd had gone, and he entered and drank from the fountain. A small man in a blue work shirt was motoring one set of stands back into a stack against the wall. A team of younger assistants removed the volleyball net with small, flashing tools, then carried off the chairs and official's tower. Efficiently the blue-shirted man swept the bleachers opposite, stopping here and there to polish with a towel anchored to his belt, then retracted them as well. The whole room changed. It was, to East, an interesting thing. He sat and watched against the wall, the two guns lumpy and hard against his thighs.

At last, the small man locked shut a storeroom, working off a large ring of keys, and then his assistants disappeared. Two black men came in with a basketball, taking the court at one end, dicing, lots of leaning and hand checks. *Damn,* they laughed. *Damn.*

One of the two left, and the second noticed East lingering by the stacked bleachers. 'What's up, young man? You looking for a game?' he called over.

East shook his head. But the player stepped closer, scrutinizing. Something changed in his voice. 'You all right? Need something to eat?'

East tried tucking his head away in his sweater. He couldn't begin to talk to the man.

'I can slide you into my dining hall. Get you some help if you need it.'

East shook his head again, stood, crept away. The guy seemed okay. But nothing was enough to trust him. And no sense in just bringing the man his trouble.

He slept the night in the gymnasium. Collapsed, the stacked bleachers made a tower of thin shelves on their backside, each one twelve inches below the next. East slid himself onto one of these shelves, waist-high. The next plank was just a few inches above his nose. Like a tool in a drawer, he thought, like a body in a morgue. It had been more than twenty-four hours since he had slept, but even in his dreamless sleep he knew that he must stay quiet.

At five in the morning East was awake. The gym must be closed, he judged, but he lay in his safe slice of darkness, mind and body still, until the first sounds careened in the hallway: a mop bucket, the metallic knock of deadbolts. His fingers straightened the guns in his pocket, and he waited until he heard the first voices, early comers. Then he slipped out of the bleachers. He considered taking another shower. But it would only be luxury. He could not stay here in the gym forever.

He drank, used the bathroom, then saw three people on the way out of the building, enduring the briefest of greetings. Frosty air. Except for its watery lights, the campus was largely dark. He felt good after the long night's rest. Eight hours, nine?

Ninety dollars and change left after gas and tolls and the food of the first day. He bought a bagel with cream cheese at a walk-in place on one of the side streets. A bagel: three dollars and eighteen cents. His first college lesson.

Today the road rose and fell. The trees twisted low and misshapen, as if storms had combed them many times. A few dark apples still dangled. He hungered, but he dared not walk into the orchards. Once he found an apple on the side of the road and picked it up. Nearly perfect, like bait in a story for children. He put it in his pocket with the gun.

He noticed tags on the backs of the signs across the road: c+w. Some of the paint weathered, some still glossy fresh. On most of the signs. Then on all the signs. He turned around and looked behind the signs on his side. Tagged as well. He was walking through territory.

A figure came walking toward him on the shoulder gravel half a mile ahead. At a shorter distance he decided that the figure was a girl. He sank his head low into the collar of his sweater. Avoided even taking a good look. A mass of brown hair pinned back. She had a down jacket on, but she was shivering too. He felt relieved when she was by him.

One house caught his interest. He saw that it had burned from the center out, not long ago. The bricks were still smoked black. The roof's peak had given way to something like the mouth of a volcano. Heavy smudge still bloomed in the air. Across from the front yard, a school bus, still caution-yellow, but its long yellow sheet metal was marked in primer gray: CHRISTIAN WOLVES. Then the plus sign. Like a cross.

Like the van. He stamped it in his mind, then crossed to walk on the other side.

Slipping. A light rain had done little more than grease the roadside. His joints were webbed with red exhaustion. He had not reckoned on the cold. Toward midday he crossed a small junction, not even noticing it until a truck hurtled past.

He touched his pocket. The apple was gone. He could not remember eating it or throwing it away. The guns were still there in the loosening pockets, riding the bruises they were making on his thighs.

The next town was two miles off, and he thought that if it had a store, he would buy clothing. If it had a place to rest, he would rest. He imagined Walter walking with him, his voice, his hypotheses: what this closed factory had made, how those trees were planted, how this kind of church felt about black boys. But Walter could never have walked this far. Walter would be home, wondering why East hadn't called. And worrying about that old lady, Martha whatever. She'd be coming back on the plane, East recalled. Perhaps today. And Walter would be beside himself with guilt over it.

He wondered if he was far enough. He felt far. He felt lost. But if there were such a thing as far enough, it wasn't a place you could walk to.

The next town was what he settled on. Far enough was going

to have to be here, at least for a while, even if he hadn't glimpsed it yet.

This town wasn't much. A couple of places by the highway, closed or indifferent, cigarette butts and harvest stubs blown clear up to the doors. Telephone books rotting in split plastic bags. East glanced up with effort at what remained of the signs: TIRES, VACUUM REPAIR. It didn't matter now. A nightclub that once had some style: a splashy sign, now a skeleton, and exterior walls studded up with white stones like a dinosaur's armor. Some sort of weird, fenced yard like an impound lot that said SLAUGHTERRANGE. COM. HELP WANTED in soaped letters in the window. A matronly farmhouse across the road disapproved of it all.

He turned down the side road and found a main street parallel to the highway. There, an old grocery, a post office full of cobwebbed shipping boxes, a pawnshop. Two stores said ANTIQUES but were falling apart themselves. The windowsills on the hardware store were rotting. A doughnut place seemed to hold the only people now, and one bar, blinking BUD, where they would be tonight. A Laundromat, machines scraped out and yawning.

And the little motel: Starlight. Two little wings of ten rooms each spread from an airy center office filled mostly with dust. Curls of neon tubing still clinging to the sign. It was the sort of motel you found on big north-south streets in The Boxes, but open there, sprawling, a clientele there to use or drink or hide, who sometimes just lived there for decades, disapproving of the others, fallen oranges rotting beneath their parked cars that never moved. But here in Ohio, the Starlight was empty, bleached sun-white and then dusted again, front door padlocked though the sign still said OPEN.

Town wasn't much. Clearly they'd run the highway just north of it at some point. But the highway had failed to keep it alive.

Boy, this is why you get on the plane, he thought.

Outside the Starlight Motel, he climbed atop a concrete planter full of poisonous-looking dirt and surveyed. Relieved now of its relentless moving forward, his body cracked with want. A passing moment of sunlight lit the houses briefly. In the offing was a church, a shingled thing jumbled together like children's blocks, a big cross, gilt and dirtied.

Two days walking in the air had thinned out his stubbornness. But the stubbornness that remained was choosing. He had chosen. *This is where you said you'd stop,* he reminded himself. Small, and no people out: everything he saw to hold against the town, to walk away from – to flee it, in fact – were reasons that, standing in the fading light, he steeled himself against.

A pickup truck with five kids in parkas in the back, sitting packed together, rumbled by slowly. All five kids turned their heads to look. Their mother gave him a single glance and blew a plume of smoke out her window, then flicked the lit cigarette butt after it.

He didn't even know the town's name.

After an hour, when his eyes had measured the town and his body had stiffened with cold, he climbed down from the planter awkwardly and walked to the grocery store. Closed. But oranges and cans on racks inside: at least that. At least the store was alive. He scrutinized the darkness inside, then backed off and read the sign. CLOSED ON SUNDAY. He had never heard of a grocery store being closed on Sunday.

Maybe, then, it was Sunday.

Next he walked to the doughnut shop. It was emptier than before, perhaps. But open. He paid his money for two large fried apple fritters, then added a cup of hot chocolate. He was beginning to treat the cold as a permanent adversary. The hot, doughy air of the shop was worth the people staring. He stood numb, breathing the steam off the scorching cup.

He used the bathroom for what he hoped was not too long. Hot water at the sink up his forearms, over his face, around the back of his neck. Carefully he dried himself. The clatter out by the main highway drew him back that way. The weird impound lot had, in the last two hours, filled with trucks and cars. The building there resembled a small barn backed up to a clumsy, bulldozed berm a story high, blocking off view from the road. A few dim lights burned cold on poles. The clatter back there was shooting. It had started just before sunset. He had heard the first shots from the doughnut shop as he stood there eating a fritter, dreaming on his feet. The first burst made him spill the rest of his hot drink on his fingers. Triggered, not automatic, four or five shots in all. He looked up, shaken: the locals in their booths had looked up too but were already back to their doughnuts.

Shots rang again as he stood at the mouth of the lot. The house. The wondering face of the girl. Involuntarily his body ducked. He looked around in the cold air – one split of dying orange in the dulling sky in the direction he'd come to know as south. A small car sat glowing its parking lights near the barn like a resting hog.

The shots weren't right – they didn't sound the same way. They lacked the knock a gunshot had. A *tump*, a different bang – he didn't know how to describe it. No houses like in The Boxes to echo off. But the same rhythm, the exchanges of fire, he could hear that – the conversation. The old music of his streets.

A target range? But there were shouts from inside too, and scrambling. An occasional yelp.

Somebody *burning* their ammo up, he told himself.

He slipped closer to the barn, finding a place to listen.

After he'd seen half a dozen men come in or out, singly or in pairs, carrying loads in heavy canvas bags like athletes used, or hunters, he got the nerve to open the door. *Slaughterrange.* An electronic beep announced him, but a noisy bouquet of Christmas bells rang too, duct-taped to the back of the door.

Long tube lights hung from the rafters hissed and flickered. Maybe the building had once been a garage: the floor was concrete and dipped slightly toward two long, steel-grated drains. The front half was given to two carpets, ratty and colorless, each of which anchored a sofa, a chair, a skid-marked coffee table, and a boxy TV. The back was a counter, antique with glass windows. Over the counter hung a range of weaponry, and a young man stood behind it.

'Hello,' said the man, standing very still. He had a strong gaze and a weak nose, a nose that glistened and twitched like a rabbit's snout. It was a U's nose, East recognized.

East said nothing. He studied the guns over the man's head. Large and gripped out, sniper guns. He'd never seen guns like this in plastic bags before, like hairbrushes at the drugstore. They were not real guns, but he did not know what they were. Some of them looked like fantasy, outer-space guns, colored green and orange like children's toys.

'Can I help you?' said the man, looking East over. East recognized the small, secret fidgets of his face. He was, maybe, thirty. Behind the counter he would have a real gun.

'What sort of place is this?'

'Best paintball range north of the Ohio River,' the man said automatically, as if it was a phrase he'd been paid to remember.

'Paintball?' said East.

The man reached and drew out a pearl of orange. He tossed it to East. 'That's a stale one,' he said. 'That one will hurt when it hits.'

East looked at the faintly luminescent nugget in his hand. 'What are you here for?' said the man. 'The job?'

East shrugged.

'Perry's not here tonight. You might catch him in the morning. He's in charge; he'll see you about it.'

'What is the job?'

'It's, like, assistant. Like a watchman.'

East detected the accent, the harsh sound inside the words. Like a movie spy.

'I can do that,' East said.

'This is a job for a grown man. You have to stay late.'

East said, 'I can do a man's job. I can stay late.'

'What are you,' the man said politely, 'thirteen? Fourteen? In school?'

'I'm a man,' East said. 'I don't go to school no more.'

'Ha. Good,' said the man. He had a telltale wetness in his nose, a bubbling. Then two men came in with canvas bags, and East watched them pay and take the tubs of colored balls the man gave them and transfer them into their guns and their own containers with funnel-shaped loaders, perched on the edge of the sofas, mumbling profanely. At last they returned the tubs and moved up a stairway beside the counter and out a door that went to the back of the building, the berm side.

'Can I look?' East said.

'Not tonight,' said the counterman. 'Come back tomorrow.' At first he'd seemed friendly, but now he'd seemed to have changed his mind.

In the parking lot East sat far apart from the other men's cars and trucks and listened to the shooting music fill the air. Dull night. No stars. He found himself starved for sleep. The strange hours.

He awoke with a gasp, leaning against the building. He had

been dreaming of the van, someone terrible peppering it with bullets: Michael Wilson, somehow, but with Sidney's face, firing out the mouth of the cabin in Wisconsin where the daughter was the dead Jackson girl aiming at them from beneath the suitcase. There was no shaking this. There was no *far enough* to settle his mind at sleep.

Leaned up against the wall was a roll of pink insulation. The wall type, fiberglass. He checked it, shook it – dry, no mice or vermin.

He found the largest truck in the yard, a jacked-up Ford with a work bed. He fed ten feet of insulation in between the huge back tires. Then he crawled in on top of it and fetched the rest of the roll around him, like a blanket, like a wrapper, sheltering under the huge round differential with its burnt-syrup smell. The cold and the lights muffled down, and he slept to the knocking of the shots in the yard beyond.

At one point in the night he woke and saw, through the hole in the end of his pink swaddling, the sky. The truck above him had gone. But he was still there.

18

THE MORNING LIGHT STARTLED East, and he struggled to unbundle himself, unwrap, to find his feet and stumble free. Pink strands in his mouth, drying at his lips. Pink fleece in his hair. All his skin crawled.

Then his head cleared. He went back, picked up the insulation, and rolled it carefully, tightly. Leaned it back up where it had been.

He walked down the highway, furtive in the cold air, and revisited the doughnut shop, for its bathroom as much as the food. He washed in the sink with the palms of his hands. A spill of salt at the corners of his mouth, streaks of wet on his sweater. The black eye slowly reshaping itself. His muscles lank and dog-tired under his skin. He could not bear to look in the mirror at what was left.

Purchased two doughnuts but could not bring himself to sit in the warm little shop, among other people. He went instead down the street, to brood by himself outside the little closed motel.

When East opened the door again, there was one person sitting in the big white building of Slaughterrange: an old man, pink like a ham, larger than the bar stool he occupied. Sandpaper bristle of ginger hair. He was holding a small piece of machinery in his left hand and rendering it with the screwdriver in his right.

'You the one Shandor said was looking for a job?' he bellowed without looking up.

East sized the man up, and he stopped short. Six foot five, three hundred pounds, maybe. The sort of man who was used to moving things. He lay down the tool and the chunk of beaten metal, and he brushed his hands on his Carhartt overalls.

'Was that you lying in the yard last night, son?'

East did not lie. 'I fell asleep.'

'Cold,' said the white man, 'to be falling asleep, under Tim Crane's truck. Where you staying?'

East said nothing.

'You the one, then, that wants the job?'

East nodded. Kept his eyes on the old man's eyes. There was something wrong with them. Sticky. Not high, but lagging a bit.

'I got to ask you a few questions.'

East said, 'I know.'

'Name?'

'Antoine.'

'You had a job before?'

'I did security. Two years.'

'How old does that make you?'

'Sixteen.'

'You ain't sixteen and done two years security, son.'

'I got a license,' said East. 'It says sixteen.'

The big man shifted on his stool. He did not ask to see the license. He was not in that sort of pursuit. 'You get high? You' – his voice became bitter, humorous – 'tweak out?'

East shook his head.

'You in a gang?'

Shook his head again. It wasn't necessarily a lie.

'Christian Wolves? Any other gang, known or unknown? You got tattoos?'

East said, 'No.'

'Do you mind showing me?' the man said. 'If you would lift your shirt up.'

East held up his sweater and the red shirt beneath so that the old pink man could see him, ribs and the two black points on his chest.

The man was embarrassed too now. 'Higher,' he said. 'I got to see your collarbones. That's where they put them.'

'Who?'

'The Wolves. Their tattoos. I don't know,' the man said.

East stripped his shirt off all the way and turned once, a dull outrage marking his face from inside. But the man, when he turned back, was looking away, with distaste. Maybe for East. Or maybe for having had to ask.

Maybe his willingness to be seen was all the man needed to know.

'Good,' said the man. 'I can show you how to work here. But I can't show you how to work. That, you got to know already.'

'I know it,' East said.

'I'm Perry Slaughter. I would be the owner. Excuse me.' Now the big man seemed to be wilting in on himself. He turned away and bent down behind the long wooden counter with the thick glass windows at the front and top. He came back up with a thin rig of plastic tubing, which he fit over his ears and into his nostrils. For a moment he stood, taking hits of something through the tube.

'You ain't happy with me, I can move on,' East suggested. 'I don't need this job.'

'Exactly why a person asks for a job,' Perry Slaughter gasped below his tube, 'because he don't need it. No, you're fine, for today at least.'

He peeled off the tubing and stuffed it back in the drawer. He regarded East suspiciously over the bristled pink of his cheeks. 'I take a little oxygen now and then,' he admitted. 'The good shit.' There was downstairs, and there was upstairs. Downstairs was the register and the counter and the cabinets full of paints, the front room, the bathroom. Upstairs, out the back door, was a covered deck with lockers and a four-man air station, chrome and shining and eager to hiss out air, and the sidewalk landing atop the plowed-up berm with its observation rail and lifeguard chair where someone could watch over the range.

The first two mornings East swept the range, raking up heavy litter and the clusters of paints he'd find, burst or spilled or trodden in. He'd board the stranded, wheelless school bus and the jeeps mired and moldering in the center of the range, picking up chunks of new-broken glass or metal. On foot, he pulled a light, knobby-tired tote behind him, emptying it into a Dumpster in the parking lot, which in turn was emptied by a black truck that stopped by and lifted the Dumpster above its head like a trophy, shaking it, the invisible driver jerking the hydraulic levers. At first Perry Slaughter had East taking directions from the other boy: upstairs or downstairs, what he should do. The other boy, Shandor, showed East the blaze-orange coat and helmet for entering the range when there were shooters, what the protocols were for sorting out problems or escorting the injured. Shandor showed him how the register worked, how to charge members, how to charge guests, how to sell time, paints, how to rent guns and headgear and check them back in, how to take a credit card, how to refuse one. Shandor showed East where the bathroom was and how to mop it out. The other boy seemed to prefer the outdoors, at least for the first string of warm afternoons, but then it no longer grew warm in the afternoon, and he left East out to look over the range.

East did either without complaint.

The men came every day, especially Sunday, new and curious, or regular, rumbling or limping, tires or boots crunching the frozen peaks of lot mud. They rented their guns or toted them in nylon bags with mighty, treaded zippers. They paid credit or they paid cash – money clips for the ones still working, pads of secret cash like squashed drink cups for the ones who were scraping by, who were no-good squandering, who were pilfering it out of a mattress or a mother or a wife. They came singly and in groups. There were posted hours, but they came before and they came after.

They paid entry and rentals, and they bought paintballs. Sometimes they bought gear – guns, helmets, pads, bags, military goggles. They bought drinks, crackers, beef jerky, chocolate bars. They lingered downstairs and stared at football on TV, from a skeptical distance or joining others on the sofas. Or they hurried up the stairs and out the back, to suit up and leave their wallets and phones and work shoes in the lockers there, pocketing the locker key or pinning it to a hip. Sweatpants, coveralls, track suits, dirty jeans. Then they went out to play, to shoot one another.

They left litter: the spent paints, the husks with their brilliant yolks. The blown bags and wrappers, the coffee cups, the tubes of liniment, the popper bottles, the bandages. The gum they chewed, the tobacco they dripped, the cigarettes they ground out, the gloves they lost. They left papers from the state and from their loans and from their joints and their wives. They left the *Plain Dealer* and *Dispatch* and *USA Today*. They left the penny-saver and the auto ads and their gun magazines and their computer-printed directions to here or somewhere else.

They scattered and held, playing their battles, dark shirts and light, red bandannas or blue, stalking one another with one paint or another. They scrambled through breaks in the land, burrowing themselves below the bulldozed hillocks and against the dead trailers and trees, the fortresses of fallen tree trunks, the one length of fieldstone wall older than anything. They hid in the school bus, or sometimes they swarmed in or out of it like a hive of bees. They revered the two surplus army jeeps painted army green mired near the trenches at the far end of the range, each with its white five-pointed star.

They scrambled and sighted, scrambled and sighted. Sometimes the men shouted at one another, coordinated, vague military directions, used phones, used walkie-talkies, working organizations in the brush. They formed teams, crews, alliances, factions. They turned on each other and then won each other back. Sometimes they ran singly, eyes blacked, sleeves peeled back in the cold, panting, waiting, shooting at anything or anyone, guarding their vantage points jealously, their long guns slung spanning their chests rigidly, extended skeletons.

They died, and they waited on the sidelines, rubbing bruises, watching the others. They died, and they came back to life.

In the beginning East got sixty dollars a day paid in cash – no discussion what a day was or how long it could last. It did not matter. Before the second week was out, Perry had made it a hundred. By then East knew the range. He knew the waiver forms and how to file them and how to talk back to someone who'd twisted an ankle or caught a paintball in the neck and now was angry, now threatened to sue. Soon it was East being asked the questions about how to clear a jammed barrel or punish an offender. Shandor had been there for four months, but Shandor did not work as hard as East or as much. And some days Perry's instructions were to tell Shandor he was not working that day.

Maybe Perry had begun to trust East, from seeing him, catching him working when he popped in for a few minutes now and then. East worked hard. Or maybe it was that Perry had never liked Shandor in the first place. Shandor was polite and handsome but evasive. He dabbed at his nose constantly. He could not remember, made things up. He had a thin, rabbity nose that was always wet with something.

At last one Monday, East asked where was Shandor, was he sick, knowing that wasn't the reason.

Perry looked away. His loud bray had, this morning, gone quiet and upset. 'All right. I'm going to tell you. Shandor won't be back.'

East raised his eyebrows.

'I put him in my truck and took him down to Columbus.'

'Columbus? To the college?' He'd overheard the talk on the sofas, the games on TV.

'The university?' Perry said. 'Nothing to do with that. It's what he wanted. He thought it would be a good place to start fresh. He had me turn him out on the street with his little suitcase and a handful of my money.'

He shook his massive head and his body wagged along.

'If somebody were to ask after him,' Perry concluded, 'now you can tell them where to look. But I can't imagine who would, outside of Hungary or wherever.'

'Why not?' East said.

'People don't connect with someone like that,' Perry said, 'who ain't from here.'

'I ain't from here.'

'Yeah, well,' Perry said. He counted out twenties for the weekend and pushed them across the counter.

East unlocked the padlock that secured the back of the cabinet. Time to start the day.

'So, you gonna hire somebody new? Cause it's hard to watch the back and front the same time.'

'I will. Right away,' Perry said. 'Never really took the HELP WANTED sign down. You need a day off?'

'I'm fine,' said East. He wasn't sure of the calendar, but he thought he'd worked fifteen days in a row. 'It's okay.'

'You tell me if you need a day off,' Perry said absently.

Perry didn't hire anybody new right away. But he began staying around. East figured he liked it: liked seeing the men and peppering them with his questions. Liked muttering in their presence and then holding forth.

Listening to Perry talk, East learned about the place. It was Perry who'd taken his wife's family's old field and plowed up the berm, Perry who'd backed the fences with sheeting to keep the noise and stray paintballs in, Perry who'd gutted the old barn and built the store inside. Plus the upstairs landing, where, through the long and dim afternoons until the lights came on at night, East oversaw the range.

Atop the berm, in his lifeguard's chair with its drop-hinged shield of spotty Plexiglas, East surveyed the men swarming like squirrels across the acres. Scrambled and sighted, scrambled and sighted. East admired some of the players, the small ones, the ones who shot less, who perched and waited, content to stand as rear gunners, hiding, conserving themselves. As Perry had told him, East ejected players whose behavior annoyed the others – cheaters, head shooters, overkillers in groups where overkill was unwelcome. Anyone with smuggled paint, with stale paint that did not break on contact, that bruised and bounced off. He protected the customers and protected the business.

Some of the men slighted East at first, or ignored him. But most came to accept him. They saw that he was always there. In the lifeguard's chair over the railing he was quiet and watched patiently, never hurrying them. They couldn't get much out of him. But he nodded once carelessly when a player asked if he was from out west, and that news got around, became the foundation of a dozen tales about who he was. He was no schoolboy. He was a runaway, an escapee. He was somebody Perry was sheltering, somebody's illegitimate son. He dealt with them directly and calmly, looked boys and men both in the eye, ended problems at once, kicked people out fairly and quietly if they had broken the rules, whether they were one-timers or regulars. He cut people off the way a bartender would. He seemed to have no fear and no body temperature: he sat out on the chair in a cotton shirt when everyone else was wearing a parka.

Some of the younger ones, kids buying paints out of their part-time jobs or the money their parents allowed them, idolized him. They called him Warlord, called him the Ancient, called him Gangsta.

The night the Buckeyes beat Michigan, a carload of Michigan guys had stopped at the range and rented out guns and snuck in a bunch of store-bought paintballs that were as stale as rocks and left bluish bruises where they hit. Then they lit a player up, a regular, mercilessly, four of them on one, fifty or sixty shots all around the back and shoulders, even when he was on the ground. East hadn't hollered or blown the air horn. He'd just switched out the lights. Then the regulars had all the advantages, knowing the range like a familiar block, like their own yard, and one of the Michigans had his teeth loosened with a gun butt. In the dark it was just an accident, and they got loud with East, and East faced up to all four, took their guns back and saw them, bleeding, out the door. That night East let the locals stay and play the TVs till five in the morning. More men arrived; they brought cold beer, they brought pizza, they watched the game again on a 1:00 AM rerun and sang through it.

They asked East to come and sit, to have a beer, but he mopped up and stayed away, keeping business.

Maybe he wasn't of age.

The shooters were white, all of them. Some of them had to forget what color he was before they spoke to him. But he had made his place. He was just Antoine, the new boy Perry had, and he was all right. Better than Shandor – they had not liked Shandor. He was something, Russian, Ukrainian, maybe, not from America. And Shandor was an addict. He was always looking past them, looking at something else. It made them uneasy, the men who came here, drank a few beers, went paintballing every day. Antoine, whoever he was, was American. Antoine looked them in the eye. He knew what he was doing, Antoine.

They respected him, stopped watching him all the time. But he never stopped watching them.

19

THE SHOOTING, SHOOTING, ALL the time. It filled his ears, was all he could hear. Then he didn't hear it anymore.

The range was just one of the things Perry ran – his deals, he called them. The range was a deal. He had another deal, plowing – city streets, in one truck, and driveways, which took another, and he got paid on state subcontract for plowing roads that the big trucks couldn't do. Another of Perry's deals was bulldozers. He could grade your yard or clear your lot or break your building up into a pile for hauling away. If you had a home and paid tax on it and you wanted to stop, wanted only to be bled for the land, Perry could start on a morning, and the place would be mud by night. He commanded Bobcats and bigger dozers and graders and a couple of backhoes, some of which he owned, some of which the state did, owned and maintained, though they stayed on his lot and bore his name in black letters on the side. BONDED. The truck that emptied the Dumpster every day, that was Perry's too.

Another deal: Perry was mayor of the town. Stone Cottage,

Ohio, was what they called it, though they'd stopped quarrying stones, and there was no cottage anyone knew. He did not want to be mayor, but the mayor controlled zoning, and he wanted to control zoning, because no one wanted a paintball range a block from Main Street. Everyone had known that was why he'd run to be mayor. But he had bulldozed them too, one by one, and on voting day a little more than a year ago, he'd won. The range opened that month.

Maybe they'd known, Perry declared, maybe they knew all along how much he'd hate being mayor of their God damn town. Four years. Maybe that was their revenge on him, what they extracted in exchange.

'You could quit being mayor. Now that you got what you wanted,' East said, head down, polishing the countertop glass. The counter was fourteen feet long, from an old candy store. It had glass in the top an inch thick. The glass got smudged under everyone's elbows, but East liked to keep it clear, keep the pans of paints visible underneath, glowing even without light on them.

'What I wanted *then*, son,' Perry said. 'There's always a new thing to want. And I'll get it too, but they'll make it hell on me.' He withdrew the oxygen rig from the drawer and slipped it on. A cannula, he called it. 'It's only fair.'

'Hell is forever,' said East bravely. 'Not just four years.'

Perry coughed wetly. 'If I make it four years,' he said, 'it will be the devil's last miracle.'

It seemed a revelation to Perry that East didn't steal money. He kept the register straight, severe, didn't take IOUs or cut deals. But he couldn't see how Perry would know that. To slip out a little – the way Shandor apparently had – would be easy. There was a lot of money. Most of it passed quietly as cash. Sometimes loose bills were offered him to extend someone's range time, to pay for a gun someone'd broken, or for a handful of stale paints, duds, for laying a hurting on the birthday boy or the boss. He'd take it. But whatever came, he put in the register, included in the deposit. The deposit wasn't in a bank. It went through the front mail drop of the farmhouse across the highway, where Perry lived.

Perry trusted him. But maybe trust was a trick. Maybe trust was the act that not trusting put on when there was no better alternative.

Maybe trust was the trick that kept him working twelve, thirteen, fourteen hours a day. Mopping, raking, sitting counter on his ass.

'Son, I know you're gonna take me one of these days. I just don't know how,' Perry hollered, laughing, as if his loudness could command this place forever.

The hundred per day still wasn't good money. Just the same, East got his handful every day, paid timely. And in this town he spent little – there was nothing to buy. An egg sandwich every morning at the shop, and fruit from the grocery twice a week. A used coat for outdoors at the resale, used jeans for a dollar or two, warm shirts. A good pillow still in its plastic wrapper. He bought gloves at the hardware – even the men with ragged coats and uncut hair wore good gloves. East studied, bought a pair new, thirty dollars. Warm, elastic, he could work all day in them without a complaint.

The old bank was built of stone with fat sandstone pillars in front but had the same name as East's bank in The Boxes. He acted trustworthy around banks, and banks so far had trusted him. Anyway, his wad of twenties was getting thick. He wasn't going to bury his money or squirrel it away, the way he'd buried the two guns behind the edge of the parking lot, plastic-bundled, in a wave of dirt Perry's bulldozer had left behind.

He asked that five hundred dollars be made into a cashier's

check. He made a new account and deposited the rest. The woman seemed confused that he didn't want to order checks.

'Just the ATM.'

'But you'll want the flexibility,' she said. 'Not everything can be paid online.'

Patiently he listened to her explain the options, the fee-free checking, the online access. She looked intense, friendly but businesslike. Her dark black bob cut hung down. A stud in the side of her nose. She might have been twenty-three. He wondered if she walked or drove in to work, if she rued living here.

At last she concluded her pitch.

'Just the ATM,' East repeated calmly.

'But you can. You could,' she countered. Her hands paused, unsure. Then she lay them on the desk. 'Well,' she said. 'We're happy to have you.'

He got up, walked to the post office, bought a pre-stamped envelope, and sent the check to his mother, without a note.

The smell of the bleach and cleanser and water East liked to mix together in the mop bucket wasn't right; it rose and curled inside his nostrils, wasn't healthy. But it smelled clean. Twice each day, now that Shandor was gone, East made the bathroom clean. Since he'd started cleaning it and mopping cobwebs, wiping fixtures clean of the dust that got in somehow, the men had begun helping out, using the trash can, pissing the floor less. They spat or spattered somewhere else, wiped their blood off the sinktop, picked their bandages up and threw them away. They began to keep it right. They put their returns on the return box, their beer cans in the recycling.

The spiders had stopped coming down out of the ceiling and claiming corners every night.

The barn, East learned, had been the old garage for the farm trucks, before Perry Slaughter had it remade. All that work – the bathroom, the storeroom up top, the stairway out the back, the antique counter with its heavy glass – Perry had bartered.

'For paintballs,' Perry said. 'Some people will do anything for paintballs, God help them.' Standing in the bathroom doorway as East mopped, he coughed and laughed both. 'When I opened it, I thought it would be a weekend thing. But they wanted to come back. Then another range opened up five miles up the road and stayed open every day. Everyone I had went away. So I stayed open every day, and they all came back.' He scratched his sandpaper chin with a middle finger. 'The guys they fought up there, they brought them all back here. Every day.'

'How these guys afford to come in here playing every day?' East said. He pressed the mop out.

Perry snorted. 'They can't. Son, it's like jerking off. It's like meth. These boys can't stop, and they can't call it what it is.'

'What do you mean?'

'This is what they lie about. Not having a girl. Not were they drinking. They come in here and then tell the world they didn't.' He looked back over his shoulder: heavy tires rolled past on the road, whining. 'It's the ugliest business I ever been in.'

'If you don't like it,' said East, 'why you got it?'

'You got to sell what you got left.' Vapor rose around Perry's boots. 'You ever heard people talk about Peak America?'

'Peak?'

'Peak. Like a mountaintop, Antoine. Like high as you're ever gonna get.'

East twisted a knot in the trash bag. 'No.'

'Well, that was Ohio, right here, fifty years ago,' Perry said. 'What a God damn country. But that's past now.' He backed out and put himself down on the stool behind the counter, and East followed him out with the trash bag and the bucket.

'All these boys,' the old man sighed. 'Their daddies, fifty years ago, they worked foundry jobs, or machinists, or they were white-collar: sales, teacher, bank. Everything. Drove to Cleveland, drove to Youngstown, had a pension, second house. Ohio exported more steel than Japan. Than Germany. Than England or Spain. The whole countries. We were making babies then, believe me. Time you turned thirty, you'd have four or five. These days, most of these boys who come in here every day, secretly, the thing they want is for that girl to turn them out. She can keep the house. The sooner she gets another man, the sooner he is free. He can't fix nothing anyway. Gets an apartment that's tiny – the size of that bathroom. That's all he wants,' Perry said. 'Works a little when he can. Got his beer and his PlayStation. Can't look his dad in the eye. That's what I mean. We were up there, and we've come down to this.'

East stood still. He thought of the road, the towns he'd walked through. 'Everything out here is pretty chewed up,' he volunteered.

'You have no idea.' For a moment Perry eyed East, licking his thumb, like someone turning a page. 'You think you want to be a dad, Antoine?'

East laughed.

Perry said, 'Maybe you are already. Sometimes you *act* like it,' he added mysteriously.

East lugged the bag out the door into the cold parking lot and tossed it over the side of the Dumpster. He breathed the cold air, scanning the trees opposite, their damp black and bare white. One large bird perched, watching the road below.

His two guns lay in the wave of dirt just there. Every day he reminded himself of them. But rain kept packing the dirt down.

Back inside, East changed the subject. 'What about you? You ever had any kids?'

'Early I did,' said Perry. 'With my first wife. Not much of a father. Sooner or later, every kid is gonna want to kick your ass.'

Wetly he coughed. 'I gave them every opportunity back then.'

East looked forward to these talks with Perry – he wasn't sure why. They went forever and everywhere, and the old man moved from mumbling to hollering about things as if they were East's fault: World War Two. Miners who died. American steel and Japanese steel. All about lumber and what happened when the trees weren't old anymore. Perry had spent his life knowing what things were made of. He would talk about those things all day. Sometimes East caught himself thinking about it, wondering about things he hadn't even known he was listening to.

Perry was dying. It was not something he ever mentioned to East. It was something East slowly stopped denying to himself. Perry took a battalion of pills each day. All colors, all shapes, counting them out from a box he kept in his pocket. Under the counter were other pills he didn't want his wife knowing about. He'd count out a handful and chase them with a can of root beer, and he'd wince and clench his eyes.

No one took pills like that if they had a choice.

Perry's cough was a variable thing, like an engine that some mornings started and on others refused. Some of his teeth were coming loose. One day he pulled one out and lay it on the glass countertop. Then he was called away on his little silver flip phone, and he forgot about it. East didn't know what to do with the tooth. A tiny blackening spot of blood peered at him from between the roots. After a while he picked it up and put it in the register.

Perry hadn't hired anyone yet. East reminded Perry how he was stretched thin, running the place by himself. After that, Perry came and worked four full days in a row – from ten or eleven in the morning to helping East clean up at closing. It was fine with East this way. He didn't need some new kid to be the boss of. He'd had plenty of that.

One morning, before the range opened, Perry invited East over to the tall, yellowing farmhouse to eat. East did not want to go but did not know how to refuse. So he sat down to breakfast with Perry and his wife, sitting in a straight chair where the wicker curling around the back didn't make it any less uncomfortable.

Perry served out eggs and ham and potatoes and talked to various ends.

His wife, Marsha, sat mostly mute. She asked East a few polite questions about not much, then broke off, as if she'd prodded enough.

Perry talked about her as she sat, occasionally nodding assent. The land had been hers, her family living on it a hundred years: grapes once, and apples and cucumbers and pumpkins and squash and corn. Animals that fertilized the soil, soil that fed the animals. 'That's done for,' Perry said, and she got up then, cleared her plate, and sat back down with a glass of water into which she'd stirred something that sank and swirled.

Her sister had gone to California and was never heard of again. Two brothers were killed at war and the third driving drunk on the highway. When you could no longer hire men to work the fields, then not boys either, waves of Mexicans kept the farm for ten or fifteen years. But now the Mexicans were gone, and the farms up this road were farms no more: it cost more to run them than any crop could bring in. The windbreaks had grown out and filled the old furrows.

The paintball range, East guessed, was something Marsha had agreed to without knowing what it was, without knowing how high the bulldozers would cant the walls, or that a large red and white banner reading SLAUGHTERRANGE.COM would be her view out her front window thereafter, that her home would rock each afternoon with the sound of gunshots and idling trucks. She too had said yes to her husband with only a vague idea of what his bulldozers would do. And now, East could see, she was a woman whose business it was not to look out the window at how her money was made.

The walls of the dining room were lined with photographs of the white people who were Marsha's ancestors. Fierce faces in gray, the women with hair in elaborate plaits, the men always a little smaller than their suits. The children he could barely look at, wondering if they were the doomed ones.

East thought of the pictures in the gun house in Iowa. The same fierceness, white people with hard eyes, keeping still the faces that their hard lives had made.

After Perry picked up the dishes and washed them, still holding forth from the sink in the kitchen, East half bowed quietly and thanked Marsha before leaving her quiet dining room. He had barely heard a dozen sentences from her, but he knew he had wandered into a battle about what was left, about what could and could not be sold. He could see the fragile stacking it was not in his interest to upset.

His ATM card arrived. This new ATM, he could feed cash right into it, no deposit envelope. It counted it up. East was suspicious, but the machine was always right.

The little eye in the window above the keypad, observing him, the camera under the roofline – he didn't even hide his face anymore.

'Warmest day in thirty years of Decembers.' Perry was drinking off a bottle of Old Crow. 'There'll be a front down from Canada next,' he added. 'Then I'll have to be out in the plow. I'll get someone in here to help you.'

'All right.' To East the promise was already empty. To get Shandor any help, it had taken *him* walking in half dead.

They sat together in canvas chairs at the end of the landing, away from the building, where the sky paced above them, great clouds, barely tinted from below, coiled like the entrails of some great creature.

'Another hour,' Perry said, 'these clouds will run out, and we'll have nothing but stars. If you can stay awake.'

And truly, the shelf of cloud passed, unveiling a long, clear black road of sky. The number of stars was more than East had ever known. Like something scattered. He doubted his eyes.

Perry slugged from the bottle, sleepy and content.

'You ever do astronomy? The constellations and so forth?'

'What's a constellation?'

'You know, in the stars. Say, the Dipper. Say, the North Star.' Perry turned his bull neck around with difficulty. The north was behind him. 'You know the North Star? Underground Railroad stories and all that?' He pointed vaguely. 'By the Dipper, there?'

East laughed. 'What's a dipper?'

Perry's finger stopped tracing in midair. 'A water scoop. A dipper. What do they call it? A ladle. There. Handle, handle, handle, then the box of four stars.'

'Which box you mean?'

'Damn, son. That one. Then the last two point at the North Star.' Perry took another drink and stopped before he said something else.

East wasn't sure. But did it even matter? So many stars. This is what old men did, sitting out in chairs, staring at these. In the morning, when East woke up slumped and startled in his chair, Perry's whiskey bottle sat empty on the ground. But he had gone.

The cold front rolled in as Perry had said. For two days the clouds gnarled and darkened; then it snowed, the sky trying to blot out the world.

East had seen flurries before – twice since he'd left The Boxes, and once when he was there, a strange cloud that came south off the mountains and glittered the air over The Boxes for five minutes one January day. But never anything like this. The road a foot deep, the trucks slipping, helpless, thunder roaring behind the farmhouse. No one came, and he was glad that they didn't. He didn't trust it to be safe, going out.

Perry came through about noon in the small plow, turned off the highway, pushed clear a rectangle of the buried lot. He jumped down then and left the truck idling outside.

'Jesus,' Perry chuckled. 'Not bad for a Saturday. I think you can take the rest of the day. I'll put a sign up, pay you anyway.'

East could not contain his alarm. 'It's supposed to be like this?'

In the disastrous cold, Perry seemed as young and happy as East had ever seen him. 'Yeah. It's supposed to be just like this.'

The men were just as pleased to go shooting in knee-deep snow. That Sunday after the Browns game there were twenty, thirty guys. Perry brought in a large red plastic drum of coffee, handing out cups. 'Don't know what I did round here before this boy showed up,' he said to the older ones who just came to lounge away the evening, talking not about paintball but things they'd done and why their knees and backs and hearts didn't work. Why they were retired but none of the younger ones would ever be able to do that. Why staying here in Ohio was what they'd do even if it was a bad idea. They'd be in it to the end or be damned. That was what they told each other.

The Browns game was replayed late, and the men stayed and talked and watched them lose again. Their season would end in a couple of weeks. But it was over a long time ago.

East swept the stamped-out snow from their boots out the door, mopped up the melt, repeated it once or twice an hour until at last they stopped coming. Menial work. Sometimes he tired of it, felt a bubble of resentment. But it was also true that Perry's praise gave him a soaring, stinging pride. With Fin, he supposed, it had been more or less the same way. It was the first time in a while he'd let himself think of Fin.

Sometimes when he was looking out over the range, watching the men hide and mass and surge and shoot, he thought of Ty, thought of The Boxes. But he no longer could find the phone number Walter had given him, and he didn't try to remember it. What was in The Boxes was safe without him.

At the top of the stairs, the back door led onto the landing, the lockers, and the air-compressor station was to the right. To the left, latched and rarely used, was a little storeroom. A utility sink, a green skylight. All these weeks, East had been sleeping there. He could lay down a certain double sheet of cardboard on a pallet – it was comfortable, smooth, had a give to it. He had the pillow, a used blanket. And along the roadside he had found a box that a dishwasher had come in, still clean and dry. He could fold it flat, slide it behind the cabinet in the day. At night he opened it and slept underneath, the dark string humming quiet in his chest, in blackness, encased.

If Perry knew about this, he had not let on.

Sometimes in the night East dreamed of the Jackson girl. Or of the judge's daughter, screaming. Or of being here at the range with Walter and Michael Wilson, the three of them searching, hunting somebody. Or of nothing, just the yellow line broken on the road, a line of nothing, of questions. Sometimes in the day, watching the men stalk one another, he dreamed these things too.

But one day in December, when the players had left because of a steady rain, Perry came and called East to dinner. Refusing didn't seem to be an option. Perry counted the bills into a leather folder, then counted back change for tomorrow's register and hid it where they always did. East swept quickly and locked the back door. Then they hurried across the road, bent under their coats, Perry explaining. Marsha had a son. He couldn't make either holiday, Thanksgiving or Christmas. This was going to have to do. He had come in that day from Philadelphia, Pennsylvania. 'Sorry,' Perry concluded, 'to spring this on you.'

East took this to mean it was not Perry springing it at all.

The son was named Arthur. He was tall, an attorney – as he pointed out – and he sat to Marsha's left. They were already sitting when he and Perry came into the dining room. Perry brought the food from the kitchen and then sat down on East's side of the table. The room was dim, like for a celebratory dinner, but an overhead light shone down on the table, bright enough that someone might clearly read a document.

Marsha had made the butternut squash, green beans, and wild rice, Perry pointed out.

'But the turkey is from IGA,' said Marsha soberly. 'They do a nice job.'

East nodded. He couldn't tell what this was about. Perry stood and carved the turkey with a long knife burnished black. The son said a tight little prayer, and meat was served onto the plates. It was warm and tender, the first real meat East had eaten in almost a month. He felt his stomach get confused about it, cramping dully.

Marsha waited until they had all refilled their plates before she spoke.

'You need to put Antoine in a decent place,' she said. 'Not on a sofa that others crouch on all day.'

So this was the ambush he was in for. The lawyer son was Marsha's version of a gunner. Had she come in and looked at the range, at the storeroom? When he was out, getting breakfast, maybe? Did she guess that the sofa was his bed? Or had she found his nest, his box and bed?

'That is a garage, not a decent place for a human to live,' Marsha said, 'but you have one living there. I look out at night – he does not leave. I look out in the morning – he does not come back.'

Perry, mayor of the town, looked down at his fork, then made parallel digs through his mashed potatoes. 'All right. I didn't know where he was staying. I didn't know. Say the quarry hires a guy: they don't ask, where are you staying?' He coughed again and removed something from his cheek with cupped fingers. 'Antoine. Did I know where you were staying?'

East stirred. 'No, sir.'

'They know if they want to know,' said Marsha. 'And if they ask. If they keep paper. If their records are at all legal, they know.' Her son the lawyer gave a listening nod.

'There's paper enough,' Perry said. 'Precious little, but enough.'

'If your luck holds out,' Marsha said, spearing a green bean. 'But you knew, Perry. You knew, and you didn't even take him anything to make it comfortable. A bed, a hot plate. You could have tried to make it nice. I mean, we must have a dozen toasters in the attic. Arthur gives me one every year.'

'Not every year,' interposed Arthur.

She looked at East then, sad half-moons under her eyes. A silent apology. Maybe she was sorry for watching. But she was watching.

Perry served himself two rolls from the basket. 'We'll see what's possible.'

Then she addressed East. 'What brings this on is, we received the notice. The state: they'll inspect. Within a month. And if they find you staying there, they'll revoke the permit and close the business.'

'Which would not make her unhappy,' Perry said, chewing. 'Which would not break her heart.'

'Antoine.' She spoke up – the loudest sound East had ever heard her make. Her eyes darkened. 'He has to find you a place to live. I will make him. There are decent places.'

'Not for what he's paying now,' Perry grunted.

'If I have to remind you who owns the land and the building,' said Marsha, 'I will.'

Perry wandered the subject around, mentioning an apartment building he knew, owned by a lady down near Chillicothe; down there they used to make truck axles, and they were once the capital of Ohio. Now they had a storytelling festival.

But Marsha cut him off. 'They don't make truck axles now, do they?'

'No, Marsha, they don't.'

'You haven't ever gone to the storytelling festival, have you?'

'No, dear. I have not.'

'It's in September. Almost a *year* away.'

Perry coughed. The dinner had been an effort for him even without the conversation. He was sick, East had recognized from the beginning, but always florid, forceful somewhere back inside. Now he was tired inside.

'All right,' he said under his breath. 'I'll find you a place. I can help you pay for it.' He stared at the meat piled before him, then at his wife. 'Not tonight. Maybe tomorrow.'

So the attorney son served himself more wild rice. He hadn't had to say a thing. East wondered if he considered it wasted time, coming out here. But his sitting by Marsha's side had given her courage.

Everyone finished in silence. East chewed his last green beans slowly, one at a time, crushing each little seed out and finding it with his tongue. His plate when he handed it over was as clean as if it had never held food. He stood and pushed his chair in square with the table, as if he'd never been there.

It had been difficult, sitting there. A conversation he could never really speak up into. But he would remember this meal – the good food of a family. Even this one, so far from his own, or what had once been his own.

It was the talk of the apartment that unsettled him – the moving, giving up space he knew for something different, threatening. He ruminated and could not sleep. The box was hot with his restlessness. He tipped it off him and listened to the wind creaking the skylight in its frame. He stretched his legs and drew them in again. Finally he sat up and found his shoes.

He locked the front door behind him and walked into town. In the night, the air had warmed, and the snow had thawed to gurgling mush. In the one bright window, a handful of people sat hunched at the doughnut counter. They all looked over at the one at the end, who was telling a story. It was three o'clock in the morning. The street smelled like the sweet, frying dough. The people didn't look up as he passed the little slurry of light.

Near the gas station hung two black pay phones. East picked up a cold handset and stared at the powdery buttons.

It had come back to him, the number off the flyer, seesawing out of that woman's body. He could see it now. He dialed.

'Abraham Lincoln, please.'

'Oh, baby,' the operator purred. 'He ain't been to work lately.'

'I got to talk to someone,' he said. 'What can you do for me?' She could have been the operator from before. He couldn't tell.

Some males paid a lot of attention to women, but he hadn't paid much.

'If you work there,' he said, 'you know about Abe Lincoln. You can get him, or you can't.'

She said, 'Hold on.'

The music was high, quavering. Vampire hip-hop. A car slushed by and stopped at the doughnut shop; two men and a woman climbed out, all talking at once.

East heard the different, male breathing first. Impatient. Maybe just woken up.

'Yeah. Who is it?'

'Who's this?' replied East.

The male on the other end said flatly, 'No. The first question is mine.'

He remembered now the chaos of the last time he'd called this line. *They'd arrested them all.*

'Did Walter get back?'

'Walter who?'

'Michael Wilson? Did Michael Wilson get back?'

'Michael Wilson *who*?' But the bite was fake. The voice knew this was real.

'From what I'm asking,' East said, 'you know who I am. Just tell me. Are they *back*?'

He stood waiting. The line hummed. The man was waiting him out.

'Just tell Walter for me,' he said at last. 'I was out here with him. I'm still out here. Get him on the line. I'll call you back, half hour.'

'I ain't your secretary,' the voice said. 'Fuck you.'

But this meant *yes*. That East was still being listened to, the phone still connected, meant *yes*. 'Half an hour,' he said again. He hung up the phone and turned around where he was standing.

Empty street. A big truck headed down the side road over the creek – they weren't supposed to. They ruined the little bridges that weren't load-rated, Perry said. But at night they came anyway. Somebody was driving them, and that somebody needed to go home.

He bought a chocolate doughnut and ate it at a corner booth. Rivers of glaze and grease on his fingers and the rich, fragrant cake. Dark crumbs on the waxed white bag. The half dozen customers and the night girl stole glances at him. So be it.

He listened. The three who had come in were discussing a card game, bowers and the dead hand. One of the men was the redheaded counter girl's brother. The girl with the two men had just given up smoking, East observed. It was in her restlessness. He could not smell the smoke on her, but he smelled the need. He knew. The counter girl did not like the ex-smoker who was there with her brother. She said nothing. Nobody knew the one at the end, the balding customer with the round, streamlined head. He tried to insinuate himself; he laughed pleasantly at everything. He wanted to be a part of this place.

East watched the clock, counting off thirty minutes. He zipped his coat and headed for the door. 'Good night,' ventured the counter girl from behind him with her plain, flat voice, clear above the murmuring and the bouquet of Christmas bells on the door.

'Good night,' he answered.

Above, dim stars showed, like something unburied.

'I'm gonna put you through,' the operator said. 'Three-way call.'

'I just want to speak to him,' East said. 'Don't want a three-way call.'

'Shall I have him call you back at this number?'

'You got it, the number?'

'Yes, I have the number.'

So now they would have an idea where he was.

'How you doing out there?' she added. Like someone had told her.

He grunted and hung up.

East scratched the dry skin above his jaw. For a moment he considered just walking away – abandoning the phone, leaving just this trace, this much of himself. But that assumed something, he knew. That someone remembered him. That somebody was still wondering.

Walter's voice was muffled. 'Who is this?'

'How was your flight?'

'Damn.' Walter whistled. 'Man. Nobody knew what to figure about you. Was you dead or in some jail? Or did you get back here and hide out?'

'Is it okay to talk?' East said.

'Yeah,' Walter said. 'Yeah, I borrowed a phone, so be cool. But yeah.'

East was about to spill a story. But he swallowed it. 'So. Fin still inside?'

'Yeah. He's gonna be happy I heard from you, though.'

'Who's running things?'

'Oh,' moaned Walter. 'It was gonna be Circo, you know? Every one was gonna hate it. But then he got a DUI and had weed on him, and Fin, on the inside, said no. Fin hates that, you know, distractions. So it's kind of complicated, kind of in process. We're changing up. Getting out of the house business. Some dude actually bought thirty blocks, the houses, the U's, the kids, everything.'

'He bought, like, the houses? That people live in?'

'He bought the rights,' Walter said. 'Any business going on in there, he gets to own that. Paid a lot of money. And –'

The strangeness of news from home. Like a message in a bottle. 'Did Michael Wilson make it back?'

'I heard he did,' Walter said. 'I ain't seen him.'

'Why is Fin still in?'

'Aw, man,' said Walter. 'He got, like, a billion dollars bail. At first it was a hundred thousand, and we had that easy, so the judge went sky high. They ain't letting him out. Ever.'

East glanced around in the dark.

'Anybody talking about it?'

'No one saying *anything* about that,' Walter said.

East felt a twang of disappointment. In spite of himself.

Walter laughed. 'You still out there, man. That's what mystifies me. What are you doing? You need money, I can send it. Or a ticket. You could fly home now, no problem, except there's a couple things I gotta fill you in on.'

'No. I'm here now.'

'I kept waiting on you to call.'

'No, I'm here,' East said. 'So, man. What are you doing?'

'Me? I'm back in school,' Walter chuckled. 'Missed a week, nobody said shit. But I'm going to *private* school in the spring. Last semester, college prep, no more Boxes. They sending me up, I'll live there. Do a little recon, you know.'

'Like Michael Wilson at UCLA?'

'Maybe. Good school up in the canyons. Kids up there, they're either movie stars or geeks.'

East tried to imagine it. He didn't know what to imagine.

'What are *you* doing?'

'The old thing,' said East. 'Just watching.'

'What? You found a house and crew?'

'Different.'

'Different but the same?'

'Yeah,' East said.

'That will hold you,' Walter said, 'but that's little boys' work, E – you know it. We did that when we were little boys.'

East felt the sting. But it passed. 'Walter. I need you to do something.'

'What?'

'Send me something. Go over to my mother's house and tip my bed up. You'll find a wood block that don't belong, with a butterfly bolt. Get my ATM cards, and if you can, get my phone, and mail them to me.'

He gave Walter his mother's address and the street address of the range.

'I saw that area code. Had to look it up,' Walter said. 'Ohio?'

'Ohio.'

'Is it like Wisconsin, all cold?'

'Warm and mountains,' East said, 'just like LA.'

'How I'm gonna get in there, your mom's house?'

'Tell her I need it. Give her fifty dollars, man. She'll let you in like anything.' Grimly he added, 'Probably let you in for five.'

'You ain't coming back, are you?'

'I don't think. Don't tell anyone what I told you.'

'Believe me, man. I'm keeping quiet about all this. You're not coming back?'

'Don't tell nobody I'm out here,' East repeated.

'I won't say a word,' Walter said. 'But you're not coming back. I can't get my mind around it.'

Perry put the mail on the counter and regarded it sideways. Express package, addressed to Antoine Harris. It took a day and a half.

'Last name Harris,' he observed. 'First time I knew you had a last name.'

'I lose track myself,' East said.

'I must engrave you a nameplate,' Perry declared.

All day the package glowed in the cabinet, radioactive with his previous life.

That night he tore the brown paper and tape and unwrapped a shoebox that had come from under his bed at home, with a pair of his old, outgrown shoes, battered but still whole, still real. Why had Walter sent those? He almost chucked them into the trash.

The stink of his socks, the bedroom at his mother's house. His salt.

Then he felt around. Down in one toe, a flat bundle was wrapped in brown paper with the scrawl he could barely make out: COULDN'T GET PHONE. WILL KEEP LOOKING. W. Inside the fold, a thousand dollars in twenties, wrapped around his ATM cards, and one more card: a license, State of California.

The name, his own. Strange to read it there, in that official type, beneath the watermark. The address, his mother's, the birthday, his own. A few days past now – he'd forgotten it. He was sixteen now. A licensed operator.

The photo he remembered taking in a drug house a year ago, a different shirt, a new haircut. Someone had been fighting in a bedroom upstairs as he had sat straight against the backdrop and looked the camera in the eye.

Maybe it hadn't been much work to make. But Walter had made it. He wasn't sure how to feel. Was it a reward? An invitation? Or was it a rope, tying him down to a spot on the ground? With Melanie and the Jackson girl clinging somewhere along the line?

He stared at his face for a while, till he felt sleepy. He concealed the license in a small crack behind the baseboard. He reached up and switched off the light.

At some hour in the dark, the thick, cloudy, pressing winter dark, he heard the front bolt scrape, the heavy door pop open. He tipped his box back. Soundlessly he rolled his body onto all fours and then uncoiled, balanced and erect.

With a quick twist he unscrewed a stout broomstick from the push broom and carried it before him, ready.

'Antoine?' came Marsha's voice.

She was too shaky to drive herself. He helped her into one of Perry's trucks and took the wheel. All that morning they kept vigil at the hospital, in a high room that looked down upon a snow-covered drainage pond. Perry lay sliced open, a network of tubes and lines crossing him like roads and wires on white countryside.

20

His time at the range seemed to fall off the clock: the light came late, and even the short December day seemed to go on forever, across hours that hadn't been numbered yet. The regulars stopped in to ask what East knew. They weren't going to the hospital to see Perry, weren't sure they were even allowed. But they missed Perry; they wanted to talk. They leaned on the heavy glass of the candy-shop counter. Some of them told East about their fathers' heart attacks, some about their own. There was a little business going on in back but nothing that pulled East away from the counter. He rented time and guns and sold paints while the regulars loitered around him.

Some of these men had never said an extra word to East before. He hadn't been among them a month's time yet. What did it mean, that they came to him instead of Marsha, that they saw *him* as Perry's friend, his confidant? They weren't telling East about Perry – with Perry gone, they were telling him about themselves. 'Wish him well,' they said. They left cards for East to take to the hospital, sometimes group-signed: GET WELL, they wrote in ballpoint pen, some neatly, some in childlike scrawl. SEE YOU SOON.

Soon. The time had crawled to this point. It stood still for him, poised like a cat at the top of its leap. He waited for it to begin to come down. He wondered at the future of Stone Cottage without Perry. He had come to think almost protectively of the town, though he had only just arrived.

On the third day she returned. She wore a brown sweater, corded and woolly: East imagined that once her hair had been brown like that. He asked how was Perry, and Marsha asked if he knew what a do-not-resuscitate order was.

'It means he'll get what he wants,' she said dully. It meant they knew already that Perry would die tonight or tomorrow. Something seized in East's throat, and he reached the broom handle and leaned until he could speak again.

This could be decided by a piece of paper a man had signed.

'Does he know?'

'Does he know what?'

'Does he *know*,' East said, betraying something like panic in his throat, 'that he's going to die now?'

She lifted her hand and bit it. She turned, seeming very small, and he waited for her at some distance.

Again he went with her to the hospital. She drove this time, in a long old white car he had never laid eyes on before, a Plymouth.

Perry was still alive in his junction of tubing and wires, the monitors, the cannula, the intravenous lines, an undressed mountain. His eyes were turned up. They were cloudy like the eyes of the fish East would see in the Spanish markets just east of The Boxes, eyes that he never let himself look into, for what they had seen he knew he'd see one day. He let Marsha go to Perry's body; he stood waiting by the door. The nurses eyed him, this mysterious black boy: what did he mean? There were black nurses, young women he noticed in pale, flowery blue; there were black doctors and black men in hairnets pushing mop buckets along the floor. But this black boy with his bare head in this fat old white man's room, trying quietly to comfort the widow-to-be, what was that? He did not hide from their eyes.

He let Marsha have her time, and when she left his side and went to go sit at the window, where she cried with a little chuffing sound, he approached Perry's bedside.

'Have they given up on him?'

Marsha took a breath. 'There isn't much to give up, Antoine. All that wiring on him, it's keeping him alive. When they take it off, then he dies. It's that simple.'

'When they gonna do it?'

'Now,' Marsha said. 'I shouldn't have. You don't have to stay.' East looked down the pupils of Perry's eyes as if he was looking into a hole in the street, as if there were depths to the man, and in the depths there would be what the fish knew, what the fish saw: the end. The being swept up, the laying down. Sharply, as if she were here right now, he saw the Jackson girl in the street, her eyes: the seeing of the last thing and the fixing on it. He shuddered. Perry was a color part his wind-scorched red and part the opalescent white of paint, the white of the winter sky. East backed away. He stood again by the doorway, and when the two nurses returned, they had to push in past him, so much had he forgotten where he was.

'Mrs. Slaughter?' the younger of the two nurses said. The black one. The older nurse waited quietly, deferentially, much like a nun. 'Are you ready?'

Again Marsha took her moment. 'Yes,' she said quietly.

'The doctor can be here in a few minutes.'

Marsha stood and came to East in the doorway. Her body, the opposite of Perry's, female, small, her tiny birdlike bones visible in her wrists, the hands darkened with age. Her brown hair and dark eyes going gray.

'You don't have to stay, Antoine,' she said. 'I'll be all right.' Words in his throat curled under themselves. He shook his head. It took less time than East would have guessed. The needles came out of Perry's body, and the breathing tube with its scarlet cloak of mucus scraped back up out of the mouth with only a little urging. Marsha had reviewed her signatures on the paper without very much looking, and she touched Perry and moved back to the window without very much looking at him either.

'It's what he wanted,' the older nurse said by way of consolation, and Marsha laughed once, a hollow *pop*.

Out the window was the highway. Winter cars rushed past in their coats of grime.

'Push this button if you need anyone,' the nurse said.

It was as if Marsha had fallen into a trance, and East, after a minute, moved again toward the bedside. Was this it? Suddenly he was eager to know. He bent over Perry, watched though he had been unable to watch Ty, unable to stay where his brother and the ones before him lay and suffered.

Perry's breathing was soft and tinkly, glasslike, like a stone rattling in a bottle as it rolled. It tumbled and slowed, tumbled and slowed. It isn't taking long, East thought. There isn't much more. Once Perry's breath nearly ended on the upstroke. Then he let the air out – another roll, another tumble. East put his hand near Perry's hand, and he leaned and looked again down the barrel of Perry's eyes. The last thing anyone saw. He supposed he was willing to be it. He put the fingers of his hand atop Perry's knuckles, and Perry let out a half cough, out of his chest, which was high and white and furred with hairs like bare winter trees on a mountain. The stone in the bottle rolled again. The eyes swam in their clouds, their baths of white. Then the bottle bumped up on something, rolled no farther, and the mountain knew it too, what the fish knew, that last thing of things.

21

THEN AGAIN IT WAS windy and warm. Like summer warmth after the snow, like California warmth: another wave of southern air, men walking in shirtsleeves, cars with their windows open and music spilling. East kept the range closed. He was alone. No one pulled into the lot, now muddy, the tracks shimmering with melting snow under the blue sky. Melting water sounding everywhere. No one stopped. He supposed it was Marsha the regulars were greeting now, now that Perry was dead. A man's sickness you discussed with other men. When a man died, you spoke to his wife at last. But no cars at the house either. He did not cross the road. He was not sure how to approach the house or if, now that Perry was gone, she would receive him.

He worked at the building and the yard in the warmth that might not return, he knew. He worked like it was his own. He aired the building, cleaned the storeroom where the many jugs and trays of balls gave out their waxy smell. He put the stepladder up – sixteen feet, it frightened him to climb it – and cleaned the lights, replacing two old tubes that spat and flickered. These were the lights that would kill you – that's what Fin said once, dull your eyes, take the color out of paint. He dropped the old tubes into the bin and watched them break into curls of glass, puffs of white powder rising from them.

In the afternoon he put on a pair of hip boots Perry had left and wheeled a Dumpster around the range. In shadows lay thick slush like the kids drank with syrup, and it still lay heavy in the lee of the berm with its shading fence. But where the sun hit the ground, he could find the litter in the mud: chips bags, candy wrappers, sandwich papers, sweat towels, plastic flasks, cigarette packs, bloody socks, popper vials, zipper pulls, beer cans, stray gloves. Some of it windblown, most of it dropped. Each time he cleaned the range, he learned things he hadn't known: what they brought and dropped was what the range didn't sell. Cherry cigars, green tubs of chew. Wrappers from Chicken Lively – what was that? Glass pipes, someone getting high – he had ideas who. He pinched the pieces with the picker and raised them high for a look. The boots were enormous on his feet, and he tightened the laces until they bit rings around his ankles.

The streak of yellow-orange across the south. A rent in the clouds, or maybe their end.

He filled two bags with trash before dark. The bags weren't right. Some awkward, shifty plastic, thin and bulgy, not tough like the regular bags. Maybe they were for something else, not trash. But Perry wasn't here to ask about it. East lugged them out one at a time, opening the gate and scuffling down the shrubby bank to the bigger Dumpster. Then he stood outside eating a bagel dry and looking at the daylight dwindling down the road to his left. A thin, worried-looking dog came padding down the edge of the road from the east as if it were following the fading light. It looked at East and lowered its mutt head. East tossed the rest of the bagel, and it gave it a sniff, then picked it up and took it along. Silent thing, intent.

He left the boots outside the door. Inside, he put the roll of weak black plastic bags away in the storeroom and took his good gloves off.

He vacuumed the sofas and the two raggedy rugs. Swept out the corners.

The next day, just as warm. He allowed himself to sit for a few minutes at a booth in the doughnut shop. Ate his sandwich. A napkin holder of rust-speckled chrome. The morning light played over the salty lot like a single, insistent note.

He found the paint that Perry had used to paint the door and its frame white and, while the sun was bright, painted them again. He painted until the paint ran out; then he soaked the brush in thinner and cleaned the windows with a blade.

It wasn't clear what he was going to do next. It was clear to East that he was waiting for something, some sign, some sudden clearing that would allow him to glimpse his desire. Clear that he deserved to wait. Not clear that he deserved such a sign.

But the day was fresh, and the air moved through, dusty, hopeful. At dusk he sat outside again, watching the house, Perry's house. Marsha hadn't come or gone. Two days now without customers, without cold. He regarded the driveway curiously, the hump of the yard above the roadside ditch.

He tried not to feel left out.

After a little while, the dog passed by again. East saw it coming. Careful, stepping quietly along the roadside, skirting stones. It knew what it was doing.

He had saved a part of his lunch this time, egg and cheese with the bread. He called to the dog, not a word but a sort of yelp. The dog stopped, eyed him uneasily. He threw it a chunk of greasy bread, and after the dog wolfed this, it stood squarely, assessing him now. It came for the handful of food he held out.

He did not touch the dog. He could see the worn path something had rubbed around the dog's neck, part scar, part dry riverbed. Like a landmark in the fur. He watched the dog eat, eyeing him shrewdly, and then move away.

He took a shovel from the locker atop the landing, and he dug his guns out of the piled dirt where they'd waited for him.

Long before midnight he was asleep, curled on his pallet, the single pillow. He slept the long and grateful sleep of men who work – a breathing sleep, a dreaming sleep of childhood, or flying, or pathways leading somewhere. He burped and shifted, and steadily inside him, like the ocean's tide, one great muscle drew air and pushed it out, drew it again.

It was late December, a Tuesday. It had been a busy day.

The back door was open, as if someone were minding the range, as if the building were still airing. East slept. Beneath his box he did not feel the air. And he had been in the air all day, this southern air, which did not feel or smell so different from the air that he'd grown up in.

Only the noise, the sustained clattering, woke him. Like something being dragged, being broken. His eyes opened, and he lay paralyzed, as happened sometimes in dreams. *The need to move.* He could not move. *It's the middle of the night.* Like a child's excuse.

The sounds echoed up. Now he smelled the air. The nighttime wind and smell of melt, the milky smell of rock being ground. He reached up under the sink. The tough plastic creased there, formed a crevice, and into it he'd pressed the two guns he'd dug up. He dislodged one and fit his hand around it, and silently he stood.

The open back door looked out across the range toward the

shushed lights of town. Nobody there. Just the man-size furrows of the field.

He crept to the stairs. The noise persisted: was it Marsha? A clank and a sigh, a clank and a sigh. Like a giant lugging his tool kit, shifting it with every step. In his hand the gun was strange and cold. He took the corner, paused, and stepped down.

The blow came from beside, below. It smashed the gun out of his hand, sent it spinning over the ragged sofa. Again it came and smashed him off the step. He plunged down the half flight of stairs, hit the concrete, and rolled. He tried to come up – *the pavement is not your friend* – but the blow struck a third time. Some sort of club, it bit into him. It smashed him down again, and now he heard the feet scrambling around, and he gave up getting away, just covered himself, his head shoved down by a kick. He locked it between his knees, rolled, took the ringing blows on his left side. They rained on him like whip strokes.

Not the head, not the stomach, not the back, he pleaded silently. *Not the neck or the shoulder, the elbow or the arm.* Not the places he was being hit: he yearned to save them, as if the blows were making him miss every part of his body. He yearned to protect it. He cracked under two more strikes, rolled away, hid his face again, under his arm, the way a bird hides under a shivering wing. Whimpering. Dreading the blow that would break his head, that would send him to join the others.

The feet backed off then. He'd thought there were two pairs, but now he eyed the shoes circling, switching direction. The dark staff resting. Just one. The shoes rested, poised and small, as if picking out a target. Dark high-tops. He braced again and closed his eyes.

The voice came soft and exquisitely amused. 'Damn, boy,' it said. 'You hold a gun like a girl.'

Then he did not need to look.

'You ran from me, man. You *ran.*'

East opened his mouth, but his throat was stopped.

'I knew you'd run,' Ty said. 'I didn't think you'd shoot me. Didn't think of that.'

He opened his eyes, but they flooded. The concrete floor blurred, faultlessly clean. He was a fool. Left Ty for dead. But *left him for dead* was just something you told yourself. Dead had to be for real.

There was blood smudging his face; his arm was smacked open, raw. Painfully he moved it. 'Ty,' he coughed. 'You gonna kill me?'

He dared to look up. Above the sofa he saw something swinging – a nylon tote, hung on its strap from a rafter. Something in there shifted, causing the racket.

A decoy.

'Found you,' Ty said.

He closed his eyes.

'What are you doing here?'

'Found you,' Ty said simply. 'Stand up.'

East was ready to die on the clean, hard floor. Like people did. Standing didn't mean anything now.

Ty bent over him. He pulled at East's shoulder, gave up. 'I'll whip you till you get up, then,' he said, almost helpfully. A foot helped nudge East onto all fours. His arm burned, and he sheltered it from Ty.

'Take a seat,' Ty said. He pointed with the club. It was just a stick, the broomstick East had used, he saw now. Unscrewed.

'You gonna kill me?'

'I should,' Ty said.

East eyed where the gun had ended up. Somewhere way past the other sofa. But Ty would be ready for that.

He sat.

Strange, long journey across the world. The world would have its way; you could not stop it. And his brother was the world.

Ty acknowledged it too. 'Funny, seeing you again. Seeing where we left off.'

In the dark, East nodded.

Lightly Ty spun the broomstick. 'You ask what I'm doing here? Did you try to find out about me?'

'Find out what?'

'Find out *what*,' Ty snorted. 'Did I live? Did I live or die, nigger?'

'Where I'm gonna find that out?' East mumbled.

'Well, first, you got to care,' snapped Ty. 'Care enough to try. Internet, man. But you don't do that – I forget. Or call somebody. Call home. Let me tell you. They were gonna make me a state orphan. Give me to a farm lady. They asked me my name every day for a week. Then I walked out.'

'Out of what?'

'Hospital.'

'And then what did you do?'

'What you think?' Ty said. 'I went *home*.'

'How long you look for me?'

'For you?' Ty said. 'Since yesterday.'

East made a face.

'Didn't look. I waited till you popped up. I knew you'd be out here somewhere, man. Every cow you looked at, you fell in love.'

'Did Walter snitch me?'

'Naw. Walter loves you, man. He thinks you the real thing.'

'Then how?'

'You called Abraham Lincoln,' said Ty. 'That got back to me. Cause I'm on the inside now. Not scraping along begging for jobs. Fin changed his mind. I don't even see a gun most days. So I looked in the records, found out the number. Pay phone over there, right?' He cocked a finger over his shoulder, toward the town. 'Flew out this afternoon, came into town, walked to your pay phone. I asked one person two questions, and I knew where to find you.'

'You flew out here?' said East. 'By yourself?'

'East. Don't insult me,' Ty said. 'Remember Bishop Street swimming pool? You had to keep your face out of the water?'

East remembered the old, grimy, city pool. Splashing, a war of noise. Kids drowned all the time. Neither of them had ever had a teacher. The teenage lifeguards were no better – they were just the ones who'd made it that far.

'You'd dogpaddle down to the deep end with your friends. I was, like, four or five, and I'd track your ass down? Splashing and gasping because I couldn't swim. But I found you.'

'I remember.'

'Well, nigger,' Ty said quietly, 'now I can swim.'

East looked up at his brother. The light flick of his hands as the broomstick lashed this way and that, its alloy screw-tip flashing. Heels dug into the upholstery.

Almost impatiently, he said, 'You gonna kill me?'

'No,' Ty said. 'I'm not.'

'I don't believe you.'

'Maybe you shouldn't.'

The hanging bag had stopped swinging, now just twisted slowly. East reached down to mop his blood, wipe it elsewhere on his shirt. Tried not to drip it on the sofa. *Well, finally,* he thought. *Family reunion.*

'I'm hungry,' Ty said.

In the dim light, Ty looked the same. Skinnier, though. If that was possible.

'How –' East began, then stopped, abashed. He didn't believe. A ghost. A ghost didn't fly across the country to trade vengeance in for a whupping.

'How are you alive?' he finished.

'You ask? How I didn't die?' Ty spun the stick and stopped it straight up, like a clock. '*Thank* you. I woke up in an ambulance. Coughing up pink shit. All that day I chilled out on a ventilator. You know what that is? It's a machine that makes you keep breathing. Another four days with a tube going into my side. That bitch *hurt*. Hurt worse than the popgun did. That is how I didn't die.'

'How you just walk out?' East breathed. 'They didn't cuff you, suspect you? Didn't ask you about it?' He found the words. 'The judge?'

Ty squinted. 'Why would they?'

'I know they had police on that.'

'Maybe,' Ty said. 'But we kept a low profile. Did it right. To them I'm just a victim, some cold, black-on-black shit. They *much* more likely looking for you.'

East hung his head. 'So when you gonna kill me?'

'Was up to me, you'd already be getting cold,' said his brother. 'But I'm here on business. And I'm hungry. So let's eat.'

Early morning. So there was just one place to go. East walked Ty out to buy a box of doughnuts before the light. Ty waited down the street.

Even before six, the place was warm, confusing, alive. East stole a glance back from the counter. But he saw nothing but the windows reflecting movies of the inside.

He could run. He was faster than Ty afoot, or used to be. He knew the yards and fields here. He knew where Perry kept a key to the old truck.

But there was nothing in it, running. He could open a gap between now and his old life. But only a gap.

The doughnuts waited in their bins, blessed and bright. The counter clerk today was a thin boy, hair brushed straight up. He folded the box together, and East picked out twelve and paid.

'You get one more. Thirteen for a dozen,' the thin boy said. East said, 'No thanks.'

'What,' said the boy, 'happened to your arm?'

East looked at it in the light for the first time. It was a whacked mess, the sleeve soaked and blackening. His stomach slunk downward. 'Thanks,' he said.

Five people. It didn't matter who was in there or what he might have spoken out loud: they couldn't change things. But what Ty had said was right. If he were here to kill East, it already would have happened.

Though he could still take a notion.

Ty waited in a doorway, reviewing the morning *Plain Dealer*. Seeing East, he rolled the paper again and bagged it. The angle of a pistol sprang in his pants.

He fell into step beside East. 'So this your house? You standing yard still?'

'Kind of the same deal.'

'Paintball? There's money in that?'

'There's money.' It would only amuse Ty if he said how little.

'What you running besides?'

'Nothing.'

'Straight up?' Ty laughed. 'Huh.' They walked back along the highway without a word.

The day was coming up, black thinning to silver. The two boys crossed the damp lot, and East unlocked the door. The holiday bells rang. They'd been on there since he arrived, but weeks had gone by without his really hearing them.

Ty stalked around the place, examining the counter and the merchandise, trying on a pair of goggles. East stood watching until he felt time again, stretching long. He went to unknot the rope that slung the bag from the rafters and lower it to the floor.

Ty finished his circuit. 'Now you sit down,' he said. 'I brought a message.'

Gingerly East sat on one of the sofas. Ty took his perch opposite. 'Ready to listen?'

'I guess,' said East.

'Then – you're coming back. This ain't home. You don't belong here.'

East shrugged.

'The organization changed. So I came to get you. Here on, it's business.'

'Business,' East repeated blankly.

'Maybe the fat boy told you. Somebody bought The Boxes.'

'Walter told me,' East said. 'So, they sold Fin out?'

'Streets and houses. Those shit holes you stand by, man,' Ty sneered. 'Like this place. You remember how your place got taken down? That took five minutes. Police took two more while you were gone. It ain't even hard for them; they come before lunch. So, yeah, we sold them out.'

East shook his head.

'Things change,' Ty insisted. 'They paid us like fools. Businessman from Mexico. In love with America, man. Paid us one and a half million dollars.'

East whistled. 'But what's left? What's the business now?'

Ty's face tightened. 'Don't you ever pay attention, man? Houses got no future. Police like hitting them, mayors like hitting them, news likes hitting them.' He wiped his mouth. 'You the only one doesn't get it. Your boys, your crew? They back in school now. *Making* something of themselves.'

'What about us?'

'Us. We're making money. All that what Michael did at UCLA, we work other colleges now. Them schoolkids love weed. Smoke too much. Pay too much. They'll even go pick it up. Walter's back in school too. But he still works Saturdays at the DMV. They think he's, like, twenty-five. So far up in them computers now, they can't stop him.' Ty smiled. 'You know Walter just makes up people, man.'

'He makes up licenses.'

'No. He makes people. He made you, Antoine Harris. We *talked* about this.'

East's arm smarted. 'So how you gonna make money on that?'

'Shit, boy. People pay. You know what a college kid will pay to be twenty-one, have a second name? What a Mexican dude will pay to be in the computer for years going back?' Ty wiped his mouth. 'People make lives on that shit.'

'Police gonna catch you on that too?'

'Walter is smart,' Ty said. 'And careful. You don't even know his name.'

'Walter is his name,' snapped East.

Ty laughed in his face. 'You don't listen. You don't even know who you are.'

'Your brother,' East said.

'Half brother. Right,' said Ty. 'We got your mother in common. But since you always been Fin's boy, that organization gonna be yours. That's what Fin wants.'

'Fin's boy?'

Ty's face filled then, no longer just a talkative skeleton. It filled and flexed with the old hatred.

'Nigger, you know,' he said. 'Half brother. But you are what I ain't.'

People had always whispered at it. But there was nothing he could trust upon. A father wasn't anyone he'd ever known.

It wasn't anything he could use now.

'We left town for that reason,' Ty said.

'What reason?'

'Protect the core.'

'The core?'

'You think Fin gonna send the four of *us* to kill a dude?' Ty said. 'Makes no sense. Why not just two guns? Why not one?'

'To protect us,' East said dubiously.

'Get you out of town. Walter and you. Brains and blood.'

'But what about…' East said, and then it was as if he couldn't remember anyone's name. 'What about Michael Wilson?'

'Michael Wilson was a babysitter. Bad one, we found out. He handled the polite situations. I handled the impolite ones.'

'But people higher up,' East said. 'Sidney. Johnny.'

'There is no Sidney or Johnny.' Ty made a quick gesture that East didn't want to see. Something slipped, pulsed under East's ribs.

'But what about the dude?' he protested. 'The judge? Why was that?'

'An excuse.'

'An excuse?'

'Prosecution got a hundred witnesses, man. They didn't need Judge Carver Thompson.'

'Why we *kill* him, then?'

'You,' said Ty.

'Me?'

'You were the only one took that seriously. It was you who kept on. Mission-focused – I hand it to you, man. Fin says something, you do it.'

Ironically Ty bowed.

'No,' East said. 'That ain't how it was. Don't put it on me. We killed the man. What comes of that?'

'Nothing comes of it.'

'Nothing? People are dead now, man.'

Ty ran his fingers over the box and picked out another doughnut.

'Shit be crazy,' he said.

All that time, flickering again inside his skull. The van, the hours of country. Rolling under their wheels like wave tips passing his brown calves at the beach. The same feeling, the same dull roar, tires, water, the same laying out of light on the sand and fence posts and all there is. Lightly flying. He still felt it.

He shook his head out, the way he would sometimes after waking from a dream.

'How is Fin?'

'Fin?' Ty chewed slowly. 'Two days after we left town, he turned himself in.'

'He did what?'

'He walked into a police station and sat down. Tired. Living house to house,' Ty said. 'Don't think they weren't surprised, though.' He held up a finger while he worked something in his mouth. 'Come back, man. It's what Fin wants. Fin *knows* you shot me. But he don't have but one bastard son.'

East rubbed his eyes. The light of day was finding the skylights.

'Terms of my employment,' said Ty, 'is, I have your back.'

'I don't believe you,' he said at last.

'If I was gonna kill you,' said Ty, 'this was my chance. No, come back. Cause Fin is giving us hell till you do.'

East stood. He tested his shaky legs. Ty made no objection to it.

'These doughnuts.' Ty was mumbling through a full mouth. 'Good. I see why a girl like you would settle down.'

'I never heard you talk so much,' East said.

'Well,' said Ty, 'we all got to do things we don't want to do.'

In The Boxes, when someone insulted you, you insulted them back, or if someone punched you, you punched them. But everything was subject to organization. If an insult came from inside, you threw it back. If it didn't, you found out first. Found out what you could get away with. It was possible you could get away with nothing. Possible you would need to swallow your pride.

If somebody really hurt you, bruised or beat or shot you, you didn't need to ask. Injury called for injury. No need for organization. These rules of living were inside out. These rules of living kept boys polite day to day, even if they had free rein to kill.

A brother putting a bullet into a brother was unacceptable. It had happened, no doubt. One must have had a reason. But there would be a response. East had known this without consultation. He knew it the way he knew walking, he knew language. He had come to Ohio expecting to be kicked, to be gutted, for the last bullet in the world to find him and spit in his face.

He did not expect to be fetched back. He did not expect doughnuts, still soft from the oven, or to be handed an air ticket reading FIRST CLASS LAX DATE OPEN with a name he'd never heard, clipped to a California state driver's license with that same name. Same name and a picture of his face, taken back one day when everything made sense.

Ty's car was a sleek gray Lincoln, parked a quarter mile down. 'How'd you get hold of this? You're thirteen.'

Ty fiddled with knobs. 'You forgot my birthday. I'm fourteen now.'

That's right, fourteen now, East thought. Both Sagittarius, born early December.

'Steal it?'

'No, man. Just a car service.' Finally Ty exploded with disgust. 'Fuck this motherfucker. How you get defrost and heat at the same time?'

East flipped through the knobs, chose something. Ty shook his head and gunned the engine. It was smooth, new and powerful. 'Couldn't figure out the radio either,' he confessed.

East had told a lie – that he had business to close up. Money hid and deposited, debts to be collected and paid. Otherwise, he feared Ty was just going to put him on a plane, today. It surprised him when Ty simply said okay.

As for Ty, he was flying home immediately.

'Don't make me come back,' he warned. 'This car, we got one week.'

'*We* got?'

'You got six days left. More than that, I have to make a call. I *don't* want to make that call. So six days.'

'All right,' East said.

The wound was bandaged now. Ty had helped him disinfect it back at the range. The big first-aid kit had everything he needed. But picking the shirt out of the sticky, clotting blood hurt almost as much as the whupping. Ty bandaged the arm and taped it down. Squeezed it once, like a joke, and East screamed.

'See?' Ty murmured. 'See?'

Light rain fell. The temperature was dropping again.

'One thing I forgot to ask. How'd you *get* here?' Ty said.

East considered. This too, this memory, seemed like a train on a different track than he'd been on. 'Old lady rode us to an airport. Walter flew home. Then I stole her car.'

'You stole a car? *You* stole it? From a lady who gave you a ride? Cold,' said Ty. 'You get rid of it?'

'Left it two days back.'

'Two days, what?'

'Two days of walking.'

'You burned the car, right?'

'No. Left it by a police station.'

'Crazy,' Ty said. 'So why you stop there? At your store, paint guns, whatever?'

East had to remember before Shandor, before Perry, when he

was just a kid in the street. 'I got cold, man. Cold and tired. Sign said HELP WANTED, so I went in.'

'I know they liked you, didn't they? Had you pushing a mop?'

East shrugged. 'Hundred dollars a day.'

'White man stealing from you,' Ty jeered. 'I hope you stole a little back.'

'I don't steal,' East said.

'You stole that lady's car.'

'Yeah.' East's blood quickened. 'That was different.'

'Oh.' Ty's fingers tapped the wheel. 'Tell you one thing different. Bet it wasn't no white lady's car you stole.'

East shut his mouth and looked out at the dirty snow, stinging. Ty hummed. He drove fast, relaxed. Fourteen now, and he seemed to know driving by heart. He seemed to have the airport route in his head. He seemed just to pick things up like that.

East said, 'Ty. Back at the gas pumps, when you held the gun on that dude. What were you thinking? What was the play?'

'You mean,' Ty said, '*before* you shot me?'

'Before I *had* to. You were out of control, man.'

'Maybe I was,' said Ty. 'But come off it. Who was saving your ass, every time? In Vegas, from Michael Wilson, from that hick-ass town? And who did the job?'

'What job?'

'The *judge*.'

Then East remembered the judge: his name, his face. The dark shape of him moving around in the bright cabin like a rat in an experiment. 'Ty. Did the judge know you? He looked at you.'

'I bet he did.'

'He *smiled* at you,' East said.

Ty just laughed.

'You ain't gonna tell me?'

'No,' Ty said.

This shit, thought East. 'But now you're saying I'm in charge.'

'Play that,' said Ty. 'You always in charge. Fin had a hundred hungry niggers working, but you're the only one ever follows directions. Did you ever wonder how I had a gun after they took one off me?'

'You had a second one,' East said, 'they didn't find.'

'Same one,' said Ty. 'Fin gave it back. You listening now?'

'Forget it,' East seethed.

'East. You got your way. You understand that your way goes on top of my way. But your way don't stop me?'

'Just be quiet, man,' said East. The rain was letting up, and Ty took the exit to the airport. But East was in his mother's apartment again, arguing. Arguing for his life against this impossible boy.

'You stick to business,' said Ty. 'But I am business, East.' They sat hot in their seats, hating each other like brothers, till they pulled up to the terminal, gray planes hanging in the sky.

22

ALONG THE DEPARTURES CURB, the gray Lincoln stopped. NO PARKING. DROP-OFF ONLY.

Ty said, 'When you're ready to drop it off, call this number.' A sticker on the dash. 'Give them one hour. They meet you here. Or wherever you need.'

'What do I need? Credit card? Fill the tank?'

'Bitch, this ain't Avis. Just give the car back.' Ty handed East the keys. 'Walter said you don't fly. So if you *got* to drive this car back to LA, okay. But call and let them know.'

East scanned the line of windows along the terminal. Airline porters. Police. Families pulling suitcases on small invisible wheels.

'Two more things,' said Ty. He popped a compartment between the two seats. 'There's your phone. A charger too.'

East spun his phone in his fingers. The familiar weight and shape.

'Just be careful. Don't say much. Be smart. I called you. So my new phone is the last number on it.'

East stared at the phone. 'Thanks,' he made himself say.

Ty reached down into the compartment again and came up with a roll of bills.

'Three thousand dollars, if something comes up,' he said. 'This is *my* money, now. A loan to you from me. Understand? Say it.'

'It's your money.'

'All right. Take it.'

East let the money sit in Ty's hand for a long time. A debt he didn't want. But there was nothing else now.

He put it away in his pocket.

'Don't lose it.'

'I won't.'

'Plus this.' Ty fished a little silver gun out of the compartment, showed it, and replaced it. Then he took an envelope out and laid it on his thigh as he threaded the zipper on his jacket. FIRST CLASS, it said, just like East's. DATE OPEN. JOE WARNER.

'So, this is it,' East said. 'No luggage? Nothing?'

Ty shook his head.

'So. Six days. You got what you need. Any questions, you call me.'

Ty picked up his ticket. East studied him for a long moment. The sharp easiness. His long little balding head. Kidney bean – that's what their mother had called him.

'I don't want to come back here. Winter and shit. If I do, it's the old rules. There will be consequences.'

'I hear,' said East.

A hard chuck on East's arm, right on the bandage – East kept from crying out. Ty unsealed the door with a rush of wind. He climbed out and straightened his colorless jacket. Ticket folded over once in his hand, he checked the traffic behind them and then mounted the sidewalk, passing people in parkas and colorful letter jackets. East watched Ty hurry toward the electric doors, which slid open for him, just another young man on the way somewhere else.

It took East a moment: now he was expected to drive the Lincoln off. DROP-OFF ONLY. Not to slide over: to get out and walk around the big car. He did so, his hands and chest tingling. Paused at the driver's door and checked the little chrome key ring: DODGERS. The brand of home.

A girl passed on the sidewalk, small and black, leading her parents, who were all burdened down with garment bags and ski poles. East didn't look: he knew she would be the Jackson girl, all big eyes and bravery. That face swimming atop her face.

Then she was gone.

He coaxed himself onward, opened the door, lowered himself into the driver's seat.

Barely any noise. Solid. He checked the mirrors, moved the seatback up. He wished he'd watched the route more on the way. Ty drove the roads as if he knew them. East knew only one town.

If he could find his way back to the long old highway, he'd be all right.

The wind moved the trees. The rain was stopping. But the pavement was already dry.

The steering wheel was thick and almost drowsy in its softness. He would need a little sleep as soon as he could get it.

Back at the range, he spent a few hours. He polished the countertop. He cleaned the storeroom. In the evening dark he dragged items out to the Dumpster – his bed of clean, flat cardboard. His blankets – he saved his new, still-fresh pillow. The box he'd fit under at night. He slept his last night on the sofa, comfortable without the heaters. The cold didn't bother him now. He wasn't as skinny as he used to be.

The last day. East took alcohol and rubbed down the register, the bathroom, the door handles, the cabinets – any place he'd touched, any place he'd made his. He went to the bank and cleaned out his Ohio account, took cash, more than a thousand dollars. Added it to Ty's money and Walter's. At a table outside the little grocery where farmers sometimes came, he bought a handmade bouquet. Dried flowers, yellow and orange. He walked them across the highway to the leaning-forward yellow house where Perry had lived with Marsha. He stood for a moment on the porch but didn't knock. He left it on a rocking chair beside her door, with a note that said, *From Antoine, thanks. RIP.* An ambiguous goodbye. He didn't know if she'd ever get them. He doubted she'd ever step inside the range again, or her son would. It seemed to have been abandoned, except for him. It seemed to have been just the one man's dream, and when he died, it stopped. East had left it spotless. He hadn't stolen a thing.

He cleaned the two old Iowa guns inside and out. Reburied them, deep this time. He spread the three like licenses out on the counter – East, Antoine, and the new one, the person who matched the plane ticket – and studied his face: the three times, different expressions, different shirts. But each one of them him. Each one a different life.

It wasn't easy to decide.

The first he chopped to bits was Antoine. The van. The guns. The trail they'd made. He cut it to bits with Perry's wire snips. Then it was down to the new name and East.

He wondered what Walter had invented for him, what sort of life, what weakness. What sort of story, should he not come back. And he was never going back.

In the end, he and East said goodbye. Age sixteen, licensed driver, State of California. Snipped him too into tiny squares. Wrapped him in the shreds of the one-way ticket back to Los

Angeles. And left him in the trash can outside the doughnut shop, with the wrappers and the half-crushed cups of coffee. Became the new name, and no one else. He would grow into it as he was growing into the body stirring beneath him, the strange and turning body, as uneasy and teenage as it was hard and loyal. He looked different anyway now, fuller, older. The wind, the food – something out here was giving him pimples.

For a few minutes he parked the car at the range. He put his clothes and toothbrush in a grocery bag. Threw his pillow into the trunk. Wiped down counter and doorknobs again before exiting the building for good. Leaving the Lincoln visible while he did so was maybe not smart, but it would be fine. The car would do to take him east, to the dense snarl on the map, that opposite coast with its tangled cities: Washington, Philadelphia, New York. He had the rest of the week.

The sun was going down. The dog, the colorless dog, followed the border of the road, weaving. He had no food to offer it this time, but he whistled, and it came. He touched its scarred and rippled neck, and it whined. Sharp, black, careful eyes.

He opened the back door of the Lincoln, and warily it looked the car over. 'Get in,' he said.

Before he left, he stopped and ate a doughnut. The place was nearly empty – the thin boy pouring coffee, two women from the grocery store, a lady truck driver in a fur collar eyeing her cab outside. He would miss this town, not that he'd ever liked it. It was a place he'd stopped and studied. But the way he was leaving felt like leaving home. He bought a second and third doughnut and had them packed in a paper bag. Take-away to anywhere. Outside, the strange dog lay asleep and breathing in the borrowed car.

He stood outside and took a last look around. It was growing night, but the town was not dark. Lights shone beside doors and over driveways, still air. Somewhere he sensed a clatter: he listened, then caught the voices, boys in a driveway shooting hoops, the echoes clashing. He could see the plumes of smoke, the exhalations of every chimney, rising and dispersing. Each house a quiet mystery.

Nobody watching. He fingered the keys his brother had handed him, and as he opened the door of the borrowed gray Lincoln, he caught himself, just a glimpse, in the curved window glass. Alone, the first few stars in the unswept sky behind him.

Then he was gone.

ACKNOWLEDGMENTS

Thanks to many people who helped *Dodgers* find its way, including Dan Barden, who suggested that fifteen pages might not always be enough; my old friends Wendy Brenner and Kevin Canty, who kept listening and helping; Steve Yarbrough and other fellows and teachers at Sewanee Writers' Conference; and staff and fellows of the Virginia Center for the Creative Arts, where much of this book was written.

My remarkable agent Alia Hanna Habib, a brilliant reader and advocate, and my superb editor Nate Roberson, patient and sharp-eyed and wise, and to everyone at McCormick Literary and at Crown, who have seen this book through to places I did not imagine it would ever see.

No Exit Press has crafted this edition beautifully: my gratitude to Ion Mills, Clare Quinlivan, Claire Watts, Elsa Mathern, Sue Amaradivakara, and Alejandra Creixell for their careful handling of the book, and for getting it out into the light.

And to my students at Trinity.

To my parents, for the world, and to Deborah Ager, for making it sweet.

About Us

In addition to No Exit Press, Oldcastle Books has a number
of other imprints, including Kamera Books, Creative Essentials,
Pulp! The Classics, Pocket Essentials and High Stakes Publishing
> oldcastlebooks.co.uk

For more information about Crime Books go to > crimetime.co.uk

Check out the kamera film salon for independent, arthouse and
world cinema > kamera.co.uk

For more information, media enquiries and review copies please
contact marketing@oldcastlebooks.com